Dove of White Flame

Dove of White Flame

A Historical Novel About Saint Columba

Stella Durand

RESOURCE *Publications* · Eugene, Oregon

DOVE OF WHITE FLAME
A Historical Novel About St. Columba

Resource Publications
An Imprint of Wipf and Stock Publishers
199 W. 8th Ave., Suite 3
Eugene, OR 97401

www.wipfandstock.com

PAPERBACK ISBN: 978-1-7252-6454-0
HARDCOVER ISBN: 978-1-7252-6455-7
EBOOK ISBN: 978-1-7252-6456-4

Manufactured in the U.S.A.   05/01/20

All Biblical quotations are from the Revised Standard Version.

To my brothers and sisters
in the Community of Aidan and Hilda.

Contents

Acknowledgements

The author wishes to acknowledge help and kindness from the following people: John Anderson, the late Miss Campbell of Kilberry, Sir Edward Durand, Madeleine Durand, Martin Enright, Revd Mairt Hanley, Ven. Craig McCauley, Dr. Kenneth Milne, Andrea Mullen, Emily Murphy, the late Professor Liam de Paor, the Revd. Ray Simpson, Kristen Swanson, Karen Thomson and Lesley Whiteside.

Historical Note

Q uite an amount of material exists about St. Columba, but it is extremely difficult to prove the authenticity of all of it, and to unravel genuine eye-witness accounts from hagiography. Certainly Columba was the great great grandson of Niall of the Nine Hostages, the fourth century High King of Ireland, through Niall's son Conall Gulban, given as the eldest in most genealogies and his eldest son and so on down. But primogeniture was not practised in Ireland at the time. Rather the Kings and High Kings were all elected from the *derbhfine* or pool of eligible men, which was made up of all the male descendants of Niall. In the case of Columba, the hagiography could well have started within his life-time, particularly given his pedigree, for his contemporaries would have seen his becoming a monk when he had been in the *derbhfine* as a huge sacrifice.

I have attempted to do justice to most of the stories about Columba while sticking as carefully as possible to what is known of the sixth century, so as to give an authentic feel to the whole book. I ask more erudite scholars to forgive me if I have unwittingly perpetrated any inaccuracies. Inaccuracies have been avoided however. As my intention has been to try to make the whole life and times of Columba come alive to the modern-day Christian, and so the intent is partly religious, I have not approached the tales with the scepticism of the academic scholar. However, every single person in the book really lived. The only name I had to invent was that for Columba's horse. Also it is impossible to say with certainty when each church or monastery was founded.

The "Seven Erics of Kindly Blood" have intrigued some of my friends. 'Erics' or Éraics were annual levies or taxes, the word can also mean fines, or tribute. "Kindly blood" meant kinship: because the Alban Dalriadans and Dalraidans in Ériu were related by blood, they were bound by this arrangement to give help to their kin. The exemption of monks and women from participating in battles—The Law of the Innocents or *Cáin Adomnáin*—was finally enacted into law in 697, thanks to the efforts of Adomnán, the ninth Abbot of Iona and Columba's biographer

I have used the names for people and places which were current in Columba's day, but I have chosen to call the saint by his Latin name—which would also have been in use in his day as well as the nick-name of Colmcille—as it is the more widely known. A glossary is provided at the end of the book.

Prologue

A.D. 561

How that man stood out from his companions, his tall figure standing on a hillock among the princelings of the Uí Néill in their battle array. His white abbot's cowl barely concealed his strong shoulders, sitting royally on his back and contrasting with the colorful tunics and cloaks of the soldiers. His clever brow, his long nose, his grey eyes blazing anger, his curly red-gold hair.

How his late mother Eithne had wept three decades earlier when those foxy locks were shaved from ear to ear and fell to the floor of the little church, leaving but a mane of close curls at the back of his head. During his childhood, seeing that red-gold head playing purposefully about the fields or bent over his wax tablet, stylus in hand, at the house of the priest, had been happy moments for her. Such memories had caused stirrings deep in her, a strange mixture of pride and sorrow and love. Her Crimthann, her fox. Her Colm, her dove.

1

Gartán

A.D. 521

F elimidh watched his wife walk by the lakeside in the evening calm. Her hand sat possessively on the six months' swelling growth of babe within her, which was beginning to protrude noticeably. She was a woman clothed in a cloak of otherness. Descended from a South Laigin formerly royal and now poetic family, she was poetic herself in her impulses and imagination, and a great supporter of the *Filí*, the order of the poets of Ériu. Always a deep one, at all times slightly mysterious, she was increasingly so at this stage of her pregnancy. Her grey eyes held both a light and a faraway look, so Felimidh had purposely followed her to try to find out her secret.

At the same time part of him held back and wanted to respect her private aloneness, allow her to withdraw from him for a time into her veil of secrecy. Still in two minds, he called gently:

"Eithne!" She turned towards him and smiled holding her two hands out to him. Her beautiful smile was what he loved most about her, as well as her lovely long hair which blew in the breeze. Awkwardly he manoeuvred his tall frame down the grassy slope towards her and they stood together looking down into the brown shallowness of the small Lough Akibbon, companion to the larger Lough Gartán beside it. The reddy-purple foxgloves swayed in the summer evening breeze.

"You seem above all happy tonight, and above all, my sweet one, you are lovely. The babe fares well?"

"Yes. But Felimidh, this son of ours, he will not be ours alone" she said, hesitating, and Felimidh prompted her

"What is this? Tell me Eithne."

"I feared to share it, lest you be angry. The touch of God is on him already . . . I had a dream . . ." She looked at him questioningly.

He bent his dark head to her fair one and kissed her tenderly.

"Tell me Eithne, I give my word that I shall not be angry".

"It was around the time of the turning of the leaves. In my dream an angel came and gave me a large cloak covered with beautiful flowers and many lovely colors. This cloak was shimmering with light. The angel held it up in the air and the wind blew it far and wide, over the hills, far, far beyond our home, dazzling and shining as it blew. Then the angel told me 'You will have a son, who will blossom for heaven and his light and influence shall be carried far beyond the world you have known or heard of '. The next bit is what I feared telling you, Felimidh. " She faltered slightly, "He will belong to God".

Tears of emotion welled up in her eyes and her voice cracked as she continued.

"He will bring many souls into the kingdom of God and will be reckoned among the prophets of God". A silence lay between them. Felimidh fought to control his impulsive anger.

"I wish, my princess, that you had told me of this earlier. Then I would have restrained myself from all my talking over the night-fires that my son might become Ard Rí, High King of Ireland. That talk has no doubt made it harder for you to tell me of this now". He put an arm around Eithne's shoulder and guided her up the hill to her dwelling.

"You know how I long for sons. My three daughters are a joy to me, but I long to rear a son in the ways of my family. But there need be no contradiction, need there, between his belonging to God and his being a prince of the Ui Neill, or even a king, as he is in the derbhfine so has the right to be elected?"

"Maybe not" answered Eithne doubtfully. Looking beseechingly at her husband she continued "This first son of ours, who will shine like a light in the country beyond the hills, can we at least foster him with the priest Cruithneachan and then send him to all the best schools in the country?"

"If you wish it, dear heart."

When the oaks of Tirconnell had lost most of their leaves on the seventh day of December, Felimidh and Eithne's son was born at Gartán, a small but wild place of still, calm, mood-reflecting lakes and oak woods, enclosed by green hills and circled with further hills of blue grey. The small hunting lodge where Eithne was staying for her confinement buzzed with excited voices, and Eithne's women bustled to and fro with ewers and basins and towels. After the long labor, the young mother was exhausted and perspiring, yet glowing with pleasure to hold the little red form in her arms, all swaddled against the cold except for his puckered face with his grey eyes and crown of reddish-gold hair. She gazed at her baby with love.

When the cleaning was completed, Felimidh entered and was shown his son. Felimidh strode towards mother and baby and smiled proudly. The new-born babe was lying now, looking up at them all peacefully, the circle of faces gathered all around him disturbing him not a whit. For a few moments, all watched him in silence, then his tall strong father spoke.

"A thousand welcomes, my little son, to the Ui Neill family, and to the Clan Conall, little princeling!"

Then, to his young mother,

"A little fox you have brought into the world, Eithne, with his great head of red-gold hair. A fox with your own grey eyes. Crimthann shall be his name; a word for both a wolf and a fox, and an illustrious name after a great king".

He looked back again at the babe, bumping his great hairy fist into the hollow of his other hand, smiling and murmuring happily of his dynastic plans. Eithne looked tenderly towards the babe and said,

"A fox, maybe in some ways, but far more, a one to fly far and shine bright for God, I had thought Colm, the dove, would be my choice of name."

She bent down to kiss the babe.

"Little Colm", she whispered. The maids around the cradle puzzled over the two names and seeming opposition of the two parents and the different perceptions. Eithne sensed this and smiled at them.

"Do not fear, my 'Colm' will win out; but let my husband have his name-choice for now. I will speak to the priest, maybe he will let us baptize him in both names".

They then offered Felimidh the hospitality of the house—it was his house in fact, his hunting and fishing lodge beside Lough Akibbon and its adjoining larger lake, Lough Gartán. This was the quiet place where he had encouraged Eithne his young and lovely second wife to retire for the birth of the child away from the boisterousness and noise of their main Fort at Cill Mhic Néanáin, for she, like him, was of royal blood, a daughter of Dimma McNeve, sprung from the kings of Laigin.

As the days went by and the child grew strong and vigorous, and Eithne herself felt able, she and Felimidh arranged for his baptism by Cruithnechan their local priest at Tulach Dubhghlaise.

Felimidh sent messages to Ailech, to the King of the Clan Conall, his cousin, that a new princely boy was born. For was he not also in the line of the inheritance of the High-Kingship, being in the *derbfhine*? All were summoned to the baptism and the feasting afterwards at the Cill Mhic Néanáin Fort.

Cruithnechan rode to see the family in the days before the ceremony.

"The priest is here!" went up the cry, and the servants of the household ran up to hold his horse while he dismounted.

Cruithnechan was grey haired, yet still vigorous, a man who seemed to look at all people with affection, yet at times his brown eyes seemed to be seeing another world. Today he was in his smiling mood and blessed the entire household. The general chatter subsided as Eithne issued forth from her apartments and spoke urgently to the priest.

"Cruithnechan, I must speak with you about the boy's name as Crimthann, the fox, and I admit it suits him well with his coloring, but I feel . . . well, I feel he needs a more Godly name, we both want him to belong to God and become a priest".

"What name would my lady like?" Cruithnechan asked.

"Colm is one of my favorites, and it speaks of peace-making which, living with these warring Uí Néill, is much needed!" Eithne declared, knowing the priest would appreciate this touch of humor.

"Yes, Colm son of Felimidh, son of Fergus and grandson of Conall. But what does your husband think?"

"He is adamant on Crimthann and will let me choose only a second name".Cruithnechan thought for a while, then said,

"If he is to belong to God, he can take a second name in religion, so this would possibly answer the problem".

After Cruithnechan had partaken of some food and ridden off, Briga, Eithne's chief maid approached her mistress, somewhat nervously as if she had to say something of whose reception she was unsure.

"I had a strange dream, mistress, concerning the babe while he was yet in your womb. I shrank from sharing it before, for fear it was a bad omen, but now he is delivered and is healthy and strong, it would be no harm".

Eithne was intrigued. "Tell me, Briga, what was your dream?" she asked quietly, so as to promote the confidence.

"I will not disclose it to any others. You can tell me safely." Eithne assured her. "Did it concern my son?" Briga cast her eyes to the ground.

"I do not know for sure Lady Eithne, but I dreamed that all your own . . . insides . . . were being carried by the fowls of the air all over Ériu and Alba; all your bowels, mistress." These last words came tumbling out in an embarrassed rush.

Eithne, who was familiar with meanings of dreams, laughed.

"Do not fear my anger Briga. My 'bowels' signify what is within me, what was within me, my baby. This bodes well. He will be a holy man and perhaps the birds carrying them so far means that he is going to go and preach in a faraway place, Alba perhaps, to the Cruithni there".

The day of the baptism dawned cold and misty, as if the event of Tulach Dubhghlaise was an especially private affair not to be disclosed to all. The church bell ringing through the mist had an otherworldly sound about it. The wider family filled the small church with color, and in the hush, Eithne carried Crimthann Colm forward. The priest took him gently, and gazed at the child with a look of reverence as he took the water in his cupped hands and spoke the words in Latin.

"Crimthann Colm, I baptize you in the name of the Father, the Son and the Holy Spirit".

He then held the child slightly aloft for all to see, and Eithne glowed with pride and also something of awe to see the sight; both priest and baby seemed to be wrapped in an aura of silver light. Had a mist crept in to the church? Or was the hand of God on her son already? At the family feast afterwards, one by one the relatives blessed the child. One said,

"I pray that he will be a druid and advisor of Kings". Another,

"I pray that he will be a mighty warrior, feared throughout the land". Another prayed,

"I pray that he will be a peace-bringer to the houses of Uladh, Dalriada, Laigin, Mumhan, Connacht and Midhe". His young uncle Ernan was the last of the relatives as the long line was coming to an end, and he said prophetically,

"I pray that he will be a leader of men together, towards each other, and a leader of men to God".

2

Tulach Dubhghlaise

A.D. 523

The little ball rolled and rolled, and the sturdy infant ran after it and reached for it gleefully, clapping his chubby hands together and smiling in delight. His mother Eithne sat with her maids, spinning and weaving, and looking at the child with his ruddy curly head bobbing up and down and going with great determination about his business of play. Eithne smiled as her hand strayed to her abdomen swelling now with a new birth expected. Crimthann Colm was so full of energy, she felt that his need for adventure and learning and her own need for quietness in her new pregnancy could well both be met by his fostering, for he was already some months past the earliest age for fostering, being fifteen months old. Her arguments with Felimidh about who should be the foster-father had been long and somewhat of a tussle. Felimidh preferred a further-afield family who would prepare his son for ruling and defense of his people. Eithne preferred the scholarship and undoubted learning of the holy priest Cruithnechan in the nearer-to-home Tulach Dubhghlaise. She felt that this would accord better with the vision she had had in her pregnancy about Crimthann Colm's future, of the cloak that billowed far and wide. Briga's dream about the birds of the air carrying her 'bowels' to the east and to the west was still prominent in her mind. She had known at the time that probably meant he would be a great preacher. Cruithnechan too had been watching the child grow with delight and with something of a proprietorial sense, from hints that Eithne had dropped to him.

It was no secret at Tulach Dubhghlaise that Cruithnechan was to be given the little fox-dove for fostering. But, in spite of his fore-knowledge, the priest felt great joy and relief—and honor—when in the spring of the year of Our Lord 523, Felimidh rode to his house at Tulach Dubhghlaise and formally asked Cruithnechan to foster his son. It would be a fostering for education officially, but also the choice was made from the affection the priest was held in by the family and all in the area around. Felimidh had for years helped support the priest and paid his tithes and dues regularly as a Christian prince.

As Felimidh approached the house his spirits, already cheered by the Spring sunshine and the yellow primroses, was further lifted by the sound of women's voices singing about their work. These same women, Cruithnechan's daughters, were soon welcoming him and placing two small cups of mead on the table for him and Cruithnechan. As they drank, Felimidh lifted his cup and said,

"Cruithnechan, son of Cellachan, I entrust my son to you to foster and teach the things of God. Chastise him without severity, feed and clothe him and prepare him for his degree. Prepare him for the bigger school of Finnian at Maigh Bhile on Loch Cuan. Teach him all he needs to know. I personally wish to have my son trained in the things of war as well, but it seems that God also has plans for him, and we will have further sons, no doubt." Felimidh and Cruithnechan both felt happy and confident about the arrangements, although both may have had slightly differing perceptions of the child's future.

After the short chariot-ride from Cill Mhic Néanáin to Tulach Dubhghlaise to bring Colm to his foster-father, along a boreen pungent with wild garlic, Eithne had planned to lift her son bodily and hand him to the priest, but she had not reckoned with Crimthann Colm's own enthusiasm. The child clambered out of her arms as she began to lift him, and ran to Cruithnechan with a smile and arms open to be lifted up, happy to be going to live with his special friend. Cruithnechan's brown eyes shone with happiness as he lifted the child.

"A welcome to Crimthann Colm—but we must use only your name in religion now that you are given to God. In the Latin tongue, Colm sounds even better, it has a good strong ring to it—"Columba". So, welcome, Columba my son, and God's blessing and mine on you, Lady Eithne, and on the child growing within you".

The household of Cruithnechan also, and his three daughters welcomed him warmly and the place began to seem like home to Columba already. That same evening, a summer evening of soft yellow-golden clouds in a sky of pink and mauve light, Cruithnechan visited the church for a special prayer of thanksgiving for the fostering of the child and prayers for divine aid in caring for him. On his way home he was full of happy thoughts that God would enable him to teach and lead this boy well. He had fostered many children before but was older now, and so was glad he had but the one; and a very special one, he believed, having heard from Eithne's own lips the story of her dream which she had naturally told her old soul-friend and priest. His footsteps started to hasten along the road to go and look at the infant once more and check that his sleep was peaceful. He lifted his eyes from the rutted track where they had from custom been studying the bumps in the road so as not to fall. What light was that issuing forth from his own dwelling? Had some—or many—lamps been lit there? He lifted up his cloak and hastened more quickly. The glow from the house was unmistakable and warmed his heart. He made his way to Columba's cot. He slowed down and gazed with awe at what he saw. The child's eyes were closed, his face was peaceful, with a smile. What seemed to be a sphere of fiery light was hovering above his face. The room too seemed full of light and the presence of angels. Cruithnechan at once got on his knees and sank his head to the floor.

"Father, I see that you send your Holy Spirit in large measure to this boy. I thank you for this sign of grace. Make me worthy to be his mentor and give me too the grace I need!"

On another day, a year or so later, returning from the church again, Cruithnechan was surprised to find a very different scene. The child had somehow managed to climb up on a bench and must have pulled down Cruithnechan's book-satchel which was now cast aside on the floor, the strap broken. The child had the book on his knees and was poring over it, pointing to the words and murmuring as if he was reading aloud. The little fox, Cruithnechan thought.

"Crimthann! For Crimthann you rightly are when you behave in this manner. Return my book to me at once! You have broken the strap! I am angry, Crimthann!"

The child just gazed into Cruithnechan's face with his serious grey eyes, and said,

"Father, I want to know the songs you sing! I want to read the books you read!"

"You are young yet, Columba" said Cruithnechan, relenting a little.

"But learn the psalms you will! Come with me to the church and learn them there. Join in the daily offices from now on."

A period of great bliss came into Columba's life, the joy of discovering those glorious songs, the psalms of David. They had a wonderful ring in the ears, a satisfying feel on the tongue, and an afterglow. How he loved *"I was glad when they said to me let us go to the house of the Lord. Oh give thanks to the Lord for he is good, for his loving mercy is forever. Lord you have been our refuge from one generation to another, before the mountains were born, or the earth or the world were brought to be from eternity to eternity you are God"*. How he loved *"The Lord is my shepherd, I shall not want"*. How he loved *"Oh God, you are my God, eagerly will I seek you. My soul thirsts for you. My flesh longs for you as a dry and thirsty land where no water is"*. How he loved *"As a deer longs for the running brooks, so longs my soul for you oh God"*. And how he loved *"I will bless the Lord continually. His praise shall be always in my mouth"*.

Day after day the three-year-old followed his foster-father to the church, Tulach Dubhghlaise Church. Cruithnechan would look fondly at the young boy as he walked in the woods, thinking himself unobserved, touching the leaves, touching the bark of the trees, touching the flowers and listening with awe and delight to the cuckoo's call. He was a boy with an inexhaustible cruse of wonder and a sense of the holiness in all things. Cruithnechan wondered was he impeding his progress by not teaching him the arts and skills of reading and writing. He thought,

"I had best consult a wise man or a prophet to see whether or not it is the right time now to introduce Columba to writing and reading. I shall ask my friend Finnian in the spring-time, for the feast of Christ's birth is approaching, which means Columba has just passed his third birthday. It is a young age for starting to read, but he is a clever boy."

The woods around were carpeted with yellow shiny celandines and bluebells were in bud. Primroses, peeping through, were starting to perfume the air, when Cruithnechan was visited by his friend Finnian whom he had summoned to advise him. The wise man looked long at the sky, Cruithnechan waiting patiently by his side, and Columba, too, silently awaiting the outcome. Finnian, at last, spoke,

"He is ready to start. Write an alphabet for him now". Cakes were being baked that very day as a visit to Cill Mhic Néanáin was planned for the morrow to visit Felimidh and Eithne and see the new baby Eoghan who had arrived into the family. So Cruithnechan supervised the making of an alphabet cake for Columba. All eighteen letters were on the little cake, on the top and around the sides. Columba was delighted with it and tried his best to put aside the delicious smell of the cake long enough to study its symbols. Finnian, Cruithnechan and Columba packed up the food into the chariot and set out for the fort. The sun shone, and soon both they and the horse were hot and weary. Finian and Cruithnechan both agreed that it would be good to eat.

"Father, this little wood can be our eating place!" Columba cried, and let himself be helped down from the chariot. He helped carry the food, and when it was laid on the grass, he danced around it shouting,

"The alphabet cake! The alphabet cake!" Foster-father and son pored over the cake once again and studied the letters.

"Here I am eating C for Columba and C for Cruithnechan, now F for Finnian and F for Felimidh!" he said, smiling at the older teacher.

"Good, son. Now which is this?"

"That's D for the river, the black stream Dubhghlaise".

Such was his excitement that, as he ate, he explored the wood, leaving the adults to their own talk and he found a little stream. Half the cake was soon eaten and Columba came back for the other half. He recited the letters to their satisfaction and raced off to see what was on the other side of the little stream. He returned later with the cake finished and with bluebells in his hands. Finnian looked at him with seriousness,

"Have you finished the other half of the cake, Columba?"

"Yes, I ate it the other side of the river, then I picked these flowers for the new baby".

"Do you see that, Cruithnechan?" Finnian asked, "the lad has eaten one half of his letters west of the water and one half to the east? I prophesy that this child's territory will be half to the west of the sea, Ériu that is, and half to the east."

Cruithnechan responded

"Alba, maybe? Who knows?"

Eithne was delighted with the precociousness of her young son, according to Cruithnechan's reporting! But she was equally happy that he was not wanting in human warmth and affection, impulsively rushing

up to offer baby Eoghan his fast wilting bunch of bluebells. The church services and learning psalms became very much a part of Columba's life then, so much so that the local children nicknamed him the "church pigeon" or "church dove"—"Colmcille."

Whenever they traveled around the area in the chariot, Cruithnecan and Columba would recite psalms by heart at the tops of their voices to help the journey pass more quickly. The day they went to Ragmochu to visit Bishop Bruga, another of Cruithnechan's friends, they sang the ninety-first psalm together and then Cruithnechan instructed Columba from it. *"He who dwells in the shelter of the Most High who abides in the shadow of the Almighty, shall say to the Lord, my refuge and my fortress . . . He will cover you with his pinions and under his wings you will find refuge. His faithfulness is a shield and buckler. You will not fear the terror of the night, nor the arrow that flies by day . . . for he will give his angels charge of you to guard you in all your ways".*

Cruithnechan had been invited by the Bishop to preside at the Holy Eucharist as it was a special occasion. In his excitement the elderly priest faltered over the words of another less well-known Psalm, and in the short silence which followed Cruithnechan's loss of memory, Columba's small voice piped up with the missing words, on and on to the end of the long Psalm, to the amazement of the assembled company.

All birds—above all swans—butterflies, trees, rocks, and mountains, were always a delight to him. Then under his feet he loved the rich tapestry of wild flowers, stones, acorns, ash-keys, bilberries or frauchans, blackberries, mosses and grey-green lichens; and above his head the sunrises and sunset colors to thrill him, the ever-moving pictures in the sky that the clouds were making, and the jewelled velvet of the night sky with the stars. With Cruithnechan, before he was sent to bed, on clear nights, he would learn some of the names of the constellations of the stars and repeat with his foster-father the psalm, *"The heavens declare the glory of God and the firmament proclaims his handiwork".*

And so the years passed happily, out of doors as well as indoors, perfecting his skill at writing, and reading, but then carried off by Felimidh to learn more war-like skills, singing the psalms in church with his beautiful voice, an instrument of expression for his real love and devotion to God, and then, running in the woods gathering galls and holly-leaves for ink and lichens for colors. One day Columba asked his master,

"Why are your daughters not married, father?"

"My son, they have chosen to give their lives to God, to offer him all they have, their best gifts, their womanhood; and to serve him all their days by prayer and caring for the sick."

Columba was deeply impressed.

"Can I give my life to God?" the child asked, simply, and wide-eyed. Cruithnechan smiled,

"Of course, but not yet, Columba. When you reach the age of choice—fourteen years."

These same daughters were in their hut one day at prayer and heard the familiar young voice of Columba saying his lessons out of doors. But the voice was getting louder and louder and they were perplexed and ran out. Columba was on his knees on the grass, in a little copse of trees, while Cruithnechan was lying on the ground seemingly asleep and Columba was shouting his lessons in his master's ear, as if to waken him. They came closer and saw that Cruithnechan had the pallor of death on him. They looked at the boy's loving concern for their father, they felt in their spirits that God did not want Cruithnechan dead now, so they prayed inwardly for some time and then said to Columba,

"Wake your Master, now". Columba looked at them, puzzled but trusting, and shook Cruithnechan by the shoulders, saying,

"Wake up Father!" Cruithnechan opened his eyes and smiled and let himself be helped upright, and all five returned to the house with great rejoicing. That evening, Columba was in bed praying and saw his angel, a very young man, seemingly made of bright shining light. Awe-struck, Columba asked,

"Are all the angels in heaven as young and shining as you?" But he was disappointed that the young shining angel went away and he did not see him again for a long time after that.

When the time for Columba's age of choice, fourteen birthdays, was come, the angel did visit him again. Columba had been kneeling in prayer, conscious of the importance of the following day, wanting so much to find the right path to follow for his life. He was becoming increasingly certain that his own wish to give his life to God as Cruithnechan's daughters had done, was also what the Lord Jesus Christ desired of him. The young shining angel was beside him when Columba opened his eyes, and Columba had the distinct impression that his special guardian angel was offering to help him in his life for God, to give him graces and gifts, and that he was asking him to choose what virtues he would like. Columba thought for a few moments before replying

"Chastity and wisdom. I would like these best," Columba replied without very much hesitation. He realized that he would need supernatural help in both these areas—in chastity to overcome his very natural interest in the beauty of the female body, and help him be firm in his resolve to offer his own virginity to God as a costly and precious gift; and wisdom for he was very aware that a Christian man of God must exceed the Brehons, the Druids, and the poets in wisdom, if they were to build Christ's kingdom in Ériu and make it a Christian land—indeed, to make all five Provinces Christian. Drifting in and out of sleep, following this vision, he dreamed of himself trying to repulse three very beautiful girls, all trying to embrace him. They were indignant and said,

"Do you not know us?"

"No, I do not!" Columba exclaimed in his dream. The three maidens replied,

"We are three sisters who are given to you as your brides by our father".

"Who is your father?" Columba asked, puzzled.

"Our father is God, Jesus Christ the Lord, and saviour of the world".

"An illustrious father! But what are your names?"

"Our names are Virginity, Wisdom and Prophecy. We are going to stay with you always now." Understanding dawned on the young Columba at last that these were the graces and gifts that the angel was giving him and he slept soundly after that. To Columba's surprise he found that Finnian of Maigh Bhile had arrived whilst he had been sleeping and he was summoned to the church for a celebration of the Holy Mysteries. During the course of one of the most glorious celebrations with his brothers and sisters and his father and mother present, among many others, Columba was called up to the altar by his master and foster father, Cruithnechan, with Finnian—now Bishop Finnian—standing beside him, Columba was asked publicly,

"You are now fourteen years of age. What is your choice in life?"

Columba knelt, but his face was not downcast, but looking up and radiant.

"To give my life to God's service, to give him my strength, my body, my substance, my virginity—to take the vows—to be a monk, a soldier of Christ."

"Are you willing to be obedient always to a superior, a cleric, a soul-friend, to the end of your life?"

"Yes, I am," said Columba, "so long as that cleric or soul friend is himself obedient to Christ and following his way."

"Well spoken", said Cruithnechan quietly, though Bishop Finnian looked rather more disapproving. Now some acolytes came forward carrying a natural colored woollen tunic and also a cowl with a hood, made from the same material. These were placed round Columba's shoulders by Finnian. Eithne watched with emotion, tears streaming down her face, as Cruithnechan then carefully shaved the beautiful red-gold curls from the front of her son's head, shaving from ear to ear, so that no curls remained on the front part of his head. Columba himself was hardly aware of lack of beauty, he was just hardly able to contain himself for joy as the service proceeded. A very, very special day for him.

In his bed that night he slept but little for happiness and expectation of his new life at Maigh Bhile where he was going soon to study. He slept eventually and awoke puzzled, having had a dream of a large cauldron, into which Bishop Finnian was throwing young men of all shapes and sizes, all dressed in black. Then Finnian was stirring them round and round, and praying, and there was much steam and smoke, and then he lifted them all out, bleached white as new lambs.

3

Maigh Bhile

A.D. 535

Well it was that Columba had summer months with his family after completing his studies with Cruithnechan before starting at Finnian's school at Maigh Bhile, because helping with harvesting and playing chasing games with his youngest brother Cobthach, and joining in with his younger brother Eoghan's training in the arts of war, toughened him and prepared him for what was to come. For Bishop Finnian of Maigh Bhile would take no weaklings at his college. Staring at Columba with his steely blue-grey eyes that seemed to see right through him he said,

"You have to be a man before you can be a monk, a soldier of Christ."

He had to dig his foundations and search out suitable stones and then tree branches he had to break himself, a tough job with the sap still in them. He had to make himself a temporary abode or tent to sleep in for the first days until the hut was completed and thatched. As he worked on building it he prayed one of his favorite psalms, *"Lord you have been our dwelling place from one generation to another."* He prayed that his own hut would be a place where he would be dwelling very closely with God. Thus he started his studies on almost sleepless nights. The other students were totally unaware of his struggles because no time was allotted for the task and it had to be done in the half-light of dawn before the other students were about and the bell had rung for morning offices. Columba had to sleep on stones at night to wake himself early enough, and in the early days his ill-made thatch blew off several times in the wind and he awoke soaked to the skin. Of course the other students had themselves undergone the same rigours but he was surprised that they didn't seem to notice or come to his aid. One day he saw two rather friendly students walking by,

"Comgall ! Cainnech ! Give me hand here !"

They walked on without saying a word, leaving Columba both annoyed and perplexed. But a monk who was a senior in the school, Mobhi, nicknamed Clarinech or Flat-face, stood for a little longer as he passed by and just said quickly and quietly,

"Columba, we are forbidden to help. Try tying your thatch down." Then he walked on.

This advice was welcome and Columba decided to consult Mobhi once again when the time came to improvise a plow to break up the hard soil on his patch of land.

"Can I borrow your plow, Mobhi, to plow my patch?"

"I have none Columba"

"Whose plow did you borrow?"

"He's gone from here now."

"Whose can I borrow?"

"You'll have to make your own. Take a forked branch and tie two handles to it so you can pull it face down to the soil. Use your wits!"

In spite of this seeming hardness, Columba warmed to Mobhi and admired him for not offering him an easy option, for not treating him like a prince.

Sunday was fishing day, a day of leisure from studies, the one chance in the week to make friends with the other students. Cainneach and Comghall lost no time in recruiting the tall strong Columba to help them in their boat. Those two inseparable friends soon became three inseparable friends with the addition of Columba. Out on Loch Cuan in the boat one day Columba asked the two of them,

"Where has Finnian got his knowledge? Where has he studied?" Comghall answered,

" Were you not told? He has studied in Alba with the great Ninian at his school in Whithorn."

"I have indeed heard tell of Whithorn. That is where the white house is, the Candida Casa full of light that I have heard of. Was Mobhi there too?" Cainnech enlightened him,

"No, Mobhi is a royal prince; he has got all his learning from Finnian and is Finnian's best helper in the school." Comghall was two years older than Columba and was a Cruithnian as was Bishop Finnian himself.

Cainnech was also of Cruithnian blood, but his family now lived near
Columba's own territory of Tirconnell and the two became staunch and
loyal friends. Columba's skill as a calligrapher was soon widely known at
Maigh Bhile and he busied himself copying books for much of each day.
The studies themselves were a joy to him, the Scriptures which he already
knew and loved but also classical literature, poetry, a smattering of law,
philosophy, science, grammar, rhetoric, and astronomy.

During Columba's second year at Maigh Bhile, Mobhi was appointed Master of the novices and old 'Flatface' as he was affectionately known
watched Columba with interest. Mobhi was waiting to see if Columba's
royal blood would lead him to extravagances; if his vast energy would
lead him to passion; if his zeal would overstep itself or would he be under control. Finnian one day, while he and Mobhi were putting away the
communion vessels on Sunday after the service, asked Mobhi,

"What manner of man do you estimate Columba to be?" Mobhi
replied,

"I deem him to be a man under the control of Christ and his Holy
Spirit."

Finnian asked,

"Would he be suitable to be ordained as a deacon?"

"Yes he would, and very soon" was Mobhi's reply.

Columba was on duty as sacristan one hot summer Sunday. The
church was warm even in the morning and as he lit the candles he felt a
joy at the celebration of his Lord's Resurrection and Last Supper. All was
proceeding peacefully until all of a sudden Mobhi, who was preparing
the elements, came to the other priest, who was helping him prepare the
altar, with an anxious face.

"We have no wine! Bishop Finnian will be angry for our store was
to have been carefully watched." A vision came into Columba's mind of
the very previous day, a discourse on the Gospels *"Greater works than
these shall you do in my name"*—words of Jesus. Jesus made water into
wine. With enthusiasm, Columba went quickly to the altar and took the
container into his hands and ran out of the church to where there was a
spring. Kneeling by the spring he blessed it and prayed,

"Lord, honor your promises! I beseech you to help us! Make the
water I will draw from this spring into wine, as you did at the wedding of

Cana." With haste Columba filled the vessel full to overflowing then knelt on the grass again beside the well and prayed,

"In the name of Jesus Christ of Nazareth I command you, water, to change into wine!" Now this is where faith comes in, he thought; and returning to the church presented the vessel to Mobhi.

"Here is your wine." The two priests marvelled.

"Columba—did you do this? Praise God for a miracle!"

Columba knew it would not be fitting to take the praise and muttered,

"It is from Bishop Finnian." Bishop Finnian celebrated the sacrament as if nothing was amiss. The wine tasted . . . much as it always tasted! But Mobhi guessed. Only Mobhi and Columba knew what had really happened and Mobhi was not one to blow his own or anyone else's trumpet. But privately Columba was very pleased and felt he had learned that miracles are possible, faith brings them about, God's power is what works them. He would try again!

It happened that in church that evening they said Psalm 116 and near the end of the Psalm came this verse which stood out for Columba—*"Precious in the sight of the Lord is the death of his saints."* Suddenly Columba had a strange feeling in the pit of his stomach and knew in his bones that Cruithnechan's rising again was near. So it was no surprise to him when a few weeks later the message came that the old priest, his foster father, had died. But in spite of his foreknowledge Columba was moved with emotion and grief for he loved the old priest. He ran to the Bishop,

"Bishop Finnian, may I travel to Tulach Dubhghlaise for the funeral of Cruithnechan son of Cellechan, for he was my foster father and I loved him dearly?"

Bishop Finnian's steely-blue eyes softened,

"Columba, we will travel together in my chariot. Such a servant of God deserves a good farewell."

It was impossible for the bishop to be stern with this young man whose honesty and directness matched his zeal for God's church and the Bible and his wonderful memory and scholarship; impossible not to love him as he loved Cruithnechan.

Cruithnechan's burial was a community occasion. His coffin was carried with great honor and respect by his tall and strong foster-son among others. Felimidh and Eithne watched their son proudly. Bishop Finnian spoke with them after the burial:

"Columba is well ready to be made a deacon now. He has learned almost all I have to teach him. Give him one more year with me and then he will do well to go to Abbot Finnian of Cluain Ioraird. Abbot Finnian's monastic school is attracting people from Britain and Gaul and beyond and this will stretch his mind more than my school can."

Columba had joined them for this conversation and looked earnestly at his father.

"Father I have need first to learn more of poetry. Even one year," he said beseechingly. "Gemman would be my choice, he is a true Christian bard, and I would benefit greatly from a year with him first, before starting at Cluain Ioraird, if you would grant this wish."

"That can be arranged son. Have you thoughts of being a poet as well as a monk?"

"Why not?" Columba asked, "As David wrote psalms to praise God's creation, we Gaelic Christians can too; poetry is not just for the Fili, it must become a blessed and Christian thing—can you see that? We must take the best of our culture and baptize it!"

"Well spoken, son" said the gentle Eithne, her eyes alight as she caught her son's vision.

Returning to Maigh Bhile together in the chariot, both Finnian and Columba were silent for much of the journey, occupied with their own thoughts and memories of Cruithnechan. However, Finnian, as they were nearing Maigh Bhile, said to Columba:

"Cruithnechan was your soul-friend, was he not?"

"Yes, he was, and I shall miss him painfully."

Finnian said gently and tentatively,

"You will be needing a new soul-friend now. Had you thought of anybody?"

Columba answered

"No I had not"

"Mobhi, whom you call Flat-face, is a very holy man. You could do no better than to take him as your soul-friend."

Columba answered his master.

"I would be happy indeed if he would accept me. I too deem him a very holy man."

The promise made to Columba's parents that he would be made a deacon soon was indeed fulfilled. Columba took the step with great seriousness. He spent the whole night before the ordination in prayer in the chapel and meditated a long time on the psalm which he felt expressed to him the great, great closeness of his bond with his Lord Jesus Christ. This psalm was number 139 and he prayed the psalm again and again during his dark vigil. "*O Lord you have searched me out and known me, you know when I sit or when I stand, you comprehend my thoughts long before. You discern my path and the places where I rest: you are acquainted with all my ways. For there is not a word on my tongue: but you Lord know it al-together. You have encompassed me behind and before: and have laid your hand upon me . . . Search me out Oh God and know my heart: put me to the proof and know my thoughts. Look well lest there be any way of wickedness in me: and lead me in the way that is everlasting.*" As Columba read about the encompassing of God he knew in his heart with a sense of awe that God knew all about him, every little bit, all his conflicts and doubts, all his pride and delight in power, all his weaknesses and his strengths and his many temptations and he knew that God still loved him in spite of knowing all that. He imagined God's loving presence as a cloak that was around him. He imagined too the hand of God laid upon his head and felt in the darkness of that church that God himself was ordaining him by the Holy Spirit in advance of the morrow's ceremony.

The third and final year at Maigh Bhile was one of growing out of his old school. His boat-building and sailing ability was practiced on Sundays with Cainnech and Comghall. He learned to be a better farmer, a faster calligrapher, he learned the psalms more completely by heart, and had read every book in Finnian's library. He looked forward to going to Cluain Io-raird in the future for he had heard that Virgil and Horace as well as many other books were obtainable in Abbot Finnian's library. Columba's work as deacon was acceptable and yet he sat awkwardly to it. This tall strong red-gold-haired young man with the hypnotic grey eyes and air of leadership about him, fitted ill into a role of subservience although he was humble enough. The two conflicted in him. Columba realized this himself and talked lightly and jokingly with Cainneach of his own Crimthann-nature and Columba-nature, his fox or wolf and his dove.

Living at the head of Loch Cuan in such beautiful surroundings with distant mountains nearby, hills, shores, woods, the sea with all its moods and the ever-changing sky, Columba's ache to learn how to write his joy in God's creation became strong indeed. His favorite psalm was "*Bless the Lord O my soul, O Lord my God how great you are, clothed with majesty and honor, wrapped in light as in a garment. You have stretched the heavens like a tent cloth and laid the beams of your dwelling place upon the waters, you make clouds your chariot and ride upon the wings of the wind; you make winds your messengers and flames of fire your ministers . . .*" Oh to be able to write like that! he thought.

Gemman was an old man by the time Columba came to him. Columba's heaviness at having said goodbye to Bishop Finnian of Maigh
Bhile and all his companions especially Cainnech and Comghall and
very especially Mobhi who had become his soul-friend on the death of
Cruithnechan, grew lighter the nearer he got to Gemman's house, sixty-
five miles or so south of Maigh Bhile. On the journey Columba passed
a lake with a swan and seven cygnets, and he rejoiced at this sign of
good omen. Reaching Gemman's house at last he saw Gemman's hands
raised in greeting and his gaunt old face which enclosed a pair of smiling
humor-filled green eyes.

"Welcome, Columba! There is a bed for you in my guest house, but
you will find I prefer you to sleep under the vault of heaven as often as
possible. We will study too in the woods and the fields. My method is to
expose you to the music you find all around you as much as possible. You
must become part of the rhythm of nature if you would write with rhythm."

Columba was delighted to find that Gemman had a good library
of both classical Latin literature and also some Gaelic poems which his
pupils had begun writing down for him.

Gemman sensed Columba's potential but was sad that his pupil
could spend only one year with him, en route to Cluain Ioraird; and that
poetry obviously would only play a subsidiary role in his life. However,
he was determined that this talented young man should be admitted to
the ranks of the *Fili*, for although only seventeen years of age, he was undoubtedly possessed of the poetic gift among his many other varied gifts.

However Gemman found that Columba was rather different to himself. For example he found that Columba did not always see the things
that Gemman saw in nature. Columba would so often see the invisible in
the world of creation. He would see places as peopled with angels or with
demons and he would see messages in things, the holy in every bush. His
natural reaction to the beauties of nature was prayer rather than poetry;
but he could write good poems when he tried. Gemman knew that as
Columba's teacher if he could manage to change Columba's reaction to
beauty into a reaction of writing poetry rather than his religious Christian reaction of prayer that the result would indeed be great, the result
could be wonderful poetry. But he agonized with himself: had he the
right to make this change in a man who was given to God?

One chilly early spring afternoon Columba and Gemman were happily and busily reading out of doors, wrapped in their cloaks for warmth, and absorbing the rhythm of nature. Columba sat watching the sun blessing the grass, seeing it as God's love blessing all. He personally felt God's love coming through the grass to him. Columba felt blessed by this great love poured out through every blade of grass and every pebble and every rock, every flower, every grain of earth and every tree. Suddenly his reveries were interrupted and his and Gemman's peace rudely shattered by screams, the high-pitched and fear-filled screams of a young woman. These screams were issuing forth from beyond the hillock and so the woman could not be seen. Trees were hiding her from their vision. But soon a pounding of footsteps was heard—two pairs of footsteps. Columba stood up and scanned the distance. At last the girl came into view, her dark hair streaming behind her as she ran in panic, a desperate look on her face visible even at this long range of about 200 yards. Columba saw a man chasing her and realizing help was urgently needed, he ran towards her, his cloak and his arms outstretched. Gemman was not far behind him in spite of his age, and the two enveloped the poor maid in their cloaks calling to the man to leave her alone. The man, a strong and war-like looking dark-haired man, dragged the girl away from Columba with eyes of anger. Columba and Gemman were completely taken off guard, not expecting such treatment. Columba rushed again to protect the girl and found to his dismay that the man's knife was in her breast and she was already gasping for breath. That beautiful girl died there on that grassy hill. The two poets were shocked to silence for a few moments and just stood there gazing at the beautiful face of the dead girl. Then Gemman indignantly called out,

"This must not go unpunished!"

But already the killer had started running away from the two poets. Columba gently laid the girl's body on the grass and stood up, clothed in a blaze of light, and declared loudly,

"The moment this maiden's soul reaches heaven, the soul of her murderer will be in hell!"

Gemman looked astonished but Columba merely knelt to pray, as they both witnessed the killer stumble and fall and fail to rise.

"The famine of bread that is in the land this year is driving many folk to violent deeds, Columba", Gemman observed as they toiled along to the church with the two bodies. Columba replied,

"It is. We must pray for a plentiful harvest this coming autumn. I sorely miss the fish we were able to eat at Maigh Bhile. But let us share the pig my father has sent us with all the village when we have buried these two and all of them have joined us to pray for heaven's justice for their souls."

Even if Columba's ability to write poetry had not improved vastly from his time with Gemman, his oratory and declamation came on by leaps and bounds; his voice grew more powerful with each passing day, and the village folk would all stop and pause in their work to listen when they heard his great singing of the psalms each evening: *"These things I remember as I pour out my soul: how I went with the throng and led them in procession to the house of God, with glad shouts and songs of thanksgiving, a multitude keeping festival."*

The culmination of his year with Gemman came with his recitation of reams of Bardic verses from memory at the Annual *Fes* or festival at Teamhair. He passed this stiff examination and was admitted to the ranks of the *Fili*—the poets of Ériu.

4

Cluain Ioraird

A.D. 540–542

Cainnech was downcast. He sat on his stool with his head in his hands. Columba was now beside him, having come with the express purpose of persuading him to join him at the famous Abbot Finnian's monastic school at Cluain Ioraird. Cainnech looked at his friend with agonized features,

"Columba, I long to learn more as much as you do, I would dearly love to go to Cluain Ioraird, and also to receive priestly orders. But Columba, my family has fallen on bad times. They cannot pay the tribute. I cannot ask them to support me in this venture."

"Cainnech! Cainnech! Let some joy show in your countenance please! Do you truthfully believe I would let you miss this experience just for lack of a few pigs and cows? Of course not! My father will pay for us both—and Comghall too if necessary."

"Really, Columba? Would he agree to that? I would like to say simply 'thank you!' But can you make offers on your father Felimidh's behalf?"

"Maybe not entirely, but in this case surely I can. For have not you and Comghall been my teachers in the arts and skills of sailing and building currachs? Also, I need a bodyguard."

"Why?"

"Well, for my travelling from Tirconnel through the dangerous territories between there and Cluain Ioraird—the Ui Neill living further south are not my best friends, remember, and there are murderers about! Remember I told you of Gemman's and my experience in the spring. If I go with two friends we will be a match for anyone. Leave it to me, Cainnech!"

His friend's face brightened,

"And Comghall?"

"We will call on him together—when we have arranged with my father. Come on Cainnech, you are the silver-tongued one, you can persuade Comghall."

"Yes, but you are the golden-tongued. Besides, I believe he wants to set up his own school now."

"Not until he has studied at Cluain Ioraird. That is not to be missed. I know he is older but he must learn from the disciple of Gildas the Wise and Cadoc as well as from our master the disciple of Ninnian."

After success with Felimidh and a tender farewell to Eithne and Eoghan and young Cobthach, they set off. They found Comghall at Beannchor, an area north of Maigh Bhile. He was living in a village there and thinking about his future.

"I think this site would be perfect for a monastic school, Columba, do you agree? What do you think, Cainnech? Share your thoughts on this."

Columba spoke for them both,

"We both think yes, but not quite yet. Not until after Cluain Ioraird!"

Comghall's features readily fell into a smile.

"Just the clinching argument I needed. I had sought God's guidance about the possibility of going to Cluain Ioraird. The family are more than willing to provision me, but I hesitated, waiting for a sign, and here it is!"

The three joined in harmoniously, agreeing together on a project which would involve them all, for they had missed each other's company in the intervening year. So in a chariot laden with piglets and apples and sacks of oats, not to mention books, inks, vellums and herbs, the three set off in fine mood for Cluain Ioraird. They delayed in Ulaidh only for a brief visit to Maigh Bhile to receive Bishop Finnian's blessing. Their old master beamed on them, his normally hard features soft with affection, and he said,

"My children, I will surely see you again before too long, for I plan a journey south. I can leave the school in the capable hands of Mobhi."

The journey passed without them encountering any danger but in much pleasant companionship.

"Where shall we spend the night?" Cainnech asked anxiously as the darkness was falling.

"Have faith my friend, God knows our need and will provide," Columba replied, falling into his tacitly accepted role as leader. Sure enough half a mile further on they came to a small village with lighted huts and a priest came out to meet them and offer them food, warmth and beds for the night. They accepted with grateful hearts and, on telling their host the object of their journey, he was helpful and encouraging. They asked him could they cut sticks for building huts at Cluain Ioraird and he sent some local youths to guide them to the best spot. Columba had brought an axe with him, now knowing from experience what joining a monastic school involved.

Having cut and stashed away their sticks and fed Pegasus, Columba's rather unaptly named horse, then shared a simple meal with their host and bidden him farewell, their steps as they walked towards their host's guest-house were slow, as if unwilling to bring this pleasant day to an end. It was a clear night, the moon was shining and many stars could be seen. Without even consulting each other the three friends walked with a single mind to a spot where they could observe the sky without any of the huts of the village intruding on their vision. They all three looked up in silence for a long time at the starry heavens. And then they all suddenly together started saying the words of the 8th Psalm *"O Lord, our governor, how glorious is your name in all the earth. Your majesty above the heavens is yet recounted by the mouths of babes and sucklings. When I consider your heavens the work of your fingers, the moon and the stars which you have set in order, what is man that you should be mindful of him or the son of man that you should care for him?"*

On arrival at the huge monastic settlement at Cluain Ioraird by the river Boyne beside the large Bog of Allen, the friends were surprised at the size of the place in spite of the fame of it already having reached their ears. Senachus, Abbot Finnian's assistant, welcomed them and asked them their business. He eventually fetched the eighty-four-year-old Abbot Finnian, himself, who came out and bade the three welcome. Abbot Finnian stood tall and gaunt at the door of the church. In answer to their inquiry about becoming students Finnian replied with a searching and yet affectionate look at all three of them,

"It is not my desire to turn away any seeker after knowledge, I ask only that they obey the rules of the monastery. But you yourselves are already professed monks I see. Are you priests?"

"I am." Cainnech replied.

"I am also, "Comghall replied.

"And I am a deacon," added Columba.

"Well my sons, build yourselves huts and at the next bell report for divine office in the chapel. It will be an honor for me to have you study here with me."

"Thank you Abbot Finnian. You will find my horse Pegasus is useful for helping with farm work too. Where shall we build our huts?" Columba asked, seeing how crowded the settlement was.

"Here at the door of the church," Finnian replied in a tone implying that he was doing them an honor having seen that they were already priests and deacons, and that Columba by reputation he knew to be a Prince of the Ui Neill.

Abbot Finnian had already gone inside when the three looked at each other in puzzlement. Columba spoke first,

"No, my friends, we cannot build here at the church door. For my strong feeling is that this church will be rebuilt before too long."

He closed his eyes and was silent for a few minutes,

"Yes! I prophesy that this church at Cluain Ioraird will become as big as ... this!" he called, indicating a size three times as big as the present structure with his arms.

"So let us still build at the church door but at the door of the future church!" So they set to work with a will.

The bell for chapel sounded deep and mellow, calling across the ranks of wattle huts over the huge vale and across the meadows and hillocks, over the waters of the Boyne. As it continued to ring, figures converged on the church from all directions, from the fields, from the individual cells, from the cookhouse, from the scriptorium, from the guest house, from the farm. It was a joy to Columba, and to Cainnech and Comghall, to join in the singing of the Psalms with such a huge assembly. Such an ocean of voices, ebbing and flowing in the verses of the Psalms must surely have been heard for miles around. Columba's powerful voice as he sang with abandon added to the effect, and several pairs of eyes looked in his direction to see the owner of such a voice. Columba was as oblivious of the compliment as he was of the curiosity, being completely absorbed in his worship of his Creator.

As chance would have it, the spot that Columba, Cainnech and Comghall chose to build their huts of wattles and thatch, was in the Scottic or Gaelic quarter of the settlement—for there were many other quarters too with many Gaulish and British students. A friendly Gaelic face, with a soft Ulidian voice, appeared when the bell for refectory sounded.

"I am Ciarán. Welcome to Cluain Ioraird! I had best explain that there are two Ciaráns among Finnian's pupils. I am known as 'the Carpenter' for I am a carpenter's son. Where have you studied previously?"

"We all three have learned the liberal arts at Bishop Finnian's school in Maigh Bhile on Loch Cuan. And you?"

"I have been tutored by Bishop Erc, and also I have spent much time with the Holy Enda of Aran on his island."

" Tell us of your Finnian, we have heard much hearsay" asked the three newcomers.

They walked together to the refectory and Ciarán smiled round at the three friends and said with great sincerity,

"He is a truly holy man, who is very austere in his self-denial. We too are only permitted porridge, bread and water for daily food though we may have fish and milk on Sundays and on feast days."

Comghall obtained Ciarán's attention and said,

"I have heard he wears a chain about his body. But where did he learn his philosophy?"

Ciarán replied

"He has studied at Menevia with the holy David and with a friend of the Holy Cadoc and Gildas the Wise. He is a kind and generous as well as a holy man. He allows us to have milk on our porridge quite often. Did you hear of his proposed journey to Rome?"

The light-hearted and pleasant tone of his voice made Cainnech feel he was warming to this young man and also Cainnech felt that a story was coming up, so he said,

"No we haven't—please tell us!"

"He had a great desire to go to Rome, having learned all that David, Cadoc and Gildas could teach him, but an angel stopped him saying, 'What would be given you at Rome, will be given you in Ériu.' He then traveled all over Ériu continuing the work of Patrick and strengthening the church and while already an old man founded this college at Cluain Ioraird and now students are coming from all over Britain, Gaul and even beyond."

The three were suitably impressed. What impressed Columba particularly was the comradely and free atmosphere in the settlement, and the way Kings' sons and peasants all joined together in plowing and sowing, in baking and cleaning, in serving at table and washing, and all the tasks of a community, with simple comradeship. All work was seen as God's work.

Two other students from Ériu joined them in the refectory for the sparse meal and introduced themselves,

"We are the two Brendans; and now you make the second Columba with Colm the son of Crimthann and we have two Ciaráns as you probably already know."

They soon got to know their fellow students who were Scots and spoke Gaelic, and one of the Brendans explained to them about Ciarán. Ciarán it seemed was actually in possession of two nicknames because he was 'Ciarán the Carpenter' because of his father's profession, a respectable enough profession; and he was also playfully called 'Ciarán, the Half-Matthew'. The reason for this was that he was one of the kindest and holiest students, greatly loved by Abbot Finnian. When a new student, known as Ninnid the squint-eyed, had arrived and could not find a book in which to study and went round all the students saying 'May I share your book? Can you give me a book to read?' nobody would take any notice of him, except for dear Ciarán, who when asked could he lend his book said 'Certainly.' He was halfway through reading the verse of Matthew 'Do to others as you would have them do unto you' and said, 'Look I am just reading that I should do unto other people as I would like done unto me and I would like books lent to me. Here, you may have this book.' And Ninnid, whom nobody else would bother with, was helped in this way and when the others got to hear of it Ciaran was nicknamed 'Ciarán Half-Matthew'. Finnian himself came to hear of the incident too and his reply was "not Ciarán Half-Matthew will he be in future, but Ciarán Half—Ériu."

Ciarán watched Columba as he listened intently to all of Finnian's teaching, Columba's grey eyes full of visions of heavenly truths, his imagination alight and his fervor fired. One of the remarkable things about that intelligent young man was that he took in all and made all his own; he more than just listened, he acted on what he learned. Having heard about the apostle's healing of the sick, he just assumed he too could heal the sick—and did so—and they became healed. This tall strong princely character was a natural leader, and liked by all as well as admired by all.

Ciarán fumed inwardly then suddenly realized what he was doing, that he was becoming jealous that Columba was also a favorite in the monastery.

Hanging his head in shame he made his way to his soul-friend the Abbot Finnian to confess his jealousy among his other sins.

". . . Columba is the best singer, the quickest writer, the cleverest student, the most liked student, the most energetic worker on the farm: is there no end to Columba's virtues? . . . Oh father, I have been so envious and jealous of my brother in Christ. I ask for God's forgiveness."

Finnian looked lovingly at Ciarán and said,

"I understand, Ciarán. God understands. And as you are penitent and sorry, God forgives."

Then Finnian's eyes lit on some carpenter's tools lying around the church, as the church was actually already being extended at this stage, in fulfilment of Columba's earlier prophecy.

"But Ciarán, look at this axe, this plane, this level—you have given up this craft of your father, a respected craft it is, for God."

"Yes, I have," Ciarán answered, wondering what this was all about.

"Now think, my son, of what Columba has given up . . ."

"Yes. Courtly life at Ailech, fighting in battles, a princedom, maybe even a kingly crown, the chance to be elected High-King even, being of the Derbfhinne, a great grandson of Niall of the Nine Hostages. You are right."

"Yes, maybe even a High King's crown, Ciarán. Try to see him as your brother in Christ. He wants to be your friend I know. I also know you were one of the first to welcome him here to Cluain Ioraird, and I thank you for that. God bless you my son."

Ciarán's friendship with Columba blossomed from that moment, and when the time came after a year and many months for him to say goodbye to Columba he was truly sad. For Ciarán, Cainnech and Comghall had decided to move up to Glas Naion to study with Mobhi Clarinech, for Mobhi was just starting up a school there on the banks of the Tolka River, and they wished to support him and to benefit from that good man's holiness too. Before they left, Abbot Finnian called both Ciarán and Columba to him and said to them,

"I am happy that you two are friends. I had a dream about both of you last night, or maybe a vision: I dreamed there were two moons in the sky, one of them was silver (here he looked at Ciarán) the other was gold (here he looked at Columba). Now the golden moon went into the north of this island and shone so brightly that Ériu and Alba both gleamed in its light. The silvery moon moved on westwards until it stopped by the Shannon River and Ériu at her center was gleaming from its light. When I woke from this dream or vision I knew straight away that the two moons were Columba with the grace of his noble kin and his wisdom and Ciarán with the wonderful radiance of virtue that he has and his good deeds."

Columba missed his three companions greatly, but his temporary sadness was greatly relieved when one day an old friend came visiting the monastery. This old friend was Gemman the Bard, come to visit Abbot Finnian with a poem in hand, a poem of praise. Gemman came and reported his visit to Columba—

"Columba, I have written an *amran* for your master here and he is very kindly paying me for this *amran*, not in cattle or silver or gold or barley but in—what I have requested—prayers of blessing, for the land where I am living has become infertile and we need a holy blessing to be said upon it. Others have been resorting to druids for this but I have insisted on coming to see the holy Finnian of Cluain Ioraird for I know that his prayers will avail."

"I am right glad of that, Gemman, and you are welcome here! It is good to see you my old friend and master." And the two embraced each other.

Columba looked up from his writing in the Scriptorium one day to see his dear master Abbot Finnian enter leaning on a stick. Finnian was making his way purposefully to Columba's seat. Columba straightway offered his seat to the Abbot and when Finnian had regained his breath he smiled at Columba and spoke to him,

"Columba, hard at work, redeeming every minute! What a man of energy and hard work you are! I am told you even waste no time while grinding corn with your quern and working in the fields, but are reading some book all the while; a man after my own heart." He paused and Columba waited respectfully and silently.

"Columba, I am in need of help within the monastery. We need a bishop living here for many duties among the monks, ordinations to deacon and priest among others. I have chosen you to be the one. As you know I am not a bishop. So now go to Midhe to Bishop Etchen and ask him to consecrate you as domestic bishop for the monastic college of Cluain Ioraird."

Columba was completely taken by surprise. He would not deny that he was ambitious enough to wish to eventually become a bishop one day but he had not yet had his priesting conferred upon him. He replied to Finnian,

"But abbot, I am only a deacon!"

"That is to be regretted and it is time that was put right. Explain to Bishop Etchen that I wish it. He is my friend and will understand. Prepare yourself first my son by spending the night in a vigil of prayer."

Columba did spend part of the night in prayer but he suffered far too much from excitement at the prospect of being made a bishop to settle to any very serious praying. His mind raced round and round but he kept pulling himself back and putting his mind to prayer once more. Psalm 143 came in and out of his mind and he prayed,

"Hear my prayer, O Lord, in your faithfulness consider my proposition and in your righteousness give me answer. Bring not your servant into judgment: for in your sight can no man living be justified . . . O let me hear of your merciful kindness in the morning for my trust is in you: show me the way that I should go for you are my hope . . . Teach me to do your will, for you are my God: let your kindly spirit lead me on a level path".

He found during this night spent in the darkness of the church (for he would not waste rushlights on lighting his prayers) that the enemy was more vigilant that he was and was ready to attack him on his weakest points and play on his pride. Looking back at the events later, a mature Columba would see that God could have had a hand in this twenty-year old upstart meeting his nemesis. For he became that night so puffed up that the pricking of the huge ball that his pride had become, like a giant pig's bladder, seemed almost inevitable.

Columba set out at the first light of dawn, accompanied by his nearest friends the two Brendans, in his chariot. Both Brendans were also to be ordained priests. They came to Bishop Etchen's church in Midhe and got out of the chariot. Columba marched imperiously into the church—no sign of Bishop Etchen there. A very small hut was nearby, and Columba looked in there, but it was empty of all but a straw pallet, and stone pillar, and one leather book—satchel. They drove on until they came on some local people, who were busy with a horse and cart.

"Where is your bishop, Bishop Etchen?" Columba called out, without bothering to dismount from the chariot. The younger Brendan started to blush from embarrassment. The local man answered,

"He is over beyond that wood. He is busy plowing." So they drove on and Columba said to the older Brendan, in a fever of excitement,

"This is a bit of a comedown, for a Prince of the Ui Neill to be consecrated by a plowman. Let us test this man and see if he truly is as holy as his fame."

Bishop Etchen watched them coming and Columba almost got the impression that he had heard the last words Columba had spoken even though they had been fairly far away. Etchen had clear blue-green eyes in a freckled face framed with sandy hair, and an air of being completely unimpressed with Columba's demeanor, his horse and chariot, and his shouted message.

"Let us borrow your plow, good bishop," Columba said.

Bishop Etchen immediately handed over the plow without a word, and he attached another smaller plow which had been lying nearby to his oxen who continued on their straight line of plowing.

"Oh, I shall need an ox to pull it as well," added Columba. Bishop Etchen unhitched one of the oxen straight away and led it over to Columba, and looked at the two Brendans who had walked away to one side wishing to have nothing to do with this episode. Then suddenly to everybody's surprise Etchen went to the edge of the small wood that was nearby and whistled. A stag trotted out immediately and Bishop Etchen hitched it to the plow alongside the one ox that was left, and they plowed together. Etchen walked behind the plow looking at Columba who had now become red with mortification. Etchen spoke again,

"Can I do anything else to help you three young monks? Do you want orders conferred perhaps?"

Columba turned to Brendan,

"He is a holy man. He passes the test well. Let us proceed."

Columba then came shamefacedly and said to Bishop Etchen,

"Abbot Finnian of Cluain Ioraird has sent us to you. He wishes the two Brendans here to be made priests and myself a bishop as he has need of help in the monastery." Bishop Etchen with great calmness said,

"I will come. Await me in the church." He then continued plowing.

The three made their way to the church, tied Pegasus to a nearby tree and spent their time in prayer. Etchen eventually appeared having washed himself and put on clean robes. Some local people gathered in the church and soon there was a crowd of witnesses to the ordination.

"In the name of the Father, the Son and the Holy Ghost, I ordain you Brendan to the Holy Order of Presbyter in the Church of Christ. In the name of the Father, and the Son and the Holy Ghost, I ordain you Brendan to the Holy Order of Presbyter in the Church of Christ. In the name of the Father and the Son and the Holy Ghost, I ordain you Columba to the Holy Order of Presbyter in the Church of Christ. You are sent forth to preach the Gospel, to baptize, to celebrate the holy mysteries of the body and blood of Jesus Christ, and I sanction you all three to found monasteries and to fulfil the office of abbot, with the empowering of the Holy Spirit upon you and the love of the brethren in your hearts, and the truth of the Scriptures on your lips, and the presence of the Holy Three to go with you wherever you go. God bless you, my sons."

Columba bowed his head and accepted the ordination. His original intent to prompt and whisper 'Bishop?' melted away in the holiness and light that came from that good man. They walked outside after the service and Etchen turned to Columba and looking at him levelly said,

"I thank you for bringing me a horse and chariot, it is the very gift that is needed for a poor widow who cannot get to the church, for she is a cripple. Now her son can drive her. That is a kind act you have done this day. And have you finished with my plow and ox?"

"We return them with humble thanks Bishop Etchen."

"I am glad that you purpose now to live in the poverty in which Christ lived. But you may stay and sup with me before you leave, we have a celebration to make, have we not?!"

"Yes we have!" Brendan agreed. Columba added,

"Yes Bishop Etchen. In honesty I will admit to you that I had expected to be walking away from this place a bishop; but strangely, having encountered you, I am now content to be but a priest."

"And an abbot" Bishop Etchen interposed.

"Yes, for the rest of my life. I will never seek to change that. But I do prophesy," he added, a little bit more of his former vehemence creeping in on top his new humility, "that no person shall ever again come to have orders conferred upon him in this church." Words regretted as soon as spoken.

So that particular bladder of pride was pricked and burst. Never more did Columba seek to arrogate to himself status; the few times in the future that he was tempted to do so he had but to remember the good, solid, firm, Bishop Etchen, and humility returned. He bowed his head and went to say farewell to Pegasus, stroking her rough brown neck and telling her to serve the bishop well.

The return journey on foot gave ample time and space for reflection. They stopped in a small wood and gathered for themselves a feast of a supper of hazelnuts and blackberries. A flock of geese flew west above their heads, and they all three followed them with their eyes.

"Seeking the Isles of the Blessed!" Brendan exclaimed with enthusiasm, looking at the younger Brendan for his response.

"Yes, I too will fly west one day!" responded Brendan the younger, with determination in his voice."

A happy year of learning the joy of celebrating the Eucharist followed, and of building a new friendship with the two Brendans and Rhodan: the older Brendan who later became Brendan, the Abbot of Birr; and the younger Brendan who later became Brendan, the Abbot of Clonfert. This second Brendan would often share with Brendan, Rhodan and Columba over the talk in the refectory particularly on Sundays when silence need not be observed, his visions for sailing westwards from Ériu to find the island of paradise.

Columba had previously been visiting Mobhi, his soul friend, at regular intervals using his chariot, but now that he had no chariot and was taking to a life of poverty and walking everywhere by foot, he decided that the easiest way for him to keep in touch with his soul-friend would be for him to go and live with him at his new monastic school of Glas Naion and so he took sad farewell for the moment from his dear Abbot Finnian.

5

Glas Naion

A.D. 543

An accident in childhood had disfigured Berchan's—or Mobhi's—face for life. His friends knew well from Maigh Bhile days that behind that pale ugly mask was a beautiful and noble soul, moreover a soul, who never took offense at being nicknamed 'Flatface'. No sooner had Mobhi left Maigh Bhile and set up a school on his own at Glas Naion near the ford of the black pool on the river Tolka, than pupils started arriving. The master had appeared, expecting a few pupils, and there were fifty of them eventually. Columba was now planning to be one of them, his extra year helping Finnian at Cluain Ioraird now over and Finnian having declared that he had taught him all he knew.

Momentarily regretting his new poverty and lack of a chariot, Columba plodded on, trying to avoid the muddiest spots in the road. He soon felt spurred on by the prospect of a happy reunion with his three best friends. He was relieved that he was able to spend one night at the house of a poet friend of Gemman's which was roughly half-way, and he sat before his host's fire, his wet clothes steaming, grateful for the warmth. So he arrived in daylight on a grey windy day, a strong west wind behind him, almost blowing him to Glas Naion.

As soon as the monastery was in sight he stopped a few moments to take in the sight before him. A sizeable river was flowing between two gently sloping banks. There was a large wooden church on the north side, impressively large; the usual larger houses for eating, writing, cooking, and for the abbot himself, and guesthouse; then irregular groups of wattle and thatch huts, about forty or more, some on each side of the river where there was enough level land free of trees on which to build.

At first Columba wondered how the river was crossed, as he saw no boat. Then as he drew closer he saw that the river was shallow and stony at the point where one would normally cross between one set of huts to the other on the southern bank, and he soon saw three monks crossing this ford and coming towards him; then a voice, which sounded tiny in the distance but which also sounded familiar.

"Columba! Welcome!"

He peered at them, it gradually dawning on him who they were.

"Ciarán! Cainnech! Comghall!" he shouted, and they all three ran towards him. When they had finished embracing each other and laughing together they led Columba to the abbot. Mobhi had heard the commotion and was already at the door of his house. Columba approached him with awe, and after Mobhi had embraced him as an equal Columba dropped to his knees on the muddy grass and asked him for a blessing.

"You can bless me now Columba, now that you are a priest!" said Mobhi with a smile.

"You are still my soul-friend," answered Columba.

"May God's blessing be with you my son. May your time here in Glas Naion be protected by the angels, may it be inspired by the Holy Spirit and may it be a time of growth and maturity and preparation for future fruitfulness."

"May we show Columba around, Mobhi?" Ciarán asked.

"Show him his hut that the three of you have constructed and then I shall lead him—you all—to the church, for the hour of vespers will be come by then."

Columba looked very surprised to hear that a hut had been built for him, especially in the presence of a monk of Maigh Bhile trained in Finnian of Maigh Bhile's tough school. Mobhi laughed—

"Do not fear Columba, we have not gone soft here; we merely honor you as an expected arrival and a special friend. But we all here are soldiers of Christ, we have done our training. The time has come now to gather in what we have learned; to pray and prepare ourselves for the future battle; and to learn from each other about the best way in which to bring the light of Jesus Christ's Gospel to all parts of Ériu—and not only Ériu but Alba and Britain too."

The bothy hut passed its inspection and Columba only insisted on removing the hay-stuffed pillow and searching for a suitable stone to replace it, to the surprise of his companions. This was his only modification. Next they went to the church, and when they entered in, it appeared even bigger that it had on the outside. As they all looked with awe on the ambitious structure, Mobhi sprang a surprise question on them,

"If I were able to offer you this big church, filled with something of your choice, what would you choose to fill it with?"

Cainnech immediately looked at Mobhi and said,

"Books of course! Enough books of the sacred scriptures and other religious writings for the sons of life to learn, and for teaching all of Ériu."

Ciaran frowned for a moment, and he said,

"No, I hear singing, and would like it filled with choirs of singing men who would fill this church with praises all day long and who would make the hours of the church be a continuous sound of praise."

"And you Comghall?" Mobhi asked. Comghall hesitated for a few moments then replied,

"I wish it would contain all the suffering and illness that afflicts the people, all the leprosy and sores, so that I could bear them instead of the people, for Christ's sake."

"Well spoken Comghall! And you Columba?" asked Mobhi.

"Without a doubt I shall have it filled with silver and gold." Columba declared.

Four heads all turned to Columba at once; surprised at such an answer from their holy and prayerful, spiritually-minded friend.

"Silver and gold? Why?"

"Be practical! Be sensible!" said Columba. "I'll need it all to purchase wood to build churches, schools, monasteries and infirmaries, and to buy medicine and herbs. I'll need it to provide the churches with reliquaries for the saints' relics, shrines for the holy books, croziers for the bishops, also chalices and other cruets of the altar. I want God to have the best that can be offered. Would we use earthenware crocks on God's holy table when we sup from silver in our own houses? So I need silver and gold. These things do not materialize from nothing!"

"Yes, a good choice, Columba" Mobhi praised him, "We were getting a little carried away with ideals and you have recalled us to reality . . ."

A bell started pealing outside,

". . . and the reality now is vespers" Mobhi continued.

"And after that supper!" Comghall whispered with a wink to Columba. "Today is a feast day."

"Is it? What feast?" Columba asked, unaware of it being a feast day to his knowledge.

"Haven't you heard of the Feast of the Return of the Prodigal Son?" Comghall answered with a grin.

Soon their strong young voices lifted in praise filled the church almost as if in fulfilment already of Ciarán's wish. Maybe it was coincidence, maybe it was accident, maybe it was planned, but the Psalm appointed for that evening was Psalm 133: "*Behold how good and how lovely it is: when brothers live together in unity*".

The rhythm of Columba's days at Glas Naion was soon established, a disciplined sharing of the day between prayer, labor in the fields to grow their own food, study and the copying of books—an ever-urgent task if Cainnech's wish were to come true. They devoured books with their minds at such a rate, it was hard to keep up the supply and there was ever a sharing and borrowing and copying between different monasteries round about. Mobhi had had a long row of wooden nails hammered onto the walls of the new Scriptorium, in faith that they would all be filled soon; only half so far had leather book satchels hanging from them.

That September was a month of unseasonable weather: of thunder and sudden storms, trees losing their leaves early and rain. The Tolka River that divided the two halves of their settlement swelled to three times its size on one day of very heavy rain. When the bell pealed—very far-away sounding through the wind and rain, much weaker and feebler than usual—for matins at midnight, Columba and his three companions rose to cross over the ford to the church. But no ford could be found. The water was deep and rushing past them at quite a speed. Cainnech, Comghall and Ciarán sleepily said,

"Mobhi will not expect us under these conditions; we will say our hours in our own cells" and they returned each to his cell.

Columba stood still debating within himself and prayed,

"Lord, is it safe? I want to worship you. I have a strong desire to be with my brethren on the other side, and they are expecting me to lead the singing. I commend myself to your keeping."

He heard the bell stop and made a dash through the racing waters, which came up to his chest and ran up the hill to the chapel oblivious of his coldness and wetness and arrived dripping wet but almost on time to take his place and join in leading the singing. He smiled as he remembered the dripping wet nights in his half-constructed hut at Maigh Bhile, his initiation. So there was a soldier's training for him here too; a soldier expects to endure hardship, and how willingly when for the sake of praising Jesus Christ his Lord.

Mobhi summoned Columba to him one day. Columba went gladly, pondering as he went that of all men, Mobhi was the one whose orders he most gladly obeyed. He knew the man liked him, cared for him, understood him, was partly as a father to him, but above all a spiritual advisor. Finnian of Maigh Bhile had been his stern taskmaster; Finnian of Cluain Ioraird had been his beloved, saintly abbot and role model; Mobhi was truly his *anamchara*, his soul-friend. The cell was dark but lit by the small rush lamp. Mobhi smiled at Columba:

"Columba, you are long overdue for confessing to me. Take time here in the quietness by yourself, away from your work, your own cell, your companions, and search your heart for what you feel you should confess. I would like you to take in the whole period since we met. This is an important part of your preparation for your future work for God."

So Columba sat in silence, and in prayer "*Search me O Lord and try me and see if there be any wickedness in me.*"

This was a painful process. He prayed: "Holy Spirit show me the ways in which I have sinned". Some hours later Columba felt ready at last to make his way to the church and Mobhi received him lovingly.

"I confess in the sight of God and to you my brother Mobhi that I have sinned in word in thought and in deed especially guilt lies in my soul because of my pride, my laziness, my vanity, my gluttonous thoughts, my anger and my lack of self-control, my ambition . . ."

And so the list went on.

"Columba, we shall take your ambition first, for I feel this is something important in you. Ambition is not really a sin, unless it is ambition for yourself and not ambition for Christ."

Mobhi looked to Columba for his response. Columba hung his head. He then told of the episode with Bishop Etchen, and was glad of Mobhi's nod.

Mobhi said:

"Well how about your ambition now?"

"I do not know. I think it is for Christ now and His kingdom."

"Have you tried to get rid of these sins?"

"Yes—by mortification, by prayers day and night."

"Have you admitted that you cannot of yourself get rid of them? Have you asked for the Holy Spirit's help?"

"That is what is lacking Mobhi—may God have mercy on me," said Columba.

"He will. He does. He gives fresh beginnings, Columba. See your time here as a fresh beginning. May he wash away both sin and guilt and fill you freshly with his spirit. May it be a fountain bubbling up in you to fill the thirsty in this land of Ériu—and even beyond."

"Thank you Mobhi," said Columba humbly, "I have missed your direction sorely since my last visit to you."

"Why was it so long?" asked Mobhi.

"I gave away my chariot, Mobhi. At Bishop Etchen's suggestion. I now walk everywhere, and this is a life of greater poverty than I had formerly been used to. Bishop Etchen is a holy man and I was happy to follow his example."

"Ah Columba, I understand. But tell me, I am anxious and eager to hear—what did you learn from Finnian? What is the harvest of your three years at Cluain Ioraird?"

"Virgil, Cicero, Plato, Aristotle . . ."

"No!" interrupted Mobhi, "Not the books. What did you learn from him spiritually?" Columba considered this question for a long while.

"That a truly holy man is a humble man and a loving man."

"I see Abbot Finnian's character there!" Mobhi remarked.

"Yes, he made a deep impression on all his students. You are right in thinking that we all gained more than book learning and scholarship from him."

"What things?" asked Mobhi. Columba looked round the church as if for a trigger to memory.

"God's asking is always matched by his enabling. I learned too that mortification can breed pride as easily as it can holiness—it must be slow death to self, for filling with God's spirit to be possible. I learned in copying Abbot Finnian's life to be stern with one's self but loving and forgiving to others—to do in fact to others what I would like them to do to me. I also learned to accept all life as a gift from God and then to offer back all we have and are and can do back to him. I learned while there from my brothers the trees who are strong for their roots are deep and they face the light. I also learned or rather I should say I am still trying to learn to face my demons. I am learning all the time, Mobhi, to honor my promises and my vows to God, but also learning to expect him to honor his promises to his children in the Scriptures and thus to give him all of me to belong to him and not hold it back. Oh, Mobhi, I learned so, so much more it is really hard to know where to start telling you, I have learned so much. I will just say to end that not least of the things I learned was that there is an inexhaustible well of power and love and grace available to us from God and that it is not in a high inaccessible vault of Heaven, it is here in the earth in which he dwells, he who created it."

"And here I hope you are also learning things," said Mobhi hopefully. Mobhi went on:

"We try to teach students that to have a flow there must be a connexion which is why we begin and end all we do here in prayer, in joinedness with our Creator and Redeemer so that we can stay joined the easier. Also we are trying to teach you to listen to God's voice without fear in your hearts but in total willingness to obey, and to obey joyfully."

This claim to teach the students new skills was no idle promise on the part of Mobhi, for each Monday saw, weather permitting, serried ranks of students sitting cross-legged on the grass while Mobhi taught them much about prayer. As they sat there peacefully, their natural wool habits pale against the green grass, he taught them the listening to God in the stillness and quietness of their own hearts and he taught them not just the theory, but he actually led them in the practice of deep contemplative prayer. He sorted each one out with their spiritual problems; he advised; he answered their questions. He was looked up to by each and every student, for they all knew that what Mobhi taught was what he had experienced in his own life.

Cainnech and Ciarán came to fetch Columba one day from the fields for it was time for lessons, colloquies, discussions, teaching. They fetched Comghall where he was at another place and together made their way back to the settlement from the fields. All four were excited because the subject that was to be under discussion this afternoon was one that was dear to all their hearts. In the gathering dusk, where they sat, the farm work over and so no waste of daylight hours being incurred, they sat and listened to the wise words of their mentor. But Mobhi on this occasion was concerned not just to give his own ideas but to let each of his students contribute something.

"So now, let me hear what your ideas are about how we can best carry the wonderful gospel of Jesus Christ to those who have not heard it. Let us hear your ideas on spreading Christ's kingdom on earth—to those in Ériu as well as those in Alba, Britain, Gaul, or wherever else we are called to go with the Gospel. Cainnech, I feel that you have something to contribute. Will you tell us first what you think?"

Cainnech stood up and turned around and faced his fellows and said,

"Well, I think the best way to bring the Gospel is to do what our Holy Father Abbot Finnian of Cluain Ioraird has done: for each of us to have twelve disciples, twelve monks who are particular friends and brothers of us who we live together with and then as we get strong as a little band, as a little family of brothers, to ask each of those twelve to gather a group of twelve more monks around them and so soon already the number will be halfway to a thousand by the time these next twelve have asked another twelve to join them. We will be halfway to three thousand. So this is a good way, I feel, to be reaching a number of people with the Gospel."

Comghall spoke next. He obviously felt quite strongly about the ideas he wanted to share and was raising his hand to attract Mobhi's attention.

"Yes, Comghall. What would you like to contribute?"

said Mobhi. Comghall took a deep breath and started,

"I feel the important thing is to heal the sick. This is what Our Lord has told us to do. We cannot be preaching the love of Jesus Christ and his death for us if we are not showing the love of Jesus Christ in the actions he has taught us to do. I feel this is an important thing that we should be doing. There is so much leprosy in Ériu still, so much sickness, so much superstition, so many people living in pain and whom we can help with our knowledge of herbs, and with our care. Also there are people who are needing food and shelter. I feel these are the things we should be bring-ing as our Gospel before we have the right to be actually preaching the words." They all nodded.

A monk called Fergus spoke next. And Fergus said firmly,

"Well I still believe preaching is our first and most important task. Although I would like to say that I believe preaching is not just for those who are not converted yet, those in Alba. I believe preaching must be done all around Ériu. For although holy Patrick founded a wonderful church here, it is many, many years since his church was founded and many people have been falling away from their beliefs and falling back into superstitions, falling back into the old ways. Preaching is needed here in Ériu desperately. I feel this is the important thing that we should be doing."

"Ciarán—have you a contribution?" asked Mobhi.

"Yes," said Ciarán. "I believe we can teach the scripture along with oth-er things; that we should teach literature, teach science, teach philosophy, rhetoric, grammar, all the usual liberal arts, and teach the Scripture and worship and using the Psalms in church alongside all this so that the studies of the students are flowing into prayer so that they are studying what they will make into prayers for themselves. This is my idea."

Next a monk named Conor spoke up and Conor said wise words,

"I believe it is important to build on what people already have in their hearts. I believe we should find out what people's beliefs are and respect them, and try to bring them further along the pathway which they are already travelling. I feel that although some of the old ways are superstitious and silly, many aspects of the old way of the druids' teaching was good and it was in search of God. So let us build on where people already are in their beliefs and show them that the road that they have been travelling is the road to Jesus Christ. I believe once they have met Jesus Christ as a reality in their lives they will no longer feel the need for superstition and those practices of the old religion which are bad practices."

Mobhi then noticed that no more people were clamouring for attention, and yet his soul-friend Columba had not yet spoken.

"Columba, you have not contributed yet. Can I hear your ideas?"

Columba stood up and spoke in a humble voice,

"Mobhi, I feel that to each of us God has given our own way of bringing the Gospel. Different as we all are, we will find different methods and different means. I believe the way in which he wants me to bring people to Christ is twofold: I believe he wants me to preach and I feel I will preach the better for having been here at Glas Naion. But I also feel that my particular way is that God would have me keep in touch with all the head people, with all the princes and small kings, provincial kings, and the Ard Rí. I believe that it is not for nothing that God has called one who is blood related to every royal person in this land. I wish to use this for God. And as well," Columba went on, "I believe he wants me not to shirk interviews with those who are opposing our work. Just as I wish to face my own demons, I wish to face any Druid master who is opposing us, the Arch-Druid in particular," he said looking around and seeing quite a few fellow students nod who knew well of the Arch-Druid Fraechan.

"Also I believe that Cainnech, Comghall, Fergus, Conor and Ciarán have all said things that are worthwhile and true. We must get new monasteries but I think that is all I want to say for my contribution today." Columba finished. Mobhi smiled,

"Thank you. Those ideas are good; and each of them of course will succeed only when we prepare well in prayer beforehand. But let us now pray—it may be that the Holy Spirit has some even better ideas."

So they sat in silent contemplation for some time. The depth of their silence was broken only by the occasional call of a wood dove and the rustling of grasses in the breeze and the faraway shouts of some children in the village—sounds which only served to make the silence seem all the more tangible.

Only a matter of months had passed since Columba's arrival, when the peace of one early morning was violently broken by wails and screams coming from the village, just a few hundred yards downstream. Some of the monks hastened there to see what the matter was and to see if they could be of help. They returned twenty minutes later with long faces and were in conversation with Mobhi for some while, the other students hanging around waiting to see what had happened. Not long after this Mobhi had the bell rung and then called all the students together and addressed them with a solemn face,

"The Plague of Yellow Straw has broken out in Glas Naion village! This is serious news!"

There were murmurs all around and then silence again. What would they do? Mobhi spoke again,

"I must close my school and send you all to your homes, sad as I am to have to do this," said Mobhi. "Go now as far as you can from this place. Put herbs in your books, take great care in washing and stay away from places where the plague is rumored to be."

"And the village?" someone asked.

"I will stay and tend to them."

"Let us at least meet one last time for prayer."

"I feel it is cautious," said Mobhi "to say 'Go! Go now!' But yet I too would dearly love to celebrate the sacrament once more with you all my brothers. Is this your wish?" They all said in unison

"Yes!"

"Then let us gather once more around the Lord's table and be fervent in prayer for the village families who have been struck. I shall help bury the dead when you have left; there is no sense in having anyone else in contact with the plague. Conor and his brother Aedan who have already had contact with it in the village may stay and help me if they are willing."

Mobhi sensed that the celebration of the Holy Mystery of Christ's body and blood was a joy that was tinged on this occasion with apprehension. He preached a short homily on the words from an Epistle of St. John 'Perfect love casts out fear'.

"It is natural," he said in a tone of great understanding, "to fear what can remove with one stroke all the years of study and training and all our preparation in God's sight to go about his business. But we must remember that if he has chosen us for his work, he will look after us. Trust him!"

Columba now had a sad farewell to make to Mobhi now he was ready to depart for Tirconnel. Mobhi's flat hooded face was working with emotion he could scarce control as he said goodbye to his students.

"Columba, I want you to promise me one thing. On return to your kinsfolk you will be offered land. Do not receive a gift of land until you have received my permission to do so. This is important."

Cainnech was heading for Alba, feeling that this was where he felt drawn. Ciarán was heading to the Shannon River in the midlands of Ériu, according to Finnian's prophetic dream. Comghall declared his intention to start a school as previously planned at Beannchor. So Cainnech and Comghall were able to accompany Columba as far as the River Moyola where it flowed into Lough Neagh. Here they stopped, and here they parted, and here they each prayed for one another, and with sad hearts said goodbye. As Columba crossed the River Moyola he prayed fervently that although he himself was crossing the river the plague would not cross the river, beseeching God for freedom from that pestilence for his kinsmen in Ulaidh. As he went his way, sad as he was through parting from his friends and from the sadness that had arisen at Glas Naion, his heart became a little lighter as he realized that he was setting his face towards his future at last. He realized that at last after all these years of preparation he was about to be founding his own monastery and at last going to have the opportunity to spread Christ's kingdom in Ériu. As he went, Columba spoke the 91st Psalm, *"He who dwells in the shelter of the Most High, who abides in the shadow of the Almighty will say to the Lord :my refuge and my fortress my God in whom I trust. For he will deliver you from the snare of the fowler and from the deadly pestilence."*

6

Daire

A.D. 544

"Crimthann is here! Colm! Returned!"

Eithne was overjoyed to hear these words of her husband Felimidh and she made as much haste to welcome her returning son as her being with child again would allow her. Would she recognize him? Would they still be close? Would he be distant, a stranger? Was he a bishop by now? Were the rumors and tales of his miracles that had reached them true? Of course she had his letters but none of very recent date. The sun was in her eyes as she reached the gate and she could feel Colm rather than see him. What she felt was strong arms around her, a warm embrace; and a great vibration in the chest of his voice and his sobs of joy in between his saying,

"Mother! Mother!" The two of them were almost robbed of speech by the emotion of the moment.

Renewing of friendship with Eoghan and Cobthach his two younger brothers, getting to know his father and mother better, and hearing news of his three half-sisters, their marriages and their families, proved a total contrast to life in Glas Naion, Cluain Ioraird and Maigh Bhile. It was a whirl of activity and a time in which Columba had secretly to guard his privacy for prayer, saying his hours in snatched moments in the surrounding woods, his fellow worshippers the birds and on one occasion a squirrel.

"You still wear your monk's cowl, Colm. You are not yet an abbot?" Eithne asked.

"Mother, I have been a monk under obedience to the two Finnians, of Maigh Bhile and Cluain Ioraird and Mobhi of Glas Naion. But I have for the last few years been bestowed with the orders of priest and abbot. So very soon I will ask of you to have a white cowl made. I lack just the monasteries as yet, for my training is barely finished. The plague has closed Mobhi's school in an untimely fashion." Eithne drew back, her face full of anxiety.

"The Yellow Plague? Has it reached where you have been living?"

"Have no fear Mother, only a village half a mile away. I have had no contact with it, and I believe it will not come west of Lough Neagh."

"I have heard dreadful tidings of it, Colm. Forgive my apprehension. What plans have you now?"

"I long to start preaching and gathering some more men to live as monks with me, but I need to prepare first in prayer. Mostly I lack some land, a place where I can build."

"Talk to your cousin Aed, Colm. He is a good Christian as is his father Ainmire, your cousin-german." King Ainmire and his son Aed were at their capital at Ailech, on a hill above the northern coast, mid-way between Lough Foyle and Lough Swilly, where the huge complex included a magnificent stone cashel from ancient times, which they used to call the Grianán, or women's sun-palace. The cousins received Columba with courtesy and warmth.

"We will have a feast in your honor, Columba! But you are a monk, so how will we best celebrate your coming among us?"

Columba grinned,

"I can celebrate a holy eucharist for you all as well as a feast." Aed responded to this enthusiastically:

"Yes please, that will be an honor, to have a member of our own family celebrate for us. We will talk at the feast tomorrow about the possibility of some land. I expect you are needing somewhere to build yourself a monastery. I shall possibly be in a position to offer you something."

"Thank you very much, Aed. I look forward to the banquet."

Aed was Ainmire's son and Columba himself was in between the two in years but on the whole nearer in age to Aed. Columba was extremely glad that the banquet was to be preceded by the Holy Mysteries for he felt slightly unsure of himself as he had been out of this courtly life for a long time.

There being no church of a size to accommodate all they held this in the open air using a rock as an altar. Columba celebrated the sacrament with great joy. Afterwards seated at the feast with a frugal meal on his plate which he was set to make last for the whole of the evening, Columba looked around. The hall was full of colorful clothes, glinting of metal shields in the firelight, beautiful women as well as handsome warriors. One particular beautiful young woman was looking in his direction. Columba felt as a priest that he should look away and he did so but when he stole a glance once more at her she was again looking at him and smiling in a friendly fashion. Columba was rather non-plussed. He decided the best thing was to bring Aed into his confidence. So Columba turned to Aed and said,

"Aed, who is that beautiful woman who keeps looking in my direction?" Aed laughed and laughed.

"Columba, do you not know this lady? This is your own sister Enan, she has not had a chance yet to be presented to you. I will bring her over to this high table at once." Aed without more ado went to fetch Enan, seating her in his own place. Enan's reunion with Columba was a happy one and Columba now meeting her at closer quarters could tell that not only was she a beautiful woman but she also had the fiery spirit of his father in her, and he also, even more happily, had the impression that this woman was a woman whose heart was given to Christ.

When they were well on into the meal, Columba still eating small portions of his frugal dish, Aed turned to Columba and said,

"Columba, I can give you some land beside the River Foyle. There is a fort in Calgach's Oak Grove which is empty at present and you might find it a place in which you could build a monastery. I can make this land over to you."

"Empty?" Columba asked.

"A great slaughter took place there," Aed explained. Columba looked enquiringly at him again.

"Family feuds—the usual!"

"That would be a very great kindness, Aed. But I regret that I cannot fully accept the gift quite yet. You do understand that I wish to say yes and accept this gift; but I have to wait and think it over and pray about it for some short while. You do understand?"

"By all means, Columba. There is no haste."

Ainmire took the opportunity to speak to Columba warmly.

"Columba, your help is needed here badly. The people are going back to their old ways. We have no priest—as you saw, we celebrated the sacrament on a rock in the fields outside the fortress. We rejoice that you are back among your kinsfolk and also we rejoice that famous as you are you do not spurn us".

"Famous?" Columba looked puzzled.

"We have heard all about your turning the spring water into wine for the altar at Maigh Bhile, do not protest Columba! We also heard that you gave the credit to Bishop Finnian, but the truth of the tale has reached us even as far west as Ailech!" And Aed added,

"And also your cursing of the murderer of the maiden while you were studying with the bard Gemman."

Columba saw that it was high time for him to change the subject.

"Could I see the place that you offer me, so that I may pray about it?"

Ainmire and Aed both replied,

"Yes, with pleasure."

Ainmire then turned again very seriously to Columba and said,

"Columba, one of the reasons why I have called this feast in your honor is that I feel that although you are a holy monk and will not be wanting to spend an evening feasting and eating good foods, I feel that your presence here can be nothing but a good influence on our clan and our family. I would like to give you Columba—hoping that you would be willing to take this opportunity—the chance to make a speech or preach or say some words to the Clan Connall now about your vision for this place and about your life's mission. Will you do this, Columba?"

Columba was only too happy to do this thing and when the meal was over and Ainmire rose and a silence fell on the people, Ainmire introduced Columba to the assembled company and explained to them that Columba was here with the intention of starting a new Christian church, a new monastery. Columba then spoke. He did not speak for one minute. He did not speak for five minutes. He did not speak for fifteen minutes. He spoke for a half an hour. But to the people listening that half hour sped by as if that half hour was but one-and-a-half to two minutes long. The people were spellbound by the preaching talents of this man. But they were most of all captivated by the fire in his voice, by the inspiration in his words, by the vision in his eyes. They were also captivated by his demeanor: a demeanor which was at once that of a leader, that of a prince, that of a prophet and visionary, and—most touching of all—that of a man who cared deeply and affectionately for the whole bunch of them.

They never forgot that night, that first night when Columba preached at the banquet and transformed a carousing atmosphere into an atmosphere where people's vision was being lifted above their daily lives, being lifted higher, where people felt recalled to the love that they had once had for the Lord Jesus Christ, where people felt inspired to return to the freshness of their new-found faith. Columba made it abundantly plain that no-one would reach heaven on the faith of their grandparents or even of their parents but each must in the privacy of his own heart come to a faith in the redeeming work of Jesus Christ of Nazareth. His message was at once inspiring, challenging, and life-changing.

The next day Aed and Columba rode to the abandoned fort. Columba felt slightly guilty about this as he knew he was unable to accept the gift until he had had permission from Mobhi, but he found himself very, very excited about the prospect of starting his monastery and was wanting to see the land as soon as he possibly could. It was surrounded by an incredibly beautiful grove of oak trees. Columba stood there, taking in the atmosphere, listening to the bird-song. He looked at Aed for a long time until Aed was prompted to ask,

"Columba is there something I can help you with?"

And Columba replied,

"Aed, would it be regarded as a discourtesy if I requested to spend the rest of the day here in this beautiful place alone, so that I might pray here?"

"Not in the slightest, Columba. You are extremely welcome to spend as long as you like here. I will ride home now and leave you and the horse is yours for as long as you need it."

Columba tied the horse to a tree, and then walked round the oak grove: 'his oak grove' he couldn't help thinking of it as, and he prayed and prayed fervently that news of permission would come soon from Mobhi. He touched the barks of the trees as he walked round, thoughtfully and respectfully. These trees have seen much suffering he felt, they have witnessed the violence of the fort's conquest, witnessed too the rituals of the people according to the old religion. A sacred place.

"I must baptize it," he thought. "It shall continue to be a sacred place but one under the protection of the Holy Trinity. I can see this place becoming a really holy place. I can see people coming to it from east and west from north and south. Here we can baptize many Christians, train priests to make the Gaelic church strong once more as in Holy Patrick's day; here we can heal lepers and teach the people."

Happy with his exploration so far, in the oak wood, he walked up to the fort higher up above the oak grove. Again he stood still and took in the scene. There were houses of wood, furniture, drinking and eating vessels, all tumbled about, grain in sacks, bloodstains, signs of violence, a sense of violence in the air also, almost a ghostlike echo of sounds of turmoil.

"Holy Lord, what is it you will that I do with this place when and if it is Mobhi's will to let me accept it?" he prayed.

After a few moments an image of fire came to his mind's eye: purging, cleansing fire. Aed would not be happy with such a clean sweep but it is necessary if this is to be a hermitage, a monastery, a holy place. It will have to be cleansed for the Lord, he thought.

Anxious about Aed's possible reactions to this, he returned to his lodging, and waited, battling daily with his own impatience, and putting off the decision and the talk with Aed. Two weeks passed, during which he visited and prayed over the fort each day. Then one day as he was walking down the hill from the fort, to his surprise when he was half-way down he heard his name called from a distance. He peered through the trees. He could see two figures, who looked like monks, coming towards him, a good distance away still. He watched as they approached, and soon realized with joy that he recognized them.

"Conor! Aedán!" He hastened towards them with a mixture of pleasure and apprehension. These two monks were the two who had been left behind at Glas Naion to help Mobhi with the nursing of the sick people from the plague in the village.

"Do you bring good news or bad? Tell me straight away!" Columba asked. Conor sat down after embracing Columba and had a sad look on his face.

"We were directed here from Ailech, and to there from Cill Mhic Néanáin. Be ready Columba for bad news . . . Mobhi has died of the plague. We too have had the sickness, after we all three tended the villagers who fell sick with it. We recovered, but our beloved master . . ." his voice broke.

"When did this happen?" Columba asked sadly.

"A week ago now," Aedán replied for his brother Conor.

"God rest his soul. Had he the last rites?"

"Yes, from Conor," Aedán replied ."He was noble in his passing to resurrection and he had you in mind, Columba, for he gave me this." Aedán pulled a rope out of his bosom.

"Mobhi's own girdle!" Columba exclaimed, as he took the object into his hands reverentially. He felt with awe its worn roughness, and the crude wooden crucifix dangling from it. Conor continued explaining—

"Yes, and with the girdle came a message: 'You may accept the gift of land that is going to be offered to you in the north. You may start.' That is the end of the message. His intention was I think that you delay a bit first," Conor added.

"I know," Columba grinned, "He wanted me to restrain myself from rushing impetuously and energetically into church-building and monastery-building now that I am set loose. He wants me to take time to pray and to discern God's will first. He knows me so well! My soul-friend. Gone to his resurrection . . ." Columba's voice was husky, and he lowered his height and bulk onto the ground and the three sat in silence, scanning the distance, each hoping the tears welling up in their eyes would go unnoticed by the other two.

After a while, Columba jumped up.

"I was so engrossed in memories of Mobhi, that I have forgotten my manners to offer you hospitality."

"Have no anxiety on that score. Felimidh and Eithne looked after us well and so have King Ainmire and Prince Aed."

"What are your plans now? Can you stay and help me start up a church here in this Calgach's oak grove? I can now accept, you tell me, Aed's gift of this abandoned fort. But the land needs cleansing and I must set fire to the old fort first to purge it of violence. Can you both help me?"

"With a will! We can stay with you until you get the work established and then we thought we would travel down to Muredach's Island to see Abbot Laisren, he has a good name for holiness and prayer and we need to find a new anamchara."

"So do I!" Columba said immediately. "Let us travel to Inis Muredach together and prepare for this new work in prayer as Mobhi would have us do and then we can start the work. We will tell Aed now that we accept his gift!" Columba declared enthusiastically. Then his face became solemn. "But I cannot leave this place unpurged. Let us try to kindle a fire now and burn this fort with all its memories of violence and evil."

So they set to and found some dry sticks with which to get a spark. After several tries they succeeded in making a spark and soon they were all three bearing torches of branches, flaming at the top, into the fort. The wind that day helped fan the flames. But also—less fortunately—blew the flames onto the oaks surrounding them. As the flames crackled and blazed with an almost vindictive strength, Columba became desperately worried that he would lose his beautiful oak grove, a truly holy place. He raised his loud voice above the roar of the flames and the sound of the wind.

"Lord of Heaven, Creator of Flame, come to our aid! In the name of Jesus Christ, contain these flames that threaten to destroy the trees!"

After a while the flames died down and as Columba watched the flame he thought how the wind—the wind of the Holy Spirit—was able to fan the smallest sparks into a mighty flame. Even a little bit of faith, small as a grain of mustard seed, small as a spark from a rubbing of two sticks together, could be ignited and when the wind came it could be blown into a blaze which could encompass the whole of Ériu.

Laisren was by predilection a hermit, but already people were gathering to Staid Abbey, the monastery's shore base, to seek the hermit's wisdom and advice and to ask for healing, to get education for their sons and to read the books he had with him. So that his island retreat was no longer a desert place but more of a solitude within community. The wild weather in winter stopped boats landing, and so the solitude was more intense at those seasons.

Laisren was still living in the old monastery founded earlier in the time of St. Patrick by the Holy Muredach on the island called after Muredach, Inis Muredach. It was a wild desolate place, a wave-washed island with its small community subsisting with fishing and rearing sheep. This Laisren of Inis Muredach, with his pet name of Molaise, shared both of the names of a much younger man, the seventeen-year old hermit Laisren of Devenish, also called Molaise, as it was the pet-name for any Laisren. The Devenish Laisren was also known to Columba by reputation.

On a day of sea-mists and blustery winds Columba, Conor and Aedán came in sight of the distant island, which was about five miles from the shore. They made their way to the 'staid' or shore-base, and found a few monks there who shook their heads at his request. Sailing to the island would not be possible. Columba's disappointment was palpable, and he walked up and down, trying hard to disguise his obvious impatience. But hospitality was offered to the three and the assurance that Laisren—whom the monks called by his pet name of Molaise—would probably appear on the morrow.

While they were at the morning office the next day, as the prayers were coming to an end, Columba felt an extra presence in the small chapel. When the prayers were finished he turned round and found himself staring into the blue-green eyes of a lean, gaunt and imposing man. Columba was about to speak when Laisren spoke:

"You would not, I trust, wish to put my sailors' lives in peril?" Columba realized he knew of his impatience without being told. He felt rebuked although no actual words of rebuke were spoken. When the initial shock had worn off Columba realized he was glad. This was a godly man, and would be just the God-given restraining influence on his impetuosity that he was in need of.

Later he and his companions rejoiced in heart when after a quiet half hour together, Laisren spoke these words without turning around,

"I thank God for your safe arrival, my friends. And Columba, I am happy that you intend me to be your anamchara. Come here and talk with me. Tell me of Mobhi."

Conor and Aedán and Columba embarked on the tale of Mobhi's death, his instructions, his expectations of Columba's preparation for his mission were all heard with patience. Molaise looked serious and when he had heard of the burning of the fort at Daire—Daire Calgach, Calgach's oak-grove—said,

"Your cousin will not understand this; but pay no heed. He will see it as waste but not understand the spiritual dimensions. Stand firm, Columba."

"I will Laisren, I will."

"And Columba, you realize, do you, why Mobhi had you wait for his permission before accepting land?"

"Laisren, I do: Mobhi was my soul-friend for many years. He knew my impulsiveness, my impetuosity, and tried to cure me of it. He has been teaching me—teaching us all at Glas Naion—the importance of preparing in prayer for any great undertaking."

After they had all had ample time for soul sharing, hospitality was offered and accepted. A few days of retreat left Columba feeling that under Molaise's wise guidance he had started rectifying his besetting sins. Already he was using this familiar form of his name.

As Columba approached Cill Mhic Néanáin with his two friends on his return back, they saw someone on the look-out at the gate of the

fort, and again this person rushed out to them with an anxious air as if to be the first to bring news. So much of Columba's life in the last month consisted of people running in haste bearing news. Could this be bad news again? The manservant caught up with Columba at last, and blurted out breathlessly,

"Your mother, the Lady Eithne! Come quickly, the baby has been delivered dead but she is ill and they think dying! She is asking for you."

Overwhelming emotion gave Columba wings, and he hastened to where his mother Eithne was lying still, with her eyes closed. Felimidh, Eoghan and Enan were around her bed, Enan still cradling the wrapped form of the lost baby.

"Mother, do not be frightened. God can heal you," Columba said gently, kneeling beside her bed and holding her hand. Eithne opened her eyes and shook her head,

"No, I know . . . I . . . have . . . little time left."

She pressed Columba's hand.

"Look, over there." She pointed feebly with her thin hand and Columba blinked back the tears as he saw a white cowl folded up and placed ready for him—the white cowl of an abbot.

"Bury me in your new church, Colm, bury me in the oak grove Aed is giving you. God bless your work, my son."

Columba prayed agonizingly but knowing in his heart there was no use, her time of resurrection had come; healing was not the will of God in this case. What bitterness, that he administered the healing of God to others and yet his own mother lay dying and he was helpless to save her. Yet when he searched the faces of his father and his sister, they were peaceful, accepting. So Columba asked for oil and administered the last rites to the noble princess who had given birth to him, who had been the one who had had the faith to give him to God from his childhood, and was now dying in the prime of her age, after having made an enormous effort for the babe within her to be born safely but at great cost. No sooner was the unction administered and the prayers done, than they knew that she had breathed her last. Columba went to his father, brother and sister, and they all stood, heads bowed, arms on each other's shoulders for a long time.

Heavy rain plunged down noisily onto the oak-leaves and dripped ceaselessly onto the faces of Columba, Conor and Aedán. The three had prayed strong prayers over the shell of the fort, and now they watched as at the culmination of the prayers the heavy rain completed the washing clean of the place.

Both Ainmire and Aed expressed anger over the burning of the fort, especially the wasting of the food that had been here. Their anger was mollified somewhat by the ceremonial and honor-full burial of Eithne, wife of Felimidh. No sooner was the last sod in place over her grave than the blackbird started to sing sweetly and the wood and fort already seemed purged of their unhappy memories.

The rain came again on the day that the three oak-grove monks started work on digging trenches to build their new church and their huts. Through the rain their young voices could be heard singing strongly: "*Unless the Lord builds the house they labor in vain that build it.*"

The rain continued next day and almost all of that month. Plowing and sowing was greatly delayed that winter not to say forgotten about. When summer came the church was built and there were not only the three huts of the original brothers but five more huts of young men who had joined them to study and share in the work and the prayer. By early June, exhausted from the labor of building, Columba ordered them to take a time of resting to recover from their efforts. He ordered them, too, to let up on their fasting for a short while. The building had been all the more arduous since Columba had insisted on using hazel and alder bushes and saplings and yew wood which had to be moved from elsewhere for their building as he did not wish any of the original oak trees from the oak-grove to be cut down, but only those loose and fallen branches that were available.

"Aedán, the people here will not understand, but it is important that we baptize this oak—grove and make it into a Christian oak grove and it is also important that we respect it as an oak grove if we are to win followers of the old religion's ways to the ways of Christ's church. The name of my new monastery will, in fact, be Daire, the 'oak-grove.'"

"Columba you are right, and this is what Mobhi in his wisdom would have said if he were here now, I am sure of it," Aedán replied. Conor agreed, and pointed out,

"Columba, we have been so busy building we have taken no time to plant out barley. Harvesting time is only three or four months away. What shall we do?"

"Have no fear. Go and plant oats and barley now, I know the Lord will bless the growing of it, and He will give us a good harvest in September."

As the monastery grew, Columba's love for the place grew also, and it seemed to him as if his mother's fragrant presence hovered over the place, a benign watching spirit. The poor people as well as the sick crowded in and they were obliged to seek alms to buy bread and fish to distribute, putting the needs of the poor always before their own. Yet when the end of August and the start of September came the crops they had planted were amazingly plentiful and the harvest seemed to go on for days and days. The sunny weather likewise, so that many sacks of grain were stored in a small mill they had built beside a stream.

As always, new visitors streaming in every day brought news, and sad news among others. One such piece of sad news was the death of another of Finnian of Cluain Ioraird's special pupils, Colm son of Crimthann the monk who was perhaps another of the reasons why Columba had been nicknamed Colmcille, Colm of the Church as there were several Colms known to the people. Colm son of Crimthann had become Abbot of Terryglass and he had worked hard as his custom was—too hard in fact—and had succumbed to the Yellow Plague and had not recovered. The brothers said a mass for his soul and Columba thanked God for answering his prayer that the plague should not come northwest of the Moyola River.

The fame of Columba and his coming to Daire as his oak-grove now became commonly called, spread with great rapidity. Almost every day people arrived: to beg, to sell, to learn, to join the monastery. Columba's kinsfolk brought a young boy, ten years old, named Baithene for Columba to foster. Remembering Cruithnechan and the happy and holy influence that dear old priest had had on his own life, he gladly accepted the responsibility and Baithene his cousin was a delight to them all, a curly-haired blue-eyed lad, quiet and affectionate, willing to help and quick to learn. Happiest of days were the sabbaths Columba spent teaching the lad Baithene how to handle a sailing curragh, and Columba after five years spent inland was delighted to once more be near the sea. The banks of the Foyle estuary were a great delight to him. His thoughts and his prayers went out often to Cainnech in his preaching tour of Alba, Comghall beside the sea at Beannchor and his friend Brendan who determined to sail west from Ériu to discover the islands of paradise. He often wondered how each of them were faring.

Early in the morning before the other people were awake, Columba would rise and pray the new day in; and he would watch as the grey colorless light lifted and made way for a coming of color—the emerald green of grass, the bright pinky purple of heather, the silver grey of rocks, the pale creamy brown of the strand, the mauves and apricots and pinks of the morning sky. Yet even as he looked, so often, in the presence of his Lord, he would see a shifting, a new living vibrancy filling the interstices of color and sight, something more moving, something more like a dance. The scene would fade away leaving the dance to take its place and the song—always the singing which was inside Columba, he joining in with the angels' voices—was a song of praise.

Columba was instructing the new monks in the ways of his monastery.

"Discipline is necessary, for order brings the tranquillity which enables us to pray and study. Observe the hours carefully, there is no place here for sluggards."

He told them of times for offices, times for reading, times for prayer alone or in their cells, mealtimes, times for working in the fields, times for the almoner to hand out food for beggars. A young man piped up,

"And if a beggar comes later in the day?"

"Let him wait until the appointed time the next day", Columba ordered, almost exalting in his strictness, a spirit of rules taking possession of him. As the young monks dispersed he heard one murmuring:

"Hospitality should be the rule at all times," and was uncomfortable for a passing moment.

Some days later, knocking was heard on the gate after dark and the almoner was fetched to deal with a beggar, a wretched looking poor man. Remembering Columba's rule, the almoner did not dare hand the beggar any alms. He explained to the poor man that he was too late, the rule could not be broken; he must come again at the proper time the following day. The beggar did return the next day but considerably later than the day before. So again the almoner reprimanded him for his unpunctuality and refused to supply the man's needs.

"Rules were not made to be broken and the abbot has said that no alms must be given at this time of night."

On receiving this answer the beggar delivered a message that came as a great surprise:

"Go and tell your master that he has no right to insist on the observation of regulations that Christ has not made. Unless he deprives himself for what he spends on the poor and needy let him give to the poor at all times until God deprives him of the means."

And with this message, delivered in a rather authoritative tone of voice, the beggar departed. Columba at the time was reading in his cell and the almoner brought him the message. Immediately, Columba realized his mistake and without even waiting to put on his sandals or his cloak he ran after the departing beggar and begged his pardon.

"I am sorry! Come back! Come here! We would like to give you food and alms."

The beggar turned round for one moment, a moment of flashing insight for Columba. Then suddenly the beggar was nowhere to be seen and Columba had a strong inner realization that this man who had delivered him the message after having been refused charity was indeed Christ himself. Columba decided to humble himself in front of his brothers and told them of his error, explaining to them that although he would like all of the rules observed at all times if possible, that nevertheless they were to be always willing to make exceptions in the cause of charity. Rules must never be held higher than the demand of obeying the word of God and what Christ has commanded us to do out of love.

7

Droim Ing

A.D. 561

It was a soft, soft day. Columba thought he heard rain, but felt none. It was only the whispering of the young leaves calling the rain clouds to drop their moisture. So happy in Daire, 'Eithne's Oak Grove' as he now thought of it, was Columba, that he could gladly have spent all his days in that place. In that place where he sensed the angels' presence in every blade of grass, every leaf of the trees, and where he felt the tang of salt in the air, and always the call of the sea in his ears. But the flame of love for Jesus Christ was in his heart and the desire to spread it in his country and he knew of his people's thirst.

Thus Columba felt the time was coming now, a few years on from the start of Daire, to say farewell for the moment to his dear brothers there, to brothers old and brothers new, to his old brothers Conor and Aedán, to his new brothers Fintan, Fergus, Fionn, Urich, Aengus, Conal, Fachtna, Coirpre and Cathbad. Baithene his foster-son and cousin was almost now at the age of decision, and Columba felt that he could well bring the lad with him on travels around the country to preach and hopefully to found new churches and monasteries. Cill Mhic Néanáin, of course, must be his next place of preaching and Gartán and Tulach Dubhghlaise. Next came Ráth Bhoth and then the western seacoast. At all places, when Columba stood at some rock or hilltop to preach with his tall frame and his red-gold brows and mane of curly hair behind his tall dome of forehead and his tonsured head, the people would automatically gather.

"Look around you" he would often say, "look at those trees, these wild flowers, that grass, these oats growing, those ancient rocks, that soft and beautiful sky. Who made it? Who made all this? The one who also made the moon, the stars and the sun. He, the Great, the One Maker of all, came to us in great humility as a small baby, and as a man Jesus Christ. He lived, and walked this earth only a few generations ago, in the time of the great, great, great grandfather of Niall of the Nine Hostages. Jesus offers salvation to all who believe he died for them, for all who are willing to turn from their wrongdoing and welcome him."

Many did turn from their ways and to Columba's delight his sister, Sinech, came to live nearby with her husband, and Baithene was able to live with Sinech whenever Columba was on a lengthy journey of preaching. But when the boy had grown a little older he started to come with Columba on his tours. Columba brought him with him to Ráth Bhoth, pleased that the lad was growing so sturdily and feeling that he now was needing some physical challenge.

"Here Baithene, take off your sandals now, to save them; tie them together and tuck them into your girdle. Now—is not walking barefoot on the heather and moss one of the gifts of heaven?"

As they both took off their sandals on the grassy path, Columba put his arm around the lad's shoulders and said,

"Baithene, look—do you see that you are treading a path of jewels as royal as any king's attire—the blue harebells, the purple thistles? See, and yellow trefoil and white milkweed. And shining from the grass, among delicate pink tresses of grasses, seed heads as fine as any lady's gown. Well, Baithene, the beauty and glory of these flowers is but a tiny portion of the beauty and glory of He who made them!"

Ever practical, Baithene said,

"Teach me the names of the flowers then, Father."

As they came nearer to Ráth Bhoth on its green hillside beside the Finn river valley, Baithene getting more and more weary from the long walk, the lad was finding it hard to keep up with the tall Columba. Columba smiled lovingly at him and said,

"In honesty, Baithene, I prefer my own company on these walks. For to me they are a time of listening, of learning, of praying and saying the psalms."

"Father, I understand," said Baithene, "and I too like to listen and learn as I go along. I am happy to walk in silence."

And so the two proceeded amicably and harmoniously in silence except for the times when Columba felt the need to teach something to his young foster-son. At Ráth Bhoth, Columba found, as he was to find in many other places over the next ten years, that although the people were Christian in name they had departed from the true Christian faith and returned to many of the old ways. So fallen away from what the holy Patrick had brought them were they, that they were in need of a new preaching of the gospel of Christ. And this is what Columba did, strengthening what he found, preaching the Gospel of Christ afresh, challenging the people to give anew their allegiance to Christ and not to depend on the faith of their parents and grandparents.

One sunny morning after the office had been said, Columba was alerted by screams and yells piercing the early morning silence of that village of Ráth Bhoth. Columba hastened in the direction from which the yells were coming. He was met halfway by a lad running, a messenger running again. As he neared the lad called out urgently:

"Columba, please help us! The miller is drowned in his mill-stream!"

Columba hastened to the scene, and lifted his strong voice in a prayer even while some of the men of the village were lifting the dead body of the unfortunate man, his soaking wet garments clinging to his lifeless body. Columba moved over and knelt beside the dead man. He looked at the people's faces, a mix of expectancy, unbelief and sadness.

"Have faith in God! Do you believe God, Our Father in Heaven, has the power to raise this man from the dead?"

Silence—but a few of the women nodded.

"Do you know that in the Scriptures we read that Jesus Christ told his disciples they would do the same signs he did, only even greater? . . . He who believes, pray now in his heart and lift your voices now in a loud 'Amen' when I have prayed."

He prayed silently for a few minutes, the mill stream water quietly dripping onto his cloak from the miller's body. The crowd held their breath, many closing their eyes to pray as well. Then Columba prayed aloud,

"Lord God, Creator of All, and Giver of Life, we pray in the name of your Son Jesus Christ, asking that you would restore life to this man."

Columba laid his hands gently on the man as he prayed these words, and soon the man opened his eyes and a great peace was in them. The muscles and limbs of his large frame moved and he got up and walked towards the mill. Columba inwardly thanked God and walked towards the little building which was the church although it was in bad repair and they lacked a priest. The crowds followed him there and together they gave thanks to God who had the power to both take and give back life. Many asked Columba for baptism there and then and he stayed for many days teaching them.

Baithene asked one day, when they were back in Daire,

"What can I do to help, Father?"

"We shall see", Columba assured him. Columba gave the matter thought and had not reached an answer. However, when the evening came a monk came to Columba reporting that no plowshare could be found, and there being no smith among them what would they do. Columba turned to Baithene,

"Baithene, it will be good for you to learn to use your hands at this trade now as well as learning your lessons and copying books all day."

Columba led Baithene to the smithy which was still there from the time of the fort.

"But father, I do not know how to use these tools."

"Nor I Baithene, but the Lord does and he will guide us. Let is learn together!. We will get a good fire going first,"

Columba took Baithene's hands and prayed as he touched them that God would put into them the skill of metalworking and within a few days, with a lot of practice, the boy was jubilant, the plow was in use, and the people were thronging round his door with more tasks. And so Baithene at his young age of twelve became the smith for Daire—a lad growing in knowledge and loved by all.

A yearning for the open salt sea not fully satisfied by living by the River Foyle came on Columba, but he felt the desire was of the flesh and he asked many travelers about the needs of the countryside, to be sure of where his preaching would be needed most. Satisfied that there was a true need there, he at last sailed to Tory Island off the north coast, and founded a church there among the zealous converts.

After a preaching tour through all of Tirconnell and heading vaguely south-west, he eventually reached a spot of loneliness where the tall hills swept down to the wild sea. He was glad of the immunity his status as priest gave him, in the tradition of the Druids, the people allowing him to pass freely from place to place unmolested. He valued this freedom and aloneness for these were the times in which he could compose his poems, which he regarded as his own personal expression of his love for his Lord, his Psalms of Columba. Here too in this wild place the local people, mainly fishermen and shepherds, heard his preaching gladly and came flocking to him for baptism. Asking the name of the spot he was told that it had no name but was merely the glen, Gleann, in the mountains and that now they wished to honor him by calling it Gleanncolmcille. New churches were built and old churches were repaired all over the place as he made his way further south founding several more churches.

Passing along beneath the mountain of Ben Gulban near the land of Cairbre he had a strange feeling he had been in that place before—or was it a foreboding of the future? He built a little wattle hut by the Codnach River at Droim Cliabh and spent three days there in prayer. He preached to a small crowd who had gathered there but had no success in founding anything large like a monastery. However he left a small group of Christians behind him when he went away from that place. Wherever he went he found eager converts and he found also people who were already close to God in the mystical place of the west of Ériu and who needed only teaching about the incarnation of Christ in Palestine, his death and resurrection and the chance to read the Gospels for themselves. Their fathers had heard the Gospel from the blessed Muirdeach of Inis Muredach but they now lacked a priest and had fallen away. He stayed there several months baptizing and patiently teaching the converts to read and write. He wished heartily he could organise a monastery but no young men came forward, only families and farmers. Maybe one day he would found a monastery in that place, he thought. He left them constructing a church when he pushed on south. Now his hope was to hug the seacoast so that he could eventually find an island where he knew there was a very holy hermit. Enda was the name of the hermit and his ambition to meet with Enda was not successful for many years to come. He did not manage to find it on this particular pilgrimage.

Next Columba went to Rathcroghan to visit his kinsman Duach the King of Connaught and had good speech with him and with his young son Curnan with whom Columba delighted in playing—as he delighted always in playing with and speaking with all young people and children. The coast was a great delight to Columba when he finally reached it, for the beauty of it was outstanding and he thrilled to climb the high Reek of Patrick overlooking the lovely Clew Bay.

Columba entered into the spirit of Patrick's pilgrimage up to this ancient fort and holy place. This place was wreathed in clouds the day he climbed it and he felt it was like a Mount of Transfiguration. Once a place of merrymaking and dancing at the feast of Lughnasa—harvest season, Lugh's festival—Holy Patrick would have sained it already, for now it was holy without a doubt. The fort was no longer in use and Columba felt an awe-full sense of nearness to the living God there. A verse from Scripture came back to him: "*It is an awe-ful thing to fall into the hands of the Living God*" and yet also the verse "*in Christ we are made acceptable to the Father*". The mountain also put him in mind of Mount Sinai, and Moses beholding God's glory there. He praised God that as a Christian he with unveiled face was able to behold that glory as St. Paul had said and so be transformed into his likeness by the spirit. Much, much transformation was still needed in his own life, and not only transformation but transfiguration. He heard again strongly in his mind now the words spoken from the cloud on that Mount of Transfiguration: "*This is my beloved son. Listen to him.*"

Listen to him. Yes, listen. Listen. Listen in silence, listen in solitude, listen in the living temple of the woods, the strand, and the mountains. Teach me Lord to listen and to obey; to hear your words, your will and to put that vision you give me into reality no matter how hard I have to work to do so and no matter how much opposition I meet.

Times of striding down golden strands, the music of the waves in his ears, the shifting blues and greys of the hills and clouds all about him, were transforming times. Footsore and weary, he determined the time may have come now for him to obtain a chariot, for to keep in touch with the new churches that he had founded he would need a quicker means of transport than his own two feet. He decided to discuss this with his soul-friend Molaise. Home he went, visiting his soul-friend Molaise on the way. Molaise saw indeed the necessity of a chariot and discussed the whole notion of poverty with him, helping him to accept that the humiliation of eating bread and water when he was invited to kings' houses was going to be a necessity for him if he was going to have a chariot for one luxury; that he must not let this be a starting to let down his determination to live in poverty for Christ in other ways.

So by the next journey he had acquired a new Pegasus and a chariot, his cousin Ainmire helping out as usual. He made his way to a place Ainmire had recommended in the center of Ériu, a place called Dairmhá or the Plain of the Oaks. Here he had good conversations with Aed the son of the prince of Tethbagh. This Aed was very happy to give him a good and rich tract of land on the plain of the oaks which Columba was equally happy to accept straight away having a feeling deep inside him that this place was going to be one of his most important foundations.

Many journeys, many years passing, many new churches, many baptisms, many monasteries. Besides the large monasteries of Daire and Dairmhá, there were smaller churches at Sórd, Ceanannas Mor, Rathlin Island, Tory Island, Lambay Island, Drumcolm, Skreen, Kilglass, and Drumholme to name but a few. His kinsfolk of the Laigin royal blood helped him too. Ainmire kept him in chariots and charioteers for Molaise had told him of Bishop Etchen's holy example and they both felt that already Columba had learned enough the lessons in humility that Bishop Etchen had intended. Molaise was amazed that the man could have achieved so much on foot and both men felt more than willing to let him have the help of a chariot from now on. Molaise was also amazed at his next report from Columba that he was having such an effect on kings and princes that they gave him gifts of stock and tools and lands for building monasteries on and yet in spite of this fact he had no pride because of it but just a love, a humility, and leadership, also a zeal that made young men follow, a zeal that fired them with the same love for Jesus Christ that he had and the same vision of God living in His creation.

The young men trained by Columba had this same desire to awaken men and open their eyes to their Lord's presence all around them and to goodness, prayer and holiness. Molaise felt humbled by his position as Columba's soul-friend and felt that he himself needed to confess to Columba and yet he also felt instinctively that Columba did need a senior, did need a control over his impetuosity, he did need someone to oversee his spiritual growth or rather to channel it for it resembled a waterfall more than it did a plant. Both Molaise and Columba laughed the day they shared this insight. Columba told Molaise that he resembled the island on which he lived: still and peaceful in the sunshine, full of treasure but given to sudden storms, inaccessible in many weathers.

Columba happened to be at Cluain Ioraird visiting his dear old Abbot Finnian, now aged ninety-five, in time to be told that a synod of abbots was to be held not too far away at the Hill of Uisneach. Columba attended this with Finnian and was able to be a support and attendant to the aging abbot. Bishop Finnian of Maigh Bhile was also there.

"Greetings, Columba!" said Bishop Finnian.

"I hear, Bishop Finnian, that you are just back from Rome. How was your visit to that place? I long to hear news of it."

"Columba, I thought that you yourself intended to visit Rome?"

Columba replied,

"Yes I did intend to but there was too much work for me to do here in Ériu. I had no time for pilgrimage, maybe some other time."

Bishop Finnian pressed Columba to visit him at the place where he was staying, a monastery founded by him at a place called Droim Ing. Columba accepted the invitation with alacrity, being extremely eager not only to learn about his travels but also to see a book of Psalms that Finnian had told him he had brought back with him.

"The Blessed Jerome has made this wonderful new translation of the Psalms, Columba," Bishop Finnian told him with enthusiasm, "and he has made this translation with the greatest of scholarship. We know well his first Psalter which was a translation into Latin of the Septuagint Bible, the Greek version of the Old Testament. But now this new Psalter is the revision that the Blessed Jerome has made after studying Origen's Hexapla, that elaborate edition with six different versions in parallel columns. Jerome has made a comparative study of the Greek and the Hebrew sources and he also has written in rubrics, little one-sentence spiritual interpretations, he has written in titles, he has written in liturgical notes. So I can tell you, Columba, this Psalter is an actual treasure!"

There were many happy reunions with his former fellow-pupils from Cluain Ioraird, all abbots now, although Ciarán was very sadly missed owing to his death the previous year. His great monastery of Cluain Mhic Nós was still being built—seven years it was in the building—but Ciarán had died the year after it was founded, which was a great sadness to all. The new Abbot pressed Columba to visit him on some future occasion.

Bishop Finnian was at the door of his lodging when Columba arrived at Droim Ing. He said to the monk who was standing beside him in the door,

"I see Columba approaching, and as he comes, just as he came to me at Maigh Bhile many years ago I see the angel of the Lord accompanying his journey."

The two of them walked to meet him.

"Columba, I bid you welcome. May your staying here be blessed—a blessing to you and a blessing to me and a blessing to all our brothers here."

"Thank you Finnian!"

Columba had first gone back to Cluain Ioraird with Abbot Finnian to see him safely home before he made his way to Bishop Finnian. When he finally arrived to Bishop Finnian at Droim Ing and saw the Psalter, he was both full of admiration and full of cupidity. The Psalter was indeed just as precious as Finnian had described it. The Psalter of St. Jerome that he had so painstakingly put together; Columba felt so excited by it. Columba felt he would not only dearly like a copy to bring home to Daire for the teaching of his own monks and scholars, but he felt he must have such a copy! He felt it urgently! Now that this new translation was in existence it would be a shame not to be disseminating it further, he rationalized, and letting it be more widely known by those who cared about such scholarship and also taking spiritual advantage from the rubrics and liturgical instructions that were there.

But Columba knew his old master well enough from of old to know that he was unlikely to respond kindly to a request to copy it. In a few years' time maybe he would, but not now—not while it was so newly in his possession. So the order of Columba's days at Droim Ing with Finnian was: helping in the work of the fields, helping to visit the sick and distribute alms, joining in the monks' prayers, and reading and writing in the Scriptorium, by day. Then by night, a double life: a few hours sleep with a sharpish stone in his back to wake him in the small hours. Then when all were asleep he rose and quietly went to the church to write and write—to write with his borrowed quill on borrowed parchment by the light of a borrowed rushlight.

Columba wrote in an urgency. He saved time by adding very little decoration to his capitals at the start of each page. As he wrote he whispered to himself snatches of the psalms concerning the Scriptures from the Hebrew alphabet psalm rather like his own alphabet poem he once composed while with Gemman. *"Your statutes have become my songs in the house of my pilgrimage . . . Your commands are my delight, they are my counselors in my defense . . . I am humbled to the dust . . . O give me life according to your word . . . How sweet are your words to my tongue, sweeter than honey to my mouth . . . The unfolding of your word gives light. It gives understanding to the simple . . . Open my eyes that I may behold wondrous things out of your law."*

All went smoothly with this work of copying by night, a work which Columba did in the second half of his stay with a tame bird with which he had made friends sitting beside him. But on the last night when Columba had just reached Psalm 148—only two more psalms to go—something happened. He was racing with his pen and pushing himself: he felt he could just get it done before the bell for prime if he hurried. Scratch, scratch . . . careful not to spill the ink . . ."*Praise him all his angels. O, praise him all his host. Praise him sun and moon. Praise him all you stars of light. Praise him you highest heaven.*" O sweet Lord, help me complete this task! Help me so that my monks too may have the benefit of the scholarship of the holy Jerome . . ."*Let Israel rejoice in him that made him. Let them praise him in the dance. Let them sing his praise with timbrel and with harp, for the Lord takes delight in his people . . .*"

Columba did not hear the sound of someone approaching the door from outside, as he was so engrossed in his task and also so on the edge of sleep, a weariness dragging him down while his strong will was pulling himself up. He sensed the presence of someone only when he heard a slight noise on the other side of the door, the church-door which he had carefully locked. Angry, mostly with himself, he sent the tame bird flying off to the keyhole.

"Go and look through the keyhole!" he commanded the bird. Immediately a yowl of pain could be heard the other side of the door. The bird had put its sharp beak through the hole and injured the eye of the person who was looking through. This was not quite what Columba intended. But soon the noise was gone and Columba returned to his writing but only moments later still totally engrossed in trying to finish the Psalter, he felt a presence beside him and looked up. There was Finnian behind him, Finnian's harsh voice saying,

"Columba! Crimthann, rather, you young fox! How dare you copy my Psalm book without my permission!"

"What was the point of my asking permission if I were certain it would not be granted?" replied Columba equally angrily, his grey eyes blazing. Columba had started bundling the loose pages into a leather book-satchel hanging at his side.

"Hand my psalter over this minute and also your copy!" Bishop Finnian commanded. Columba hesitated at first but Finnian looked him in the eye in such an authoritative way that Columba felt it hard to withstand his old Master. He fought within himself. Finnian then spoke again, equally sternly.

"Columba I have healed the lad's eye who brought me the message. Harder it will be to heal your breach of trust and the effrontery of what you have done. Now hand over my Psalter and also your copy." Columba very slowly and very reluctantly handed the Psalter and the satchel of vellum manuscripts over to Finnian, saying,

"You may keep the copy of the Psalter for now but I would like to take this case to law. Let Diarmit, Ard Ri of Ériu, judge between us. The word of God is too important for just one man to own it."

Finnian saw the wisdom of this and feeling that he had an excellent case himself, he calmed down somewhat, but there was still an anger and tension between them. Finnian said,

"As an abbot of older years to you Columba and as your former teacher, I would like to impose a penance on you of prayer and fasting for a week."

They then joined in vespers with the other monks who had been waiting tactfully at the door of the church and not venturing to enter having heard the Abbot's voice raised in anger. After vespers each went to his own cell. In the morning when tempers had cooled a little, they discussed the Fes Teamhair. There had been much talk about this triennial fes or festival which was now taking place. The abbots had not received invitations to attend the fes this year, and the reason for their lack of invitation was fairly plain in the mind of Columba. So he was pleased that he was going to have an opportunity to witness for himself the doings of Diarmit, son of Cerbal, Ard Rí of Ériu, who, it was rumoured, had now three, if not four, wives, and was taking all his advice from the Arch-Druid Fraechan. How many of the old ways was Dairmit receding back into, this nominally Christian king? The Fes at Teamhair would already be in progress for this fes was a week's length. Today, in fact, was the day before Samhain and the Fes traditionally was held for the three days preceding Samhain, the day of Samhain itself—which was called 'The Feast of All Souls' by the church—and three days afterwards. So if they were to reach there in time, they had better make haste. They were particularly keen to do so for it would be at Samhain that the rites of the old religion would traditionally have taken place. How deep did Diarmit's Christianity go?

8

Teamhair

A.D. 561

Finnian and Columba arose early. It was a still morning and the bare branches of the trees stood sturdily as the grey and silver clouds moved past them. Sounds of humming were heard as they approached the barn. A junior monk from the Droim Ing monastery named Cormac was busy outside the barn harnessing a horse into the chariot in which Finnian and Columba were about to go to Teamhair. Ironic it was that the servant leading them to the place would be named Cormac after the actual builder of Teamhair itself. What was called a chariot was really just a little cart. Columba's own chariot was to be left there for his return. Finnian's horse stood obediently between the shafts, his breath clouding on the cold air. Cormac would be the charioteer, and Finnian and Columba and the two Psalters were placed side by side in the back. Finnian felt he had to bring his original Psalter, for in his possessiveness of it he no longer was able to trust it in the church.

They were on the point of setting out when they heard the gate of the enclosure burst open, and a breathless monk arrived. They noticed he was wearing the white cowl of an Abbot. To their surprise it was their fellow Abbot, and Columba's fellow-scholar from Cluain Ioraird days, Rhodan.

"Rhodan! Welcome! We are on the point of departing for Teamhair. Have you pressing business or do you wish to accompany us?" said Finnian.

"I came to see the Psalter of St. Jerome, Finnian, which you told us about at Uisneach," Rhodan replied, "but it is my pleasure to find you here too, Columba!"

Columba remained silent and let Bishop Finnian do the explaining.

"The Psalter, Rhodan, is in this chariot with us. We are about to embark on a law case. Columba here has, without my permission, made his own copy of it, by working late in the church, instead of sleeping, for a whole week while he was receiving hospitality under my roof." He pinched his lips together disapprovingly.

Rhodan looked sympathetically towards Columba. Columba then explained about the law case from his point of view and Finnian interrupted and said,

"Rhodan we must depart at once. For the Fes is already in progress, and if our case is to be heard before the week of Samhain is out, we must arrive before it ends."

Rhodan looked thoughtful and then asked,

"Then may I accompany you? Perhaps I may study the Psalter a small bit on the journey with you?"

"By all means you may, Rhodan. We will offer you hospitality in as brief a time as we can and then we shall all set out."

So they disposed with the full hospitality ritual as Rhodan said there was not much point washing his feet as they were about to get dirty again on the dusty roads. Rhodan studied the Psalter huddled up in the small space of the chariot and there was a silence between the three men as they were bumped about on their journey, with their precious cargo of Psalm books beside them. After an amount of reading and studying of the glosses and rubrics, Rhodan made an attempt to ameliorate the atmosphere, as he too was sad that these two people who had had great love between them were now quarrelling. He suggested—

"Let us read some of the Psalms together!" With an over-eager smile," Do you all remember the Psalm of David about *"The Lord reigns. He is robed in majesty. The Lord is robed, he is girded with strength"*?

Rhodan's ploy was successful in creating a better atmosphere between the three men and the journey proceeded more peacefully after that.

As the three Abbots approached Teamhair, they began having doubts as to the wisdom of their coming halfway through the Fes. The place was crowded with people; there were people of every degree, every profession and both sexes. The place was a riot of chariots, horses, people and colors. Traders were taking full advantage of the gathering of people there and there were many shouting their wares so the place was noisy and smelly as well as crowded. Abbot Finnian looked distressed and said,

"Columba, I hope that your kinsmen from Ulaidh will be giving us hospitality, for we have no provision made for lodging while we are here." Columba replied with confidence:

"I feel sure that Ainmire will help us, and if he does not the King of Connaught is also my friend and kinsman. He will surely help."

While wondering what to do, they providentially encountered Prince Curnan, whom Columba knew well from his visits to Connaught at Rathcroghan. Curnan welcomed Abbot Columba with pleasure and surprise and Columba said to Curnan,

"Curnan, we are seeking hospitality. We have only just arrived. Will your father be in a position to offer us lodgings and the means wherewith to wash and some sustenance before we go to the hall?" Curnan bowed,

"Certainly! Certainly! Please come this way, I will find a manservant to look after you at once."

When they were cleaned and fed, and their robes brushed and aired, the three abbots made their way to the large banqueting hall which was where the session of the Fes was being held. At the end of the hall they could see row upon row upon row of people sitting there all in their carefully sorted ranks. Every warrior was sitting under his own shield which was hung on the wooden wall above him. The upper end of the hall on the left was full of all of the chief poets, the amran poets, augers, house builders, carpenters, professors of literature, Brehons, harpers, and horsemen, also the tánaiste or deputy professors. On the right there were the ranks of the third order poets, the historians, the raft-builders, the huntsmen, and the charioteers. In the center were the shield-makers, the smiths, pipers, jugglers, trumpeters, footmen, fishermen, shoemakers, distributors, chess players, braziers, physicians, mariners and king's fools.

In none of the ranks was there the presence of any bishop, cleric, monk or abbot—not even the coarb of Holy Patrick at Ard Macha. In the center on the throne was Diarmit, son of Cerbal, Ard Rí of Ériu, in his grandest robes, and his son Donnall sitting self-consciously beside him. A golden crown was on Dairmit's head. On his right was the Arch-Druid Fraechan. To the left and right of Dairmit the Ard-Rí, were the kings of the five main provinces or kingdoms of Ériu—Laigin, Mumhan, Connaught, Midhe and Ulaidh. Then beyond them were the kings of the petty kingdoms, not all of whom Columba could recognize. At a glance he could only recognise only the King of Caiseal and Princes of Dalriada and Osraighe.

In front of the king and the arch-druid was a large black cauldron over a fire. Columba took in the whole scene at once. The pot was empty, the whole atmosphere no longer had the clean new empty expectant atmosphere, clean and tidy, of the beginning of a Fes. It was full very much of the atmosphere that large events had taken place—the empty pot itself was witness to this. Heads turned in their direction as they entered. The steward who was speaking continued speaking and they looked for seats and not surprisingly found none, as all seats were designated extremely strictly on these occasions. However, some of the poets spotting Columba bowed to him and made space for him and his two companions so that the abbots sat among the poets. At the next recess Finnian found a steward and filed his case to be presented to the Ard Rí at the correct time. The steward informed him that two days would probably elapse before his case was heard. They also discovered what had been happening at the Fes before they arrived. The first two days had been spent with the Brehons reciting the Brehon laws, the historians reciting the history, the Ollaves reciting the genealogies, and many, many other traditional rites. On the day of Samhain on the evening of which the three abbots had arrived, the king had indulged in the rite called 'The Mating of Teamhair' and a bull had been slaughtered by Fraechan the Arch-Druid although Fraechan had very little following at the court, owing to most of the druids having become Christian. But this Arch-Druid himself was from Bhreatain and not from Ériu, and he was tenaciously keeping to the old religion and had gained the ear of the king.

They found that the dark of the halls was a cover for evil deeds. As they had stepped from the clean sunlight into the fire and torch-lit palace and saw the ranks of faces there, the feeling had not been right. The darkness was a cover for deeds that Diarmit as a Christian king, in name at least, had a right to be ashamed of. When Columba, Finnian and Rhodan saw that cauldron beside the fire which presumably had contained bull's broth now empty and then they looked to the face of Diarmit and saw defiance in it and also a trance-like quality about his son Donnall who was now clothed in the purple and crimson robes of Tánaiste. They also saw the brown eyes of Fraechan narrowing, his look towards them hostile.

Although the three abbots had been willing enough to join the queue and wait for their turn for their case to be heard, the case did appear to be heard with reasonably good speed and efficiency. However their waiting period was long enough for them to gather much in the way of news. They gathered that among the queens staying in the Griannan or Sun Palace of the women, there was without doubt more than one queen belonging to Diarmit McCerbal who by now in spite of his thin veneer of Christianity was openly practising polygamy. Right glad of Rhodan's presence Columba was and Rhodan it was who suggested that the three men should have a vigil of prayer preceding their hearing. For years afterwards Columba could never understand why in spite of this vigil of prayer, the judgment that was given did not go according to his expectation, and his wish.

"Bishop Finnian of Maigh Bhile. Abbot Columba of Daire. You are called." Diarmit's eyes gave away nothing. Finnian stood up, drawing himself up to his full tallness, and displaying the Psalter to all, while Columba held aloft his satchel full of the copy, as yet unbound:

"Columba, son of Felimidh, transcribed my book without my knowledge or permission," he said. "I maintain that his transcribed manuscript now belongs to me." Columba rose immediately, displaying his transcript of Finnian's psalter:

"But I hold, King Diarmit, that Finnian's book has not decreased in value in the slightest because of this transcript I made from it. Also that it is not right to extinguish the divine things it contained or to prevent me or anybody else from copying it or reading it, or circulating it throughout the provinces. I benefited by its transcription which I desired to do for the general good. I challenge you: has any injury accrued to Finnian by it, or has any injury accrued to his book? I maintain it was quite permissible for me to copy it!"

The Brehon law had been well-recited in the days before the Festival of Samhain and Diarmit had it fresh in his mind. So he did not feel the need to consult with any of the many Brehon lawyers sitting on his benches. He remained silent for a short while, the poets, the sub-kings, the Brehons, the charioteers, the many, many, many ranks of people there all holding their peace and looking at him for his reaction. His pronouncement was ready in fairly short time, for he had many, many cases to deal with and felt rather unwilling to spend a lot of time on this ecclesiastical case when he had his civil law occupying him for the next couple of days. So he stood up and with a rather peevish and irritable air declared,

"To every cow her calf; to every book its transcript. Therefore the copy you have made, Columba son of Felimidh, Abbot of Daire, belongs to Bishop Finnian. Next case please."

Columba rose up with his eyes blazing.

"This is a wrong judgment!" he cried. "This is an unjust judgment! No king can remain in Teamhair as Ard Rí if they deliver unjust judgments! You know the law. You shall be punished for this."

Columba turned and dignifiedly stormed out of his seat and made for the door, clutching his book-satchel tightly. Finnian and Rhodan followed on his heels, trying to restrain him. Columba had not yet reached the doorway of the large hall when suddenly he was hit by a flying object coming from the now open door. The flying object was not a weapon, it was a young man—Curnan. Curnan had a hurling stick in his hand and his eyes were blinded with tears. Running blindly into the Hall, calling Columba's name, he saw Columba coming towards him, through his tears, and he ran to Columba and threw himself against him calling out,

"Protect me Abbot Columba! Columba, I seek the holy sanctuary of the church. I am being pursued!"

Sure enough already through the doorway had come several soldiers with spears in their hands. Columba stood up and faced the soldiers, his arms around the boy, and declared:

"This boy has the sanctuary of the church! This sanctuary is inviolable, you may not touch the boy!" The soldiers hesitated for a minute, respecting the commanding presence of the abbot. Then Diarmit McCerbal on his throne, clothed in arrogance, made a sign to the soldiers, and the soldiers immediately threw their spears at the lad, who fell into a crumpled heap at Columba's feet, blood flowing from his body onto the floor. Columba was speechless. He knelt to touch the boy and pray over him. He signed him with the sign of the cross, and gave him what Christian ministry he could. Being dead, there were very few rites he could perform for the boy and the atmosphere of Samhain and a pagan Fes was hardly conducive to a miracle of healing and raising the dead. Rhodan turned to the King and called out angrily,

"King Diarmit you have already violated sanctuary in my church in Tiobraid Árann by sending your soldiers for someone who had sought sanctuary with me, and now you have done the same for Abbot Columba. I declare a curse upon this place!"

Rhodan became quite incensed with anger, carried away and started cursing and cursing Teamhair and delivering what he called a prophecy that Teamhair would soon be just ruins with grass growing between them. While this cursing was going on Abbot Finnian who had been remonstrating with Columba the while helped his erstwhile pupil to carry the body of Curnan outside the hall. The soldiers and other crowds made way for them as they left. As they reached the door Columba called out in a loud voice,

"I will avenge this unjust judgment, King Diarmit! My kinsmen of the Ui Neill of Tirconnel will help me avenge it!" Then even as they were outside the door they heard Diarmit give orders to his soldiers to prevent Columba leaving the place. When they reached the King of Connaught's lodging, they spoke to the many servants there who had all gathered and were full of anxiety and shock and exchanging news of what had happened to their master's son.

As the servants were cleaning the body of the young prince Curnan and preparing him for burial, Columba gathered from the servants what the whole story had been. In a field beyond the many encampments of the bards, poets, Brehons and craftsmen, the young princes, sons of the kings and petty kings were having a game of hurling. During the game, the person who was refereeing the game had done an injustice to Curnan, in Curnan's perception. A great argument arose over this and Curnan's anger had risen. In his blind anger he struck one of his companions who had been disagreeing with him, there in the field, with his hurley stick. Curnan had not intended to do any more than hurt him a bit to try to bring him to his senses but the lad immediately fell down dead. Curnan's anger seemingly had receded and he had felt his only chance of safety now that this 'crime' was being reported to the king would be to run to his dear friend Abbot Columba for help. Some of the servants Columba spoke to had directed him to the great banqueting hall where the law cases were now in session, and the culmination of the episode—and of Curnan's young life—was enacted in full public view.

Columba now had a difficult decision. He felt impelled to get away from this place and to rouse his kinsmen in the North and have this injustice avenged, and have Diarmit deposed from his High-Kingship for having delivered an unjust judgment. Columba knew the law, and he knew that kings were entitled to be deposed if they delivered an unjust judgment, and he knew he was well within his rights. But yet he felt the need of this young prince for decent Christian burial was foremost and he also was more than aware of the presence of Diarmit's armed guards surrounding him. His knowledge of the King of Connaught led him to trust that he would certainly arrange a Christian burial for his son. So Columba whispered to Rhodan and the two of them agreed on a plan. Rhodan, Finnian and Columba faced one another once more. Finnian said,

"Columba, I wish I could stop you doing what I can see you are intent on. My prayers are that you would desist in this course. The judgment has been given, we have let the Ard Rí be judge of this case. Why will you not accept the Ard Rí's judgment?"

Columba looked at Finnian with sadness.

"Bishop Finnian, my teacher, please understand that the actions I am doing now are not directed toward you. My anger at King Diarmit, shared surely by yourself, is for his violation of Christian sanctuary, his open polygamy, his reversion to the old ways, his using of this Arch-Druid Fraechan as his advisor instead of a Christian bishop like yourself, as well as his unjust judgment. These injustices, all of them, should not go unrighted."

"Columba, allow me to try if I can advise King Diarmit and have him accept a Christian bishop as his advisor in lieu of this British Druid." Columba shrugged,

"Yes, Finnian, do try this by all means but do not stop me now."

Rhodan took his leave of Finnian and Columba and he set off for the kingdom of Dalriada where he had many contacts owing to his own childhood spent there and many kinsmen. He was Abbot of Lorrha in Tobraid Árann and he would return there when he had done some work of rallying some of the Dalriadans of Ériu in Aontraim to Columba's cause. Columba also took his leave of Finnian in some haste as he saw guards beginning to surround him in almost all directions. One of the current royal household servants found cloak and sword of Curnan's which he pressed upon Columba. So with the book-satchel full of the pages he had copied of Finnian's psalter over his shoulder and back, and the sword in his belt, and the cloak—thankfully a hooded one—over all, he no longer looked like a monk and was able to evade the guards, by walking along with a crowd of strangers, and making himself less tall by bending his knees. Warned by the servants that guards would have, in all likelihood, been posted to chase him up to his own kingdom of Tirconnell, that is the western section of the Ui Neill, he felt he should immediately evade them by going in a slightly different direction. So instead of heading north-west he went north-east over the hills to Mainistir Buithín. This was a monastery founded by the holy Buite, an abbot whose death was on the day Columba was born so that he always had a fellow-feeling about Buite although of course they could never have met.

9

Cuildreimhne

A.D. 561

As Columba's tall strong figure strode over the hills of Ériu, avoiding the roads, his first emotion was that of thankfulness. His thankfulness at having evaded Diarmit's guards he expressed in the words of a Psalm: *"I will offer you a sacrifice of thanksgiving and call upon the name of the Lord."* But he continued, pouring all his vehement emotion into the apt words of the Psalm, *"The Lord is at my side as my helper I shall see the downfall of my enemies. It is better to take refuge in the Lord than to put the trust in man. It is better to take refuge in the Lord than to put your trust in princes. All the nations surrounded me but in the name of the Lord I drove them back . . . They swarmed about me like bees; they blazed like fire among the thorns. In the name of the Lord I drove them back. I was pressed so hard that I almost fell but the Lord was my helper. The Lord is my strength and my song: and has become my salvation."*

On the long journey his mood of thanksgiving alternated often with that of anger as he remembered again the events in that hall. The blazing anger lent wings to his feet as he made his way cross country to Mainistir Buithin. He took no account of obstacles in his way; he went straight to Mainistir Buithin without benefit of roads. Maybe just as well, he thought, that he was not in a chariot that could be overtaken by soldiers. He had ridden with Finnian in Finnian's own cart, leaving his own chariot at Droim Ing as they were presuming they would be returning together. Let Finnian keep the chariot as his payment for the copying!

As he went he prayed for God's protection, he prayed for God's forgiveness for his anger, but he also prayed for God's help in avenging his righteous indignation against this king. As he went over the hills Columba was torn by conflicting emotions. He was agonized and grieved by the death of his young kinsman Curnan, but whenever he remembered King Diarmit's soldiers violating the sanctuary his grief would be fanned to anger, an indignant blaze, and his anger mounting like a live thing inside him struggling to get out. He knew his only hope for avenging this injustice was his relatives—those who would avenge him with the sword and the spear.

Columba's strong frame exerted itself and his long legs carried him with all speed to his destination, fueled by his anger and determination. If a hill was in his path he climbed it. If a river was in his way he swam it, throwing first the sword and then the book-satchel ahead of him to the opposite bank. His tunic and cloak became sodden with water, but he ignored it, but hearing the squelching of his sandals he removed them and tied them around his neck, enjoying the feel of the bare earth beneath his feet. His thoughts were of battles, imagining the stands of tall willow herb as soldiers awaiting the command to fight. And as he went he sang. He sang from the Psalms, *"O go not from me Lord, for trouble is hard at hand and there is none to help me. Many oxen surround me: fat bulls of Bashan close me in on every side. They gape wide their mouths at me like lions that roar and rend. I am poured out like water and all my bones are out of joint: my heart within my breast is like melting wax . . . . . . O Lord, do not stand far off: you are my helper, hasten to my aid."* He also sang songs of his own composition, poems to his advisor, his Druid, Christ his Lord.

When he arrived at Mainistir Buithin, the monks there bade him welcome and washed his feet. They also cleaned the mud-stains from his habit and fed him with oat-cakes and honey and cool spring water. Then, freshly washed and with his favorite St. John's Wort beneath his armpits for freshness, he made his way on the next stage of his journey. Monks from Mainistir Buithin agreed to go southwards to Osraighe and Caiseal and they also managed to lend Columba their old farm-horse, for indignation against the violation of the sanctuary alone was giving them cause to take up arms against King Diarmit.

Over the months, over the long months that followed the Teamhair Fes, Columba worked tirelessly to rally his kinsmen and others to the cause. In each new fort he would receive a welcome, hospitality, and a willing ear. In each he gave the same report,

"Diarmit MacCearbal the Ard Rí has gone completely out of our Christian control. He has done the Tánaiste selection ritual with the broth of a slaughtered bull and sits there with Fraechan the British Arch Druid advising him. Twice now he has violated Christian sanctuary. He flaunts his several wives openly. And now he has also delivered an unjust judgment."

Columba explained the unjust judgment to them, which was of course of slightly less interest to them than the other reasons for taking up cudgels against the Ard Rí. Each king and prince would ask him,

"Are you challenging Diarmit's High Kingship?"

"I did throw out that challenge to the Brehons at Teamhair, but Fraechan had some kind of binding spell on them, I could not rouse support there."

All the kings of Ériu having been present and witnessed the dramatic event at Teamhair was indeed a help to Columba's cause. Columba spent much time in prayer to God of a beseeching nature. His times of quiet contemplative prayer made way for a more earnest fervent prayer of supplication. In these months he spent little time at his monasteries compared to the time he spent at the courts and forts of kings. He spoke to the head man of each village; he spoke with the abbot of each monastery rousing the brothers to fight for Christianity in the land, and his success in the monasteries was immediate and easy. The monks immediately saw this as a fight between good and evil. He roused Connaught, and in Connaught in particular the support was strong and full as Duach the king, besides his hurt and sorrow over his son Curnan's death was also angry, was as indignant as Columba was about the slaughter of his son. Traditional rivalries were forgotten in this rallying, for Columba went equally to the more easterly clan of the descendants of Eoghan as to his own western Clan Conall. For these two sets of the Ui Neill in the north, distinguished for their chivalry in battle and at court, were both united in their despising the sept of the Ui Neill from which Diarmit son of Cerbal, the Ard Rí, was sprung, their cousin, from a younger great grandson of Niall. In the past there had been a treacherous murder by one of those Ui Neill, one Conal, and this was not easily forgotten by their kinsfolk.

For miles and miles around the soldiers were gathering. The word had gone out by fleet messengers that Diarmit McCerbal was marching towards Cairbre. Conlaedh King of Ulaidh, as a powerful provincial king, did not feel that he in person could take part. Ainmire was present representing the Ui Neill of Tirconnel. Columba's father Felimidh and Columba's friend Aed, the son of Ainmire, were both present and had rallied many, many men to the cause. The camp of the Connaughtmen and the Ui Neill and their helpers was based on the plain below the mountain of Ben Gulban, named for Conal Gulban, the eldest son of Niall of the Nine Hostages, and Columba's great grandfather. This grey and green mountain, its limestone rising majestically above velvet green slopes, dominated the landscape for miles around, and beneath this place Columba found his headquarters. His heart warmed as he remembered his former happy days in a small cell here beside the Codnach River at Droim Cliabh. Now he found that the Christians he had baptized there many years before had built a small church. Here it was that he spent his night's vigil of prayer on the eve of the battle.

As Columba stood with Aed, Ainmire, Ninead, Fergus and Donal, they all looked together over to the other smaller mountain, the Hill of the Kings, Cnoc na Rí. On its summit stood the stone cairn in which the Queen of Connaught, Medb wife of Aillil, was said to be buried. The Ard Rí's armies were camped at the foot of this mountain, which seemed too far away, but the next day they were to realise why this was. But when Columba was alone in the little church that the Christians had built at Droim Cliabh, he was attended only by some few faithful monks. The monks, Baithene among them, retired soon from weariness from their long walk south. Only one supporter was left to see the long night through with him in prayer and tell the story of that night's events in after years. And that was the manservant that had offered himself to Columba's service.

This young lad had arrived at the door of the church the day before, a sharpened stake in his hand in lieu of a spear. A young lad from no landed family, but from poor farming folk. A young lad with a burning love of Christ in his heart and a desire to serve Columba and the church. He was a shy lad too, and at the door of the church stuttered his request,

"Holy Abbot Columba, I am come to serve you. I am Diormit. Please . . . could you use me? . . . could I be a manservant . . . though . . . I would like to be a monk." Columba smiled and put a hand on the lad's shoulder,

"Diormit, you shall be a monk if this is your wish. But you have much to learn first. I see from your spear that you are a soldier. Now:

do you wish to serve me fighting as a soldier, or is it your wish to be a personal servant of mine?" Diormit looked at him with his shy eyes, fine eyes, hazel and sensitive; he found it hard to express what he wanted to say but the lad finally managed,

"I would serve you Columba all my days. Use me as a servant, I wish this; but please may I be a monk to serve God. Can I do these two things?"

"Diormit, you may be my servant if you are adept at finding food and also if you are willing to spend much time in prayer. Tomorrow is the time for fighting, but this day is the time for prayer and vigil. Are you willing to watch with me, Diormit?"

"I am, Master." said Diormit simply.

Columba prayed until beads of sweat were dampening his cowl around his shoulders.

"Lord God, High and Lifted up; Lord, Holy Three, the strength of my life. I take refuge in you, Christ the love of my heart. I call to you to avenge your honor. Lord, I call to you to protect your church, to pull back your erring servant, Diarmit son of Cearbal, from reverting to the old ways. I call to you to strengthen your children, and to strengthen your church in this land. Lord, I am asking for victory in the battle tomorrow." He had been praying for so long that he was drifting in and out of sleep. Sometimes his own words came to him, sometimes words from the Psalms, *"With the Lord on my side I do not fear. What can man do to me? The Lord is on my side to help me; I shall look in triumph on those who hate me. It is better to take refuge in the Lord than to put confidence in man . . . I was pushed hard so that I was falling but the Lord helped me. The Lord is my strength and my song: He has become my salvation."*

"Lord let not the spells of Fraechan have any effect on our men. Lord I beseech you to help us for we fight for right and justice and we fight for you . . ."

On and on and on he prayed all through the night. Columba had no mind to sleep and had decided in any case to pray an all-night vigil for victory. Nevertheless weariness overcame him there as he knelt before the altar, and he was unable to say with certainty—nor was Diormit—if his seeing of the Archangel Michael was dream or vision; but the message of Michael came through with clarity. Out of a cloud of silver-gold light above the altar, a living light, gradually emerged a being of flame and light. This being had a sword in his hand, he was a majestic presence. He spoke to Columba:

"You ask a large thing, and a thing which concerns the power of kings as much as the prayer of monks and Christian people. Your request will be granted but it will not be your destiny anymore to stay in this land. Your closeness to kings here is not aiding the work that God has chosen you to accomplish. Arm yourself with prayers and instruct your soldiers to respect the fence that the Druid will mark out and the victory will be to you tomorrow by the right hand of the Lord. Let it be known, that he may be glorified."

The morrow dawned as a day of mist. Columba cursed the mist roundly, presuming at first that this would be a factor working against them, but this was to misjudge both the military advantages and the Lord's methods. Columba then celebrated the Holy Mysteries for them. They celebrated this on the greenness of the plain below the mountain. As Columba administered the host to the chiefs of the soldiers his heart was large within him with emotion. His foster-son Baithene had arrived with a band of monks from Daire, and Baithene now was helping him administer the sacrament. Rhodan, too, was here accompanying Scandlan, the son of the King of Ossory, a fine warrior who had rallied with many soldiers to their cause. Great was the hush that descended as Columba led the prayer of consecration. And when the eucharist was ended great was their attention as he spoke to them of the reasons for the battle once again, emphasising the importance of them respecting the Arch-Druid Fraechan's 'fence' or force-field, which was along the Codnach river, the main river of Droim Cliabh, which regrettably isolated the church from Columba's army, but the little church had spiritual protection prayed upon it by Columba.

Columba lifted his voice into its most powerful mode, a mode powerful and far reaching indeed. He held the satchel with his copy of the psalter high for them to see, as he called exultantly:

"Men and women of Ulaidh, men and women of Connaught, of Osraighe, of Caiseal, of Cairbre, of Dalriada! Men and women of the right, of justice, and of Christ's rule! Monks and sisters! We fight today to avenge the killing of Prince Curnan. We fight today for Christ and against injustice, against the polygamy of Diarmit son of Cerbal, against his mating with Teamhair, against his Tánaiste ritual, against his using of Fraechan son of Temnan, the arch-druid from Bhreatain as his advisor instead of a Christian bishop! Against Diarmit's unjust judgment! We fight under the Archangel Michael's leading into battle! Remember that we must respect the arch-druid's fence! It is a forcefield created by dark magic along the Codnach river. Not one person must cross this 'erbe' or fence that Fraechan has conjured up, for their crossing of this line will be death to them! God go with you into battle and keep you in His care!"

And then the battle began. The satchel with the copied Psalter was carried in the front ranks of the lines of Columba's fighting men and women, lifted high at all times. With shouts, with war cries, with prayers of monks, with yells of women they surged forward. As Columba ran towards the enemy beside the soldiers, and among his brethren, he knew that these men were stalwart and strong; that they were angry on his behalf. They were stout men, earthy men; like the earth, solid, unshakeable. Columba blessed them once again and prayed there once again in his mind. Under the grey sky he felt that he was at an interface of earth and heaven. His men: earthy. His prayers: to heaven. In between: heaven's answer. The events of this day seemed not of a common substance but a reflection of war in heaven.

Even as they ran, messengers came and told them that unseen by the Tirconnel men and the Connaughtmen and their allies because of the mist, the army of Diarmit had circled the cairn of Medbh on Cnoc na Rí, the Hill of the Kings three times in sunwise direction even while they were celebrating the Holy Sacrifice on the green grass below Ben Gulban. Muddled in the mist was the battle, and not all had eyes to see a shaft of brightness—sunlight, or archangels' wings—that stayed in the forefront at all times. Great heroism and bravery was shown by the victors of the battle: Fergus and Domnall, Ainmire, Ninead, Aed and Scandlan. Maglaine, who had in foolhardy manner 'transgressed the fence', was the only casualty from Columba's side in the battle. Many, many were the casualties on Diarmit's side, and Columba only hoped and prayed that Bishop Finnian would not be among them, for he had heard a message, or rumor, that Finnian had been at Diarmit's side throughout the preparations for the battle.

Columba, bone-weary, walked among the slain on the battlefield, the bodies of those who had fought for the Ard Rí. As far as his eye could see there were blood-streaked bodies. In spite of the elated feeling of the undoubted victory, there was also remorse in his heart over the deaths of these men that he had indirectly caused. His fervor and fire and blazing anger of earlier in the day was giving way to a turmoil of mind and of spirit. He went to the little hut-church of Droim Cliabh to make his prayers. He knelt before God in silence, for now he felt there was little he could say. He offered a sacrifice of thanksgiving and thankfulness from his heart for the victory of the day, and he prayed for those who were hurt and wounded. He asked God to bless Rhodan as he now walked among the wounded with his great gifts of healing and enabled many to be made well and whole again. But above all he prayed for the dead and for the families of the dead, whose names he would never know.

Then Columba fell into a prayer of silence, in which he was not exalted into a high contemplation of God, so much as that he just returned to the breast of the Heavenly Father like a child needing comforting. He felt that he had now come to the end of himself, to the end of his own resources. He felt that all he could do was turn to God and trust that all he had read and all he had experienced already of God being a God of love would avail for him.

He did not know how long he spent resting in that healing presence that started gradually to seep into the dry bones of the innermost chamber of his spirit, remaking him from inside. That process was interrupted only once—for Diormit was asleep—by the opening of the door. Soft footsteps came behind Columba, and Columba, as was his custom, did not turn round to see who had entered the church. But gradually the knowledge dawned on his outer senses, issuing from a spiritual place within, that his visitor was none other than Bishop Finnian. He felt, rather than heard, Bishop Finnian kneel down beside him in front of the altar.

After some minutes in silence together in prayer, Bishop Finnian turned towards Columba. Columba turned to look at him too, wondering what he would meet. He found in his old master's gaze such a look of love and forgiveness that Columba felt humbled and robbed of speech. Columba opened his mouth, impetuous as always, but Finnian shook his head, and in that small action Columba understood that no words were to be spoken between them.

10

Inis Muredach

A.D. 561

E arly on a clear grey day, the mists of the battle-day now gone,
Columba walked towards the camp of the Diarmit's supporters.
This camp—composed mostly of temporary bivouacs made from fallen
branches, except for a proper hut for the Ard Rí—was now much nearer
to them, since they had achieved their purpose of camping earlier below
the Hill of the Kings by their circling of it on the morning of the battle.
Columba realized that this had been a factor in his favour for it had tired
the Diarmit's fighters before the battle had even begun. Sounds of snoring
reached him. He made his way through the bodies toward the lodging of
Diarmit, intent on cementing the new peace and ensuring that Diarmit
would return fully to Christian ways.

His way was impeded by body after body.Diarmit's septs of the Ui
Neill and their allies from Midhe and Laigin, dispirited after their defeat,
had drunk themselves into a lethargic stupor and had not yet bothered to
set about the task of burying their dead.

Columba looked from right to left and was aghast at the number of
dead, the sea of corpses. The plain of Cuildreimhne beneath that majestic
mountain of Ben Gulban was littered with dead bodies: all slain in a battle
that he had started, that he had initiated, and even encouraged. About a
book, yes; but far more than that had been at stake. As well as the unjust
judgment, there had been Diarmit's power and u unapologetic paganism.
There had been Fraechan's arrogance and hostility to the Christian faith.
There had been the two occasions of the ignoring of sanctuary. All of

these were legitimate reasons. There were of course family quarrels too, usually about land, as was so common in Ériu. But it all just started with the book. It had started too with Bishop Finnian's pride, he thought, and not wanting him to keep his copy that he had toiled night after night to write. His own pride rose up, hurt over this, yet again. But his good sense told him that if Finnian's action had been reversed, this victory would never have come, Rhodan's cursing of Teamhair would not have happened, and maybe, his thoughts went on, even if it had not all been fully necessary, God could bring good consequences from an evil situation. He looked again at the plain littered with bodies. Sorrow and remorse came crowding in once more.

At the entrance to the camp Columba was somewhat surprised to find himself greeted with respect by the guards. The commander came forward and Columba asked him how many were slain.

"Near on three thousand, abbot," was the reply. "We are now rousing the men from their sleep to get about the task of burying them."

"Will they have the Christian rites of burial?" asked Columba.

"Yes. Bishop Finnian is looking after that."

Columba realized that the respect with which he with his white abbot's cowl had been received at the camp showed that the marks of Finnian's presence and his influence were already being felt. Columba was greeted by a sobered Diarmit son of Cerbal. Diarmit offered him the hospitality of his temporary abode, sending a servant to fetch refreshment. They seated themselves on small stools, and talked. Columba praying hard for God to give him the right words. Diarmit reminded Columba of their kinship, and together they vowed never to make war on family members again. Columba exacted from Diarmit a promise that he would do all he could to restore Christianity to the land, and that he would continue from now on to use Abbot Finnian as his advisor. Columba tried hard to keep the exultant smile off his face when Diarmit told him he had already dismissed Fraechan in disgust at the failure of his magic. So the two cemented their peace that day.

In his exhaustion Columba had no recollection of returning to his own camp, but his next moment of consciousness was when he awoke in the house of a stranger, and his eyes were greeted by the full light of day coming through the chinks of the door. The first sound he heard was that of Diormit coming in and kneeling beside him and saying,

"Master!"

Columba looked at Diormit, feeling so happy that this lad, in whose presence he felt above all comfortable, was his new servant.

"Diormit, how long have I slept?"

"You have slept the day and the night through" answered Diormit.

"The day and the night?!" Columba sat up abruptly.

"Brother Baithene will explain, Master. He had herbs from your sister, the Lady Sinech, to help you sleep."

Columba felt very strange in this new and hopefully only temporary mode of existence where his life was no longer governed by the ringing of bells and the regular hours at chapel. He knew that this life where he snatched his prayers and where he spent all-night vigils of prayer punctuated by days of strenuous work; where his anger and fire possessed him as he marched round the country interviewing kings and princes and abbots, was not the right mode of life for him, for it was not the life he had been called to by God.

Happily Columba also felt relieved that the outcome of the battle in which he had the supernatural help of Michael, had not been that he had to take the High Kingship for himself, for he was pleased with the strong promises he had extracted from a new and sobered Dairmit that he would restore the Christian faith in his kingdom, with the help of Bishop Finnian. His pride and anger spent, he now felt humbled. Diormit stood there quietly and patiently awaiting orders. Columba looked at him with new eyes, and said

"Diormit. Diormit. I cannot call a lad like you my servant."

"But I am your servant. I am attending to your needs." Columba felt awakened from his lethargy by the lad's readiness for action

"I shall call you my attendant then," said Columba, "but I look to the day when you shall be among my brothers in a monastery. Diormit, we shall go home to my main monastery of Daire as soon as it is possible to do so."

Columba set out soon afterwards for Daire, accompanied by Baithene and Diormit and a few other brothers. The shadows on his spirit from the battle were immense. A gloom that not all his prayers could

totally pierce had descended upon him. Although his declared intention
had been to return to his beloved Daire, and spend quiet time becoming
a regular monk once more, he also felt a great need to see his soul-friend
Molaise. Yet at the same time but also felt too ashamed to do so straight
away. He could not get rid of the inner mental picture of the dead bodies
lying on the field of battle. The desire to be healed in the peace and quiet
of his own first monastery fought within him with the feeling that his
Christian duty was first and foremost to confess to his soul-friend. The
overwhelming need for peace and healing at Daire won this battle in him,
and he decided to postpone the visit to Inis Muredach for a few weeks.

Columba shared his thoughts and plans with his companions and
they willingly agreed to accompany him to either Staid or Inis Muredach
in a few weeks' time when he felt ready: when the beauty of Daire's oak
trees, the chanting of its monks and the river Foyle had worked their
healing balm on his spirit.

So as to avoid the mountains they took the coastal route and started
off therefore with a view of the mountains of Ulaidh in their vision. Their
view was of those tall blue cliffs, falling steep and sheer into the sea, Bun-
glass, Slieve League and the cliffs near his own church of Glencolmcille.
The land was so beautiful; it swelled Columba's heart with joy almost to
the point of pain.

They walked up the coast, discussing events, meditating upon
events, and stopping at regular intervals to pray the offices. As they
prayed, Columba announced that the fifty-first Psalm was the psalm set
for this day and they repeated this psalm at every stop for prayer. The
saying of this psalm went deep in Columba this day as he prayed, *"Have
mercy on me O God in your enduring goodness: according to the fullness of
your compassion blot out my offences. Wash me thoroughly of my wickedness and cleanse me from my sin. For I acknowledge my rebellion: and my
sin is ever before me . . . Create in me a clean heart O God: and renew a
right spirit within me. Do not cast me out from your presence: do not take
your Holy Spirit from me. O give me the gladness of your help again: support me with a willing spirit. Then will I teach transgressors your ways: and
sinners will turn to you again."*

Poignant indeed was the request Columba made to his God as he
sang with his brothers,

*"O Lord God of my salvation, deliver me from bloodshed: and my
tongue shall sing of your righteousness. O Lord open my lips: and my mouth
shall proclaim your praise*

... *The sacrifice of God is a broken spirit: a broken and contrite heart,*
O God, you will not despise."

The enormity of Columba's guilt and the depth of his depression
following the battle was all that prevented him from calling on Molaise
now. Not to be doing so was a breach of both friendship and custom, and
when eventually, weeks later, he felt ready to call and see his soul-friend,
the holy man gave the impression that he resented this 'oversight'.

The journey home to Daire seemed lengthy. Weary and thirsty,
Columba knelt down by a little mountain lake that they were passing,
and he and his companions cupped hands and drank from the brown
and gloomy depths which reflected their thoughts, letting the horses also
have a drink. The day was dry, but grey; the sun was hidden. But as they
rode northwards light broke through the clouds between two hills. By the
time they had penetrated further north and reached a large gap in the
hills as they forded a river, the light was now beyond them again between
the next set of hills, beckoning them to a future elsewhere.

Columba's thoughts, of necessity, dwelt on the future as well as the
past. His life for the last ten years had been a green martyrdom of choice,
doing penance for his sins by labor and fasting. The red martyrdom of
persecution and death for Christ's sake had not presented itself to him as
an opportunity so far. White martyrdom was what was now the question
for him. White martyrdom was to renounce everything one loved for
God. He had not yet chosen this. What was it that he loved, he asked
himself. What did he love above all, but this green and mysterious land,
this country of beauty and change and magic, peopled with poets and
pagans—people close to their soil. Could he renounce this country for
God, and go away from it as an exile, and as a pilgrim for Christ? Such an
act, for him difficult in the extreme, would be indeed both red martyrdom and white martyrdom. He resolved to talk honestly about all this to
Laisren, whom he now knew as Molaise when he was ready.

Some months later Columba felt a stab at his heart in coming once
again, with his foster-son Baithene and his new attendant Diormit, to
the wild loveliness of the coast of Cairbre, between the mountains and
the sea. He was ready now to unburden himself to Molaise, for he had
had some healing while in Daire. But Daire could not direct him; Daire
could not set a suitable penance; Daire could not decide what martyrdom

he should undertake. Gulban's peak with its long line of mountains behind which changed shape every few minutes, was becoming a familiar
land-mark.

Molaise of Inis Muredach's monastery was built within an ancient
cashel, and had stone huts to withstand the winter storms, and little cells
within the walls of the cashel. The journey over the sea to the natural harbor was smoother this day than he had known and the sunshine showed
the island as a shining and holy place. How he would love to live on an
island like this!

Molaise heard Columba's confession with a stern countenance. Molaise saw a broken man before him, and so he spoke quite lovingly when
he had heard the confession and gave absolution and penance. The older
man sensed the turmoil and crisis going on within his friend. When Columba spoke to him of his idea of white martyrdom, Molaise said gently
but very firmly

"Nothing less would be acceptable, Columba, as a penance for three
thousand dead."

Molaise looked at Columba, who bowed his head and nodded in
humility and acceptance. When they were finished the formal part of the
confession and were talking things over, Molaise had some advice:

"Columba, I have had news that this year at the annual fair of Tailltu
in the kingdom of Midhe, there is to be a Church Synod. As you know
the church leaders are trying to bring ecclesiastical synods, assemblies
and conventions to all the traditional places of meeting where formerly
there was the carrying out of old customs from before the coming of the
faith of Christ to this land. So the fair at Tailltu this year will not be ath-
letic contests only, but will be a meeting of the head of the bishops and
also some of the abbots to discuss cases of ecclesiastical rulings to do
with the monasteries and the churches. Now I have also had word about
this synod at Tailltu that the matter of your part in the battle which was
fought at Cuildreimhne is to be discussed."

Molaise paused and looked enquiringly at Columba to gauge his
reaction. None was visible. So he continued:

"The word 'excommunication' was actually mentioned to me by
someone, someone living not too far from here. My advice to you, Columba, is to go to Tailltu, or rather to go to Ceanannas Mór which is
nearby, spend time there quietly in prayer and, when the Synod is con-
vened, announce your intention of voluntary exile, of what some are calling 'white martyrdom'. If, after prayer and fasting, you still feel that this

is what God is asking of you, or what you would like to offer to God, I think that the thing to do would be to humbly submit to some spiritual superior and announce that your penance has been set and that you are accepting this penance as a penance of exile. My name has been associated with you for far too long, Columba. My authority for this would be respected, yes, but may not be sufficient. I would like you to go to a quiet place and prepare yourself under another spiritual director. A holy man, Enda of Aran, would be the best man for you, Columba."

Columba was still silent with bowed head. Molaise raised his voice now and said almost crossly

"Columba, you do realize that this is important, do you not? Because our work for God in this country is going to suffer if there is not some kind of public announcement of the grave reasons for this battle and of your sorrow over the deaths of your countrymen and of your intention to do penance in the strongest and most costly way possible to you. Go to Tailltu when it convenes, my son, but go quickly now to Enda of Aran. Do prayer, do fasting and above all, Columba, with your great energies do much, much physical labor. And I am talking now, not about fishing in the sea for I know your love of boats, but of plowing, sowing and reaping the harvest on the land, and of helping with building."

And so started for Columba a year of pilgrimage around Ériu, a year of exile from his beloved Daire, as a preparation for exile from his beloved Ériu. He made his way to many holy men in those months between the battle and the synod. He called first on an old friend, Fraoch, whose church was near his route. He was received in friendly manner by this hermit in his small church in its setting of flat meadows with no mountains around just a few small rounded hills in the distance. Columba learned much from his time with Fraoch. The hermit reproached him affectionately for having been the instigator of that murderous fight, and was un-phased when his friend rose in self-defense:

"It was not I who caused it; it was the unjust judgment of King Diarmit. It was his violations of ecclesiastical immunity and his unjust judgment and his unfaithfulness to Christ which did it all!"

Fraoch, calm and peaceful in his solitude as a hermit, answered Columba,

"But as a monk, Columba, you would have done better to bear the injury with patience rather than to avenge it with weapons in your hands."

Columba felt rightly reproached and yet he also felt his humbling had barely begun.

"That may be so, but it is very hard for a man unjustly provoked to restrain his heart and to sacrifice justice."

After his visit to Fraoch he thought he would go to see another friend, Abban, whose monastery was also in the flat midlands of Ireland, was known as 'the cell of tears', for all who spent time there came away endowed with the special grace of weeping for their sin, if they had not already attained that grace. Abban approached the subject of Columba and the battle in a gentler manner. Columba spent much time with Abban entreating him to pray for the souls of the three thousand dead.

"I beseech you to pray for them, Abban. I wish you to intercede for I cannot rest peacefully in my soul until I am assured that they have reached Heaven by your intercessions. Abban, please ask your guardian angel, who I know speaks with you each day, if God will save these souls."

Abban refused to answer Columba at first, but by the time Columba had given great evidence of his penitence and increasing prayerfulness, Abban came to him and bade him farewell from his monastery and assured him that he had had a vision that these souls would indeed enjoy Heaven.

Inis Mór was the biggest island of the group of islands called Aran. Columba had no trouble begging for the use of a small coracle in which to row over to the island. As he neared the shore, the swirl of the long trailing fronds of sea-weed was like maidens' hair around the coracle, the little light boat made from a framework of hazel covered with light animal skins and tarred over. The feel of the water around his legs, when he hitched up his robes and jumped out and pulled the small craft up the sandy cove, felt strange, new and healing, as also did the cry of the sea-birds. He had imagined as he rowed out that he was sailing west to the Islands of the Blessed that Brendan was ever obsessed by, and maybe, Columba thought, this island will be a blessed island for me.

As he walked up to the enclosure of the monastic settlement, he felt like someone who has just run an extremely strenuous race which is now over at last, and help and rest and nourishment and healing is at hand. Until he landed there he had no idea just how near the end of his tether he had been. Holy Enda of Aran was a man with whom he only spent a matter of weeks, and yet his influence on Columba equalled that of Abbot Finnian and Mobhi.

A delicious smell of frying onions wafted from one of the huts as he approached. Columba turned expectantly towards it, only to be met by a stern-faced monk who looked at him as if he guessed all that was in his mind. The monk said:

"This food is for a sick villager. Know you not that today is a fast day for us?" Columba, chastened, turned his gaze away.

Enda with his dark hair and hazel-brown eyes, was a man who was unprepossessing, quiet, yet with immense reserves of strength in his quietness. The fact that he had once been a soldier was hard to credit as he was now so different. Once Enda had greeted and welcomed Columba, he asked a monk to look after him and show him the guest house. Then Enda refused to speak with his guest for three days, while the guestmaster monk set him to work instead on the digging of potatoes, and the hewing of wood. He was given much other digging work to do as well, and hauling of stones.

Then on the fourth day Enda started taking walks with Columba along the shore. Columba felt uncomfortable with Enda's silences at first but by the time so much had spilt out of him that he felt there was no more to come, he realized he was at ease at last, although the talk was almost all on Columba's side, but punctuated the odd time with wise advice from the hermit.

"Enda, I feel empty, completely empty at last, and I find it isn't at all a bad feeling!" exclaimed Columba one day.

"God cannot pour his Holy Spirit into a vessel which is already occupied" replied Enda simply.

Columba went on:

"Also I find I have no more ambition, for myself that is. I would not have admitted I had any ambition for myself before this whole episode, but I realize now that any desire to be king or Ard Rí of Ériu has gone from me completely. I realize I was wrong in thinking that my special task for God was to be always a-meddling in kings' business."

"What is your special task for God now Columba?" Enda asked quietly.

"I now know better than to delineate a task. Mine is just to be ready for his call, listening to his voice. And to be open, always open to him, open for him to pour more of his love into the world that needs it so badly, through me, and through my monks."

"But can you keep up that openness? It is fine to make promises now, but the emptiness in you can very soon be filled with other things. Can you prevent that happening?"

"I think you have given me the clue to this, Enda. To remain open to God all the time is the work of the Holy Spirit in me; I cannot achieve it myself; and the more of myself I give him the more he has to work on—I shall aim for giving him all."

"Yes, that is an acceptable ambition," Enda agreed.

What was so wonderful about it was that the particular monks of Enda's community that were his brothers, as opposed to his pupils, were like living embodiments of their master's teaching, and Columba felt welcomed, and felt as if he was being remade from within. Even the stern-faced monk, who had caught Columba smelling the frying onions, softened considerably as time passed.

Enda had agreed with Columba that the best expiation of his sin, as Columba himself was maintaining, would be for him to win as many souls for Christ as were killed in the battle. His time on Inis Mór with Enda was a vitally important time for Columba. His working with the soil of the island was a working out of all the things in his life which had need of expression. As he worked there, as he prayed there, as he mortified his body there, and as he had these long talks with Enda, his peace in Christ returned to him. His gifts of healing returned and once more he seemed to be growing into Columba the dove, while Crimthann the fox-wolf was receding. His red-gold hair was fading now to a lighter brown and threads of silver were appearing among them and the fading of the fox-colored hair seemed to be mirroring the receding of that character in him.

Lughnasa—the Feast of Lammas as it was known by the church— was approaching now and the week of the Tailltu Fair which was now the Tailltu Synod. As Columba made his way to nearby Ceanannas Mór from Aran by way of visits to his brothers and his own monasteries and other monasteries on the way, he knew now that his fate was set towards exile. He knew too that he no longer was needing to defend himself angrily from criticism, and he knew too that the protection and guidance of the spirit of God was with him. It was as if he had died a death, as if the Columba he no longer wished to be part of him had been thrown away, had shrivelled, had gone out of his body. It was, also, as if inhabiting his body was a new spirit, one who had come through the violence and turmoil of this crisis to be a man who once again was under the control of the Holy Spirit. His vessel had been scoured and cleaned out, very, very painfully, but now it was a clean and empty vessel to receive the Spirit of God in much, much fuller measure than before. So the Columba who made his way to that synod at Tailltu was almost a totally different man in many, many ways from the Columba who had been on the field of battle at Cuildreimhne.

Brendan the Abbot of Birr sat uncomfortably, with a frown on his face, on his bench at the Tailltu Synod. He felt not at all in sympathy with the words which were being spoken about his friend Columba here. One of the bishops had risen and was speaking to the assembly:

"Excommunication from the church is the only path open to us, my brothers. If we allow this violence in our country, sanctioned by the church, it will be the church's downfall. We need to send this hot-headed prince abroad for his own good".

Brendan raised his hand to speak as he wished to answer this accusation but even as he was given the sign of permission and was rising, he heard footsteps outside and the door opened. He looked towards the door. A blaze of light was entering. The blaze had three dimensions to it: it was his friend Columba; it was Columba's angel surrounding him with light and a golden aura so large that Brendan knew that this was not one angel but many accompanying him on his journey; it was also the sunshine streaming in at the door on this August day on the feast of Lughnasa. Those who had eyes to see the one, saw the one; those who had eyes to see the three, saw the three. Brendan walked straight up to Columba and embraced him. The other clerics in the company remained seated.

The chairman of the assembly said to Brendan of Birr,

"The man who has just entered this assembly has been excommunicated from the church. Why did you not refuse to rise and kiss him?"

Brendan turned to the assembled company,

"If you had seen what the Lord has shown me today concerning this chosen one of his, whom you have been dishonoring this day, you would not have excommunicated him. For not only does God not excommunicate him according to your mistaken verdict, but he even magnifies him more and more."

There was murmuring in the benches at this and the chairman replied,

"We should like to know how God, as you claim, glorifies him whom we have excommunicated not without reason."

Brendan said patiently, in a quiet voice which nevertheless commanded the respect of the company,

"I can explain. I saw a pillar, trailing fire and very bright, going before this man of God whom you despise, and holy angels accompanying him on his journey here. I do not dare therefore to treat this man with scorn whom I see predestined by God to lead many, many people to life . . ."

". . . Many, many people indeed."

This was Columba speaking now, his loud voice commanding the attention of all in the assembly.

Columba continued:

"I have come here to inform my brothers in Christ, that I am imposing a sentence of exile upon myself. It is my desire to win as many souls for Christ in the land of Alba as have been slain on the battlefield of Cuildreimhne."

The president looked around him and saw many men nod. There was a pregnant silence over the company, but a golden one, the light that had entered with Columba stayed. At last the president rose and spoke his pronouncement,

"This synod would like to revoke the sentence of excommunication. We accept this Christian monk's self-imposed punishment of exile from Ériu. Abbot Columba, it is now Lammas-tide. By the feast of Candlemas, the day after the Holy Brigid's day of Resurrection, commonly called Imbolg in this country, you must have sailed away from this land. In half-a-year's time."

Columba gazed at the president and said surprisingly humbly,

"A year and half-a-year?"

The president accepted this simple amendment and repeated,

"A year and half-a-year: Candlemas, Imbolg, of the year of our Lord 563."

When the Synod broke up Columba was mobbed by his friends. Cainnech was there, Comghall, Rhodan, as well as Brendan of Birr, and many, many others.

To his circle of friends Columba announced,

"At Candlemas in a year and half-a-year I will be going with twelve men of God's choosing to bring the Christian gospel to the Picts of Alba. Please make this known for I want people to know this is happening, so those who feel in their hearts that this call is for them may be led indeed by God to join me. We have many preparations to make, and building a boat will be one of them." He specially thanked his friend, Brendan of Birr, for his interceding on his behalf, and promised to keep him in his own prayers.

On the journey back to Daire, feeling chastened and yet also proud and full of hope and excitement for the future, Columba realized he had avoided Molaise on the day of the synod. He debated within himself whether or not he ought to try to go to the island and see him, but decided not: he wanted to get home to Daire and start preparations. However he felt guiltily uncomfortable, he realized, as he skirted the shore abbey of Staid. This state of unsatisfactory evasion was brought to a halt a few miles down the road. When he saw the cross of Ahamlish ahead of him he could see the figure of a man standing there beside it, watching Columba's approach, as if deliberately awaiting him. Molaise! How had Molaise known he would be avoiding the island? It was not the first time he had known without being told by human agency! When Columba came near enough for speech, the older man spoke strongly and even harshly, his harshness an effort to disguise his grief that he would never see this soul-friend of his again:

"Columba, your exile must be complete, and not in part. You must go to Alba and not see Ériu again. You must not set foot on her soil again. Go! Go in penitence; go with the gospel; go with God!"

11

Dunadd

A.D. 563

T he murmuring of the oak trees' leaves in the breeze lifted Columba's spirits as he walked once more in his beloved first foundation of Daire. But it was a poignant sound for him now. The sound seemed to be a welcome back from the trees, and yet knowing that he would not be there for long before setting out for Alba, made it a welcome tinged with sadness. His brothers the monks at Daire and also his foster-sons had given him the warmest possible greetings.

Baithene, his first foster-son, was shaping into the loveliest of characters, and Columba felt justifiably proud of him. His smith-work in Daire was of top quality; he was liked and respected by all the monks; and if asked what was the quality about him which most people admired none would have hesitated to say it was that monk's humility, and that it was a humility they knew came from prayer. Columba prayed that wherever he was going to end his days, in whichever monastery or foundation his last breath would be taken, Baithene would be close beside him. He felt deeply that Baithene was his coarb, his natural successor as father to his *paruchia* or family of monasteries.

But now he must occupy his mind with the business of laying plans, gathering together his twelve men with which to travel to Alba, and his plan to tour all his churches and monasteries that were scattered around the north-west and Midlands of Ériu, for it was important that he consolidate the work that he had begun. To Columba's surprise, the first very definite offer from a man who felt he was chosen to be one of the twelve was a distant kinsman of his own, Mocutheimne, son of the provincial king of Ulaidh. Mocutheimne and Columba walked together in that very oak grove where Columba delighted to be. Columba frowned and said,

"Mocutheimne, much as I respect your wish to offer to be one of my companions to Alba, I feel that it will be a hard life for a young man with the background from which you have come. Does not your destiny lie here with your father, the King and with your family here in Ulaidh? I know and respect that your life is given to Christ, but can you not do a far better work here to serve your heavenly king, than in a faraway strange country whose language you do not even understand?"

Mocutheimne looked smilingly into Columba's eyes and said,

"It is you who are my father. The church is my mother and my country shall become the country where I can gather the largest harvest for Christ."

"There is still much large harvest to be gathered for Christ here in Ériu, Mocutheimne." Columba replied.

"Moreover, are you ready for great, great hardship if you follow Christ as a member of my band?"

Mocutheimne fell to his knees on the ground in front of Columba, his spiritual father, saying,

"I swear to follow you wherever you go, for you have consecrated me to Christ, and until I am ready to go to my Lord, my life is at his service."

Columba learned something from this episode for he felt now that in some ways the unseen listener to their conversation was smiling at Columba now. He realized that the tests for discovering who was a chosen companion to travel to Alba with him were not tests of his own choosing. He humbly confessed to God that he was loathe to accept certain people because he personally felt they may not be suitable, but he admitted now before God that he himself would never know, only God in Heaven would know who had the stamina in his soul to undergo the exile with him that he was about to start. "Lord," he prayed, "teach me discernment, and teach me to accept your leading in the lives of other men."

Not long after acceptance of Mocutheimne, and the setting of him to work at hard tasks as a preparation for the voyage, two monks arrived at the monastery to Columba to offer their services. Their names were Rui and Fethuo, the sons of a man named the same name as one of Columba's friends, Rodan. Rui and Fethuo lived on the seacoast and were expert, not only at fishing and sailing and strong at bringing in harvests, but they also were good weathermen, and good shipbuilders.

"Rui, Fethuo; I accept you both into the brotherhood of our community here at Daire. I wish you to join in the life of the monastery, but I also would like you to start building the boat in which we shall sail to Alba. My kinsmen have provided some tribute with which we can purchase hides. Timber we have in plenty. I myself have done a small amount of boat-building, so we shall work together, and become companions in this venture."

They had one solemn celebration in the church at Daire to accomplish, for Aedán very gently reminded Columba that during the many, many years of his absence, Conor had still only had the title of Prior of the community of Daire and not Abbot. So Conor was elevated to abbot and Aedán appointed as his prior, in a service of solemnity and happiness. These two loyal companions of Columba's wished dearly that they could have been among the twelve sailing to Alba, a country where they had often thought they would like to preach the Gospel. But they knew in their hearts that they had no call from God to be of that company, and instead were loyal encouragers of Columba in this venture. Columba impressed upon them the need to respect the guidance he had given to them about his beloved oak trees. None of them were to be felled. But if one was blown over by the wind then it must be allowed to lie for nine days and then cut up. One third of the wood was to be given to the people of the village around the monastery; one third to the poor; and one third to the monastery itself.

The eighteen months sped by very fast between Lughnasa and the Imbolg of the next year following, when on the feast of Candlemas—the day after the first day of February which was the Feast of the Holy Brigid—they were aiming to set out for Alba. Columba was unsure what the reaction of his family would be at first, but his heart was gladdened when his father Felimidh arrived in Daire with the youngest of his three sons, Cobthach. Cobthach had been fostered with a secular warrior prince as had Eoghan. But on hearing the Gospel preached by the monks of Daire, Cobthach had turned his life over to the Lord Christ, and now felt certain that he too was being called to sail with his much older brother Columba to Alba. This was a particular pleasure for Columba and he welcomed this brother in blood who was also a brother in Christ. This family encounter also included a poignant moment, when Felimidh suddenly knelt down and asked his son's blessing as he had decided to set out to spend some time in a lone place as a hermit.

With his purposeful journeys around the country consolidating work in Ceanannas Mór, Sórd, Drumholme, Droim Colm, Glencolmcille, Rath Bhoth, Dairmhá, and other places, more volunteers came forward. Soon Cuimín the brother of Baithene, another kinsman of Columba and the Uí Neill, was added to their little band of willing missionaries. Stocky sandy-haired Cuimín seemed like a smaller version of Baithene, who was the stouter of the two. The little band now included sandy-haired Cobthach with his honest blue eyes, Fethuo and Rui with their wariness, toughness and their closeness to nature, the prince Mocutheimne with his dark good looks and passionate heart directed ever heavenwards, and of course Baithene and Diormit who was now a professed monk. Soon to this band were now added tall, strong, visionary Mocufir, the seemingly lethargic but full of inner fire Scandal, the dreamy hazel-eyed Cetea, and the tall, thin, honest, hard-working, brown-eyed, dark-haired Thorannu. So now they lacked only one man to complete Columba's band and that man must needs be a bishop, for how could they spread churches of Christ among the Cruithní of Alba without a Bishop to ordain priests for each church?

Months and months passed by and in the shelter by the banks of the Foyle where the boat was being built, the building was nearing its completion. Still there was no bishop in their party. Once the oak and ash framework of the boat was completed and the hides were collected, Columba would not allow it that Rui and Fethuo would labor alone stitching hides day in, day out over the weeks. He felt the monks who were going on this voyage should each have had a hand in constructing their boat. So in the hours of labor, these new monks gathering into the family were sent to the shed in which Rui and Fethuo were in charge of the work. Soon, with still no sign of a bishop or a twelfth member of their party, the wool grease was well boiled and was spread over the ox hides which made the outer covering of the boat.

They were glad of the wind those days while the grease was soaking into the hides, for the smell was not a fragrant one. Columba also had some of the monks at work making ropes from flax for the ship, attaching them to leather thongs and making sure that she would be fully rigged. Again, he had Rui and Fethuo train some of the brothers from the Daire monastery in boat building and several small curraghs, or curraghals, were constructed to run tight alongside the main one for ease of access to smaller islands in bad weather. Other monks began stitching leather satchels for the books that they intended carrying with them to Alba. The expert in stitching these leather satchels was Thorannu. He turned out to be capable of stitching the leather so that no one could see the stitches. His stitches which were invisible, and within the thickness of the skin of the leather, were the result of superb craftsmanship from years of honed skills. Columba constantly inspected the work around the building of the ship and often joined in with the labor. One day he declared,

"This sail needs something important added to it. It needs a cross!" All agreed to this enthusiastically.

All was now in place for the expedition—all but the twelfth man. Columba counselled his monks to have patience and to trust in God. They trusted in God for three days and used the time to prepare themselves in prayer. Looking out from the door of the church on the third day, his face set against the winter wind, Columba saw a horse and rider on the way to the monastery. Wondering if this could be the answer to his prayer he went to the gate to welcome the newcomer. To his surprise the newcomer was none other than the hermit Ernan. Ernan was uncle to Columba, Columba had visited him several times, where he had been spending his time in a small hermitage on the west coast. Ernan's warm blue-grey eyes were soft in his gaunt face as he smiled at his nephew, and said

"Columba. I heard of your enterprise many months ago. I had not thought that it would be my place to accompany you. But I find now that our Lord had other plans. Here I am, if you can use me. A new bishop has been appointed for the work which I have begun."

Columba was almost too moved to speak. He embraced his uncle warmly and said,

"Uncle Ernan! Bishop! We welcome you in the name of the Lord! We are honored that you feel you are destined to become one of our company and with great, great joy we accept you into our band. You had not known perhaps that we lacked a bishop?"

"Nephew, I knew very little of your enterprise and tried to remain aloof from it. But fighting against where the Spirit is leading a person comes to very little fruit in the end." Great was the rejoicing of all the brothers at the joining of Ernan to their company.

The farewell that Columba made to Daire was a painful one indeed, akin to cutting an umbilical cord. His returning to Daire after Tailltu had been like returning not only to a home but to a womb, and now his pain was that he was to be cast out into the harshness of a strange country without this secure connection of his own to the soil of Ériu. Felimidh and his daughters Enan and Sinech and her sons and several other kinsfolk came to bid farewell to Columba and Cobthach and Ernan and the band of monks. Aed the son of Ainmire was also present, and Felimidh and Aed separately both reminded Columba of his kinship with the Alban Dalriada royal family. Dalriada was the name of a kingdom which had two halves, it had the western sea-coast of Alba and part of the northern coast of Ulaidh. Although one kingdom originally, eventually there were two monarchs one for each half, although the Ulidian half was smaller. The capitals or main forts were Dun Add in Alba and Dun Sobhairce in Ériu.

"Dunadd, my son, is where you should head for now," said Felimidh, "for Dunadd is the main fortress of King Conal of Dalriada. He is of our blood, and speaks our tongue, and will be able to provide interpreters for you to travel to the lands of the Cruithní. God go with you my son."

Ainmire now spoke kindly to Columba:

"Bring greetings to King Conal from me. Here, take this letter. I have had a scribe write this letter to King Conal. Deliver it to him and it will also be a safe-conduct for you."

As they pushed the boat out into the waters of the Foyle, the last few men jumped in, including Diormit who was rather green in the face already anticipating his usual sea-sickness. Although fully blessed already they prayed a blessing upon the boat, on the helmsman, Scandal, and on the skipper, Rui. A few moments later Columba turned his face determinedly away from the crowd upon the shore. But he was becoming aware that the monastery and oak wood were once more coming into his line of vision and the boat was turning. Angrily he turned to Rui and said,

"Rui, what are you doing? We must head out to sea now!"

There was some little commotion and it took some while to sort out what was indeed happening and eventually it seemed that Scandal had been using his position as helmsman to ensure that they circled a rock near the water's edge, a certain rock in the lake, three times sunwise, as a means of bringing them good luck—an old pagan custom. Columba felt anger for Scandal's action rise in him, but seeing that most of his other monks were taking this calmly he decided to let it be. He was learning to control his hot temper, and nothing would be produced by a show of emotion at a time like this. He determined instead to try sometime to teach the monk Scandal in some other way how to abandon more fully the old ways.

When they first started out, the sea for February was counted quite calm, for although early February was the beginning of spring, the softer weather normally took weeks to follow on after the Festival. However, as they reached the place that was mid-channel between Ériu and Alba, the water began to swell more and more, and waves appeared to be threatening the boat from outside. At first none came into the boat, but soon the waves were spilling the odd time into the actual vessel and the monks were all tempted to anxiety and fear for their lives. The swelling waves were coming at them diagonally and causing the boat to lift and dip dramatically. Columba realized the prevailing mood and called out to the monks that they should start to sing.

"What shall we sing?" they shouted.

"The Fortieth Psalm," Columba shouted back above the wind.

Their voices, although there were thirteen of them, sounded very frail against the roar of the wind and the waves. But they sang with faith as they bailed out the water:

"I waited patiently for the Lord and he inclined to me and heard my cry. He brought me up from the pit of roaring waters out of the mire and clay: and set my feet upon a rock and made firm my foothold. And he has put a new song in my mouth: even a song of thanksgiving to our God. Many shall see it and fear: and shall put their trust in the Lord."

The storm continued for a while, as if testing the monks on the seriousness of their intent. By the time the swell was less and the waves had become smaller waves, each of the monks felt that they had, in a way, pierced through to a place of greater faith and trust that God would care for them. Soon sea-gulls were flying above them and mewing, and they realized land was not far away. Mocutheimne's presence with them now started to have a great usefulness, for he had sailed to Alba on several occasions already, and he was well able to advise them on the best route to Dunadd. Once they reached the Scottish coast and had made their way between the islands and the mainland, they navigated the river Add with no mishap. On their way down the river they saw to each side of them stretching for miles around a plain of boggy marshy moss. Mocutheimne told them this was the Crinan moss, which was as good as any fortress walls as a defense for the fortress of Dunnad. They moored their boat in the small Lough Crinan near the fort that was the harbor for it, and then removing their sandals, they hazarded a pathway along a small ridge near the fort, taking care not to trespass into that springy and possibly lethal moss.

King Conal was king of the Alban part of Dalriada, which was a kingdom or province, spanning part of Ulaidh and part of Alba, the two parts separated by sea. It was a Christian country, and Columba and his monks were met with a good welcome there from King Conal, even before he set eyes upon the letter from King Ainmire. Mocutheimne and he were known to each other and Conal had good hospitality offered to all the monks and showed them to a guesthouse within his fortress. The brothers fell thankfully upon the bowls of hazelnuts and shiny green and red apples that were set out for them pending the meal later. At the evening meal some of the younger monks would gladly have tucked into the plentiful venison and salmon had not Columba made it clear that moderation and frugality was expected, for it was still Lent.

When there was a chance for Conal to speak to Columba on his own, they withdrew from the others and climbed a small hillock and looked across the land.

"I would like to offer you a place that would be of use to you for your work of preaching and teaching. Which area would you feel to be best?"

"The place that would seem the right one," Columba replied, "would be somewhere on the line which would be dividing your kingdom from the kingdom of the Cruithni."

"I thought so," Conal said. "Mala would be good as it is central to Alba and close to Ériu and also close to Dalriada here. It would also be a stopping-off point for the isles. But sadly Mala is not a place where my rule is undisputed; there are many Cruithní in that area who dispute my kingship."

Conal was silent for a few minutes and then he stretched out his arm and pointed in a north-north-westerly direction.

"In the line of my hand here there are three islands. There is Hinba, you see the twin peaks there. There is I and there is Ethe. That first island is the biggest of the three, Hinba: there you would have good farmland, and a settled community of Christians there already. The small island beyond that is I, the island of the yew trees, it is a holy place. Our kings have traditionally been buried there for it was a holy place in the old religion, and there may well be a few Druids there still. We now call it a Christian holy place for the holy monk Oran from Lettera in Ériu lived there when he arrived here from Ériu. He died fourteen years ago, and his hermitage which was just a solitary cell of wattles may still be there, but probably in disrepair. Oran is buried on the island beside the tombs of my forebears, the kings of Dalriada."

"That sounds ideal," said Columba, fighting within himself, for the idea of an island that was large with good farmland was also appealing to him. Conal went on,

"Ethe is small, but also good farming land. You can take your choice, Columba; or if you wish you can have all three islands."

"King Conal, all three islands would be a magnificent gift! I would find it hard to repay such generosity."

"Columba your method of repaying my generosity is going to be in an entirely different kind than the gift you are now receiving. You can be my advisor. I have refused to employ any Druids or followers of the old faith for my counsels and the holy Oran had given me good advice. Now he has died I need a man like yourself to help me consolidate this kingdom, especially in the light of the threats from the Picts—which is what we call the Cruithni here—from the north at all times. Also, Columba, you will find that though we are a Christian kingdom, our churches need strengthening. We are short of priests; people have a tendency as you probably know from Ériu to fall back into old ways when they are not receiving constant and regular teaching. Oh Columba there is much, much work to be done here in Dalriada as well as reaching the Picts! We welcome you most heartily!"

They stayed many many weeks at Dunadd at the insistence of King Conal, celebrating the Eucharist at churches all around, consulting long with Conal, celebrating a joyful Easter with their friends, when they were at last allowed to share in the venison at that very special feast. At last the day came when Columba announced that the time had come for them to sail to Hinba, and they did so with joyous hearts. They were awed and impressed by the height of the twin peaks with their rounded tops on that island. Humorous Fethuo contributed the information he had gathered at Dunnad, that those twin peaks were known as 'the Paps of Hinba.' Columba, about to laugh, looked at his brothers and noticed them looking at him quizzically, and he burst into a loud guffaw. They joined him, happy in the knowledge that their father in God put no ban on God's gift of laughter. Life had been somewhat intense recently owing to their not being settled yet and the outlet was welcome, and the laughter hearty.

The first action Columba did on reaching the island of Hinba was to climb the highest of the two peaks. The younger monks followed him straightaway, and well able to match the most agile of them, Columba was in the lead the whole time. Calling out to those behind,

"We must see if there is a view of Ériu from the top!"

When they got to the top what did they see across the waves but a blue steady line, unmoving unlike the waves—the land of Ériu.

"No! No! We cannot make our monastery on this island!" Columba exclaimed.

"This is too close to Ériu for comfort. Let us proceed down the mountain. We shall try the second island, I."

So into the boat they scrambled once more. Ernan was the second last in, and was fast becoming the spiritual support and strength and stay of his nephew. Columba realized that this man, his uncle of small acquaintance, was in the process of becoming his soul-friend—for Molaise of Inis Muredach, now Columba was in exile, was inaccessible to him. Ernan turned to Columba,

"Columba, I like this island. We have been given it, so why not use it as a place of withdrawal? If we use one of the other two islands for our main monastery let this be a place of hermitage. I feel drawn to make a hermitage here in the spot myself,"

Columba replied,

"Uncle, stay here if this is your wish!"

"I will come here in one of the small curraghs once our foundation is built and ready on the main island, Columba. This is my wish, but there is no haste about it."

The sail from Hinba to I was much, much more difficult in terms of navigation. For not only were there many small islands and islets in their path, but also many treacherous rocks blocking their way to a safe landing. Another obstacle was the fact that the wind was becoming stronger and stronger: a sudden April storm. The time they had spent at Dunadd had been well spent, but the weeks had fled by almost without their noticing them. With this unseasonable storm brewing, the monks were tempted to fear. Once again their father Columba exhorted them to sing a Psalm.

"Ascribe to the Lord you sons of heaven: ascribe to the Lord glory and might . . . The voice of the Lord is upon the waters. The God of glory thunders and the Lord, upon the great waters. The voice of the Lord is mighty in operation: the voice of the Lord is a glorious voice. The Lord will give strength to his people. The Lord will give to his people the blessing of peace."

To add to the dangers of the storm and the rocks they also found that a mist was circling around them. The mist was not everywhere. It was almost like a little local mist and almost again, Columba felt, and Ernan concurred, as if this mist was a Druidic mist, a mist of the enemy sent to confound them, to dog their steps and to prevent them from landing at a place where possibly it was God's will for them to be. It took strong prayer as well as their utmost skill as sailors to be able to navigate their way around these treacherous rocks in the mist and find their way at last to a little cove where they were able to beach the boat on a stony shore. The prow of their hide boat ground loudly on the stones of that little bay. With relief at having arrived safely and navigated the dangers, they jumped out and together they pulled the boat over those rounded stones that were clinking under their feet. The stones were all colors! A field of gems! Columba drew his brothers' attention to the beautiful stones which had swirls and whorls of color within them, lines and speckles, indents and marbling, some sea green, some white, some yellow with brown-pink marblings, some with green fire within, some smooth grey, others pink, green or brown with multicolored spots. All different, thought Columba, as different as his monks with all their shapes and sizes and different characters.

Again Columba's first action was to run up a small hill to the left of him and to call out again to his brothers,

"We must check yet again that the coast of Ériu cannot be seen from here!"

Baithene was not far behind his foster-father and the two sat side by side as they peered into the mist looking for a sign of Ériu. Both looked at each other and laughed, each knowing in his heart that no sign of Ériu would be seen on such a misty day. Columba however said in a determined and purposeful voice,

"There is no sign of Ériu to be seen from this island, Baithene. This is the place where we shall build our monastery."

At the bottom of the hill the brothers gathered together to hear the pronouncement of Columba and all raised their voices together in a Psalm of praise,

"Oh shout with joy to God all the earth. Sing to the honor of his name and give him glory as his praise. Say to God how fearful are your works: because of your great might your enemies should cower before you. All the earth shall praise you, worship you, and sing praises to your name. Come then and see what God has done: how terrible are his dealings with the children of man. He turned the sea into dry land so they crossed the land on foot: then were we joyful because of him . . . O bless our God you peoples. Cause his praises to resound, who has held our souls in life, who has not suffered our feet to slip."

After their service of praise some of the brothers said to Columba,

"Look! Here is some good green ground. Let us pitch a camp here for the night!"

Columba replied,

"No. We must head inland on this island. There is no use building a camp or a monastery or anything else until we are sure that we are free of danger of attack. There may be people on this island, and we need to find out if they are friendly."

So Columba organised them into five parties to explore the island. Two monks in each direction went forth leaving Baithene, Diormit and Cobthach to make fast the boat and unload their provisions and cook a meal for them to eat on their return to the shore. Ernan walked with Columba, and it may have been providential that those two most senior and holy men were the ones who met the only two inhabitants of the island that were found. The men they met with, beneath a green and grey fortress-like rock, were wearing unbleached, uncolored tunics very similar to their own, with natural colored cowls. Their foreheads were free of hair, they were tonsured in the same style as themselves. This could only mean two things, thought Columba as he approached the men. Either they were Druid priests, or they were Christian monks. They greeted the men as they came up in their own language and found that the men were familiar with the Gaelic tongue.

"Who are you?" Columba asked.

"We are bishops, Christian bishops" answered the two men.

Columba felt distinctly uneasy and he prayed for discernment. The emanations from these men did not give him the impression that they were Christian bishops. He questioned them regarding their training and provenance, and Ernan questioned them regarding the teachings of the Holy Scriptures and of Holy Patrick and the Church, meaning to test them. They failed their test on every count, and even before Columba had finished with them they were looking sheepish and starting to walk towards the shore to a little boat which was there.

After the departure of the two strangers Columba felt a great weight lift from his chest. Ernan felt it too and the two men joyfully rejoined their brothers in the little cove, marching over hillocks and hills, rocks, moors and past a little lake in order to get back to where Diormit had a little fire going and was cooking a fish supper for them with the aid of Cobthach.

12

I

A.D. 563

F ull of cheerfulness about the speedy despatch of the two imposters and about their arrival at last on this island, small and mean in size as it appeared to them to be, Columba and Ernan strode towards Diormit and Cobthach, Columba modifying his long strides to suit his uncle. As soon as they were within earshot of the monks on the shore Columba called out,

"Baithene! Diormit! Cobthach! I see you have caught some fish for our supper!"

"Yes master, Cobthach speared three mackerel and Baithene has also unpacked some provisions from the boat" Diormit replied.

"Good! A fish meal will be so like Jesus' breakfast on the shores of Galilee," Columba said happily. When the men had all gathered together, Columba asked them,

"Who has kept a reckoning? Which of you knows what day tomorrow is?"

Ernan smiled, knowing the answer to this but not venturing it. A silence ensued, all brows knit with concentration, then Cetea called out,

"Tomorrow must be the day of Pentecost!"

"Indeed it is," smiled Columba "and we will commence our first full day on the island with a celebration of the Eucharist on that holy day."

After their supper they set up a small camp for the night, where they all huddled under the sail of the ship, stretched and made fast with stones over the two small curraghals they had brought with them. They slept the sleep of weary men. When Columba awoke, the earliest of all as was his custom, a surprise was in store for him. Yesterday the rain and mists had dulled the earth and grass of that small island and had made all seem dark. Then he had thought of the island as a mean place. But today the mist had lifted. The rain was gone and now, even as he looked, a sudden ray of sunshine came through the clouds and lit up the island. It lit up the little drops of rain gathered on each blade of grass and set them shining, but not only the small blades of grass; it set the whole island shining like a jewel.

What had been grey and colorless yesterday now became vivid with color. The brown and grey ancient rocks were topped with green and yellow lichens. The screeching mewing gulls with their sleek white and grey bodies and orange beaks contrasted pleasingly with the fresh green velvet of the sand dunes and grassy hillocks. The olive-green velvet of the main rocky hill of the island dominated all, and there was the orange-pink of many of the rocks around. Looking downwards too there were the wild flowers. A veritable treasure trove of wild flowers Columba found that May day. The tall delicate yellow petals of the wild cowslip and the joyful brighter yellow of lady's bedstraw, the pale milkweed and the white wild carrot contrasted with the purple of the honey-yielding clover, the little tormentil, rich royal purple of self-heal, the pink of orchids, yellow mayweed, white eyebright—so many, many flowers each different like the stones of the shore where they had landed. "Lord, help me to fathom and love and accept the differences of my monks," Columba prayed." Help me to be a father to them and a helper of them in finding their own souls and of winning many other souls for you."

As they celebrated the Eucharist of the feast of Pentecost, on that island with its magic light and its breeze blowing over their heads, it seemed almost as if the Holy Spirit hovered over that island and over them. His wind was everywhere, there was no escaping from the wind, just as there was no escaping from the spirit of God.

By the following day the work of digging and of building cells was in progress, and also building a church. They discovered on further exploration of the island that the stretch of water between their island and what appeared to be the mainland was only a smallish sound a mile in length.

"That is the island of Mala," Columba explained to those who had not been party to his negotiations with King Conal. Soon the islanders of

Mala started making their way to I in their little boats to inquire if they could help in any way. On being told of Columba's kinship to King Conal they went to work with a will helping to dig and bringing over boatloads of twigs and branches suitable for making the wattle huts.

The people appeared to be Christians on the whole, and being without a priest were happy to welcome this band of monks to their vicinity. Further exploration showed them the lying place of Oran's relics and Columba rejoiced in this for he needed, indeed, to build his church on the foundation of a Christian saint's remains so that it would be a blessed and holy place. He did not want to follow the custom of burying a person alive underneath a new building, a custom which he had heard was still quite common here in Alba. They constructed a vallum and built their huts, their guesthouse, their farmhouse, their refectory; the building went on for months and months it seemed. There was no end to the building but also there was no end to the visitors and the people coming to their aid, so that Columba as their father abbot had to protect the monks' privacy and silence. As Columba built his own hut he sang the 73rd Psalm, repeating again and again the final verse,

"But it is good for me to draw near to God: I have made God my refuge and I will tell of all that you have done, My Lord."

The time of Ernan's departure for Hinba did certainly come, as once each monk had his own cell and the life of the monastery was proceeding on smoothly, Ernan had no more worries for the small community. Knowing that all was as it should be, and that with two curraghals in their possession there would always be a chance for one monk to be visiting him and joining him in his solitude, he was sailed over to Hinba by Rui who then sailed back again, so that Ernan in fact became a total solitary, imprisoned by his own lack of a boat. However, it was Columba's intention to sail and join his uncle as often as he could, and also to send other monks out to the island who were in need of extra fasting, extra penitence as well as extra solitude. Particularly he planned to send Cobthach his young brother, for Ernan had been a strength and stay to him over the months since they set out. Their second curraghal was in constant use for ferrying goods and people over the sound to the island of Mala.

After an initial period of peacefulness and prayer when the buildings were completed, movement started up. Movement of Columba with some of his brothers to the outlying islands where monasteries were founded on their own island of Ethe, on their own island of Hinba and on the mainland of Dalriada in many places. There was also movement inwards, for often they would hear a hollering from the island of Mala across the sound and a brother would row across in a boat to fetch a visitor. People came having heard that the monastery had started and that the holy Columba was there. Some came for penance. Some came to confess their sins. Some came to become juniors in the monastery, others as working lay brothers. Some were pupils who wanted to live an arduous life and study the books that Columba had brought with him and some of those in turn became members of the community in time. It was not long before the community came to number ten times the number of monks it had started out with. People came from Bhreatain, Saxons of Bhreatain, as well as Dalriada and others over from Ériu.

Some visitors who came were old friends. Cormac, a school-mate of Columba's from Cluain Ioraird days, was now a hermit on another island on the western seaboard of Alba, and he came to visit in company with Moluag, the abbot of the monastery of Lismore, a neighbouring island. These visits did much to lighten the brethren's exile and gladden their hearts as they shared prayers and fellowship and hospitality with these holy fellow-Gaels from nearby.

Columba sent Mocutheimne to study hard with Uncle Ernan so that he might become a priest. Cuimín, the brother of Baithene, was their cook and also a scribe. Baithene served as their smith as well as being an accomplished scribe. Rui and Fethuo passed on their boat-building and navigation and sailing skills to new novice monks while also helping on the farm; they were as excellent at creating buildings. Mocufir was in charge of the farm in which he had the help of Cetea, strong men both. Diormit he trained as a sacristan, looking after the altar linens and also the monks' habits and cowls; and Columba's own younger brother Cobthach, who was always willing to work with his hands, was in charge of preparing the parchments and vellums, inks and other colours for the work of gospel-copying; he also was the potter and was able to build a little kiln and to fashion earthenware crockery for the monastery and the guest-house. Thorannu was the novice master, while Scandal was guest-master and also assistant leatherworker to Thorannu, helping making the book satchels and both of them also helped on the farm whenever extra hands were needed. So each man had his special job.

Cobthach was with Columba one cloudy evening and saw him staring fixedly into the sky. Cobthach looked up too but could not see anything unusual. He felt that Columba was not in a state of prayer that should not be interrupted and Cobthach was, of course, curious. So he asked his abbot and elder brother what he was seeing there in the clouds. Columba turned to Cobthach with a smile and said,

"I see, Cobthach, . . . I see . . . I see Ériu."

Cobthach became rather alarmed, as all of them had worked so hard to maintain the fiction that Ériu could never be seen from the island of I! But his fears melted when he realized that Columba was 'seeing' Ériu in a visionary way, as Columba went on to say,

"I see an Ériu of the future, Cobthach. I see the walls of Teamhair broken down and weeds growing there. I see wars. I see murders. I see invasions. I see warlike men come from outside and plundering. I see beauty and learning fall into decay. I see much that is troublesome in the future of that land, Cobthach and there is much in my visions which troubles me. Much, much more than I have told you".

"Is all well in Tirconnel and Daire?" asked Cobthach anxiously.

"Fear not, this is the future I have been seeing, Cobthach! Please bring me an ink-horn now and parchment and I will write a letter to my friend Brendan at Birr. I feel he should know of these things."

Once their guest house was built it was seldom empty. A man came one day from the southern half of Ériu, the land of Mumhan. This man claimed that he was a priest, and he was a man Columba could see was holy, and he warmed to him. After Scandal had led him away to the guest-house, and Columba had returned to his cell and the copying of scriptures there, Columba gave thought to the fact this priest was visiting and he called on him in the guesthouse and invited him to break the bread for them in the holy Eucharist on the coming Lord's day. When the service was about to begin this priest called out to Columba and said,

"Columba, will you not come here and assist me in this Eucharist, that we two might break the Lord's bread together as two priests?"

Columba left his bench and walked up to the altar of the small church. Looking into the face of the priest he stayed still for a moment, his luminous grey eyes holding a visionary look, and he said,

"May the Lord Christ bless you my brother. Break this bread alone, for you as a bishop know well how to do it in the episcopal rite. We know that you are a bishop. You did not need to disguise yourself. Why the disguise? The reverence due to you has not been paid by us because of this."

The bishop, who had in fact disguised himself, was astonished at the discernment of Columba and worshipped Christ for his gifts in the abbot. All the brothers present realized what was happening and they, too, were filled with amusement and a holy joy that their abbot should be gifted by the Spirit to discern what had been hidden. The Bishops' name was Cronan, and Cronan's visit to them took on a quite different meaning after that.

Another visitor from Ériu arrived during Cronan's visit, bearing a letter from Brendan the Abbot of Birr. Brendan had received the lengthy letter from Columba containing many details of the vision he had seen concerning Ériu, and he was writing back to thank Columba for this. However, it also contained two sad pieces of news and one was the death of Columba's dear soul-friend, Molaise of Inismuredach. The other was the equally sad news of the death, at an advanced age, of holy Finnian of Cluain Ioraird. Great was the mourning of many of the brothers at these two pieces of news. Bishop Cronan celebrated a mass for their souls in the little church on the island of I.

13

Inverness

A.D. 567

O n one of those mornings when the sun made the island of I shine like a precious emerald set in the blue sea, Columba in his cell looked up from his writing, and saw a young monk named Colman coming towards him. Colman had on his shoulder a churn full of fresh milk which he had just carried from the harbour, as their milk came from Mala since they had no cow themselves. Colman set the churn down at the door of Columba's hut, and called out:

"Abbot, would you bless the milk?" Columba raised his hand and made the sign of the cross in the air and said

"May this milk be blessed, in the name of the Father, the Son and the Holy Spirit". To Colman's surprise the milk immediately seemed to sting his hands as he held it. The churn shook violently and the lid's bolts fell off it, the lid leapt to the ground in spite of the surprised Colman's frantic efforts to control it, and most of the milk was spilt and lay in a puddle on the ground at Columba's door. Colman put the vessel down with great care, feeling upset at the spilt milk and perplexed by this sudden storm within his churn previously so peaceful. Colman knelt and said to Columba,

"Father I am sorry, forgive me . . ."

"Stand up, Colman," Columba said to him. "Today you have been careless in your work, because when you started pouring milk into your churn there was already a demon lurking there and you failed to make the sign of the cross upon the churn before you started pouring the milk in. It was the power of this sign just now that the demon was unable to endure and that is what made the trembling as the whole vessel shook and the demon took swiftly to flight, spilling the milk. Look here, bring the churn closer to me now and I shall give it a fuller blessing again. Never neglect to bless your work and your tools. All of life is meant to become holy—do not confine your faith to the services in church!" So Columba blessed the milk-churn once more. Colman thankfully lifted it up, finding it rather heavier than he expected. On his way to Cetea's cookhouse with it he looked inside, and found the churn was a good three-quarters full of milk.

Columba continued writing for a while and then lifted his eyes to look out towards the sea-channel between I and Mala. His eyes misted over with his usual visionary mist for a number of minutes and then he walked to the door of his cell and called,

"Brothers!" Two of the newer monks appeared, Silnan and Lugne.

"Lugne, Silnan, will you two take the small curragh and row over immediately to the island of Mala? Last night a man came from the island of Colossus and he is now hiding underneath his boat, covered with hay, among those sand-hills over there at Mala and he intends to cross over the next night under cover of darkness to the little cove where we have our seals breeding. That greedy robber intends to kill some of our seals by stealth and fill his boat with them before returning home to Colossus. Approach him quietly, and then bring him to me!"

So off went Lugne and Silnan and later that day Columba found that they did indeed find the thief hidden exactly in the place that he had described to them. The thief looked penitent and had a hang-dog expression. Columba fixed his eyes on him, and said gently

"Look at me. Why do you break God's command not to steal? And why do you keep taking the property of other people? If you have need of extra food, come over to our island, ask us, and you shall receive what you need. We are ever ready to give to the poor, but we will not tolerate stealing: that is against the commandment of our Lord Jesus Christ. Silnan! Lugne! Will you give some food to this man and row him back to his own boat so that he will not go home empty—handed?"

Later on, having prayed much for that thief, the abbot again gave orders that some more food should be sent to him. The report came back to him on this occasion that the food had arrived just too late, for the thief had been suddenly overtaken by death. The gifts that were sent were

consumed by the mourners at his funeral, which Columba was happy to
know had been a Christian funeral conducted by Baithene.

Walking from the refectory a few days later, Columba heard voices
speaking in a language that he found hard to understand. He realized
this was the Pictish language and felt frustrated because he did, indeed,
understand the odd word, for Cainnech and Comghall had taught him
a fair amount of the similar Cruithnian language when he was younger.
But hearing the language was a providential event, for Columba started
feeling that it was time he made preparations for going to the land of the
Cruithni, known as Picts here in Alba. Columba felt roused from the
peaceful regularity of his life as abbot of the monastery. He had made but
short forays to the mainland and the other islands roundabout to bring
the Gospel and to found new churches. There was a rhythm to his life,
and the rhythm was becoming comfortable. He felt he should be alone
with his Lord on this subject and so he walked to the far side of the island,
to the south-west with its cliffs so as to be well away from those working
on the farm, those fishing, and other people in their little cells and huts
and hermitages.

When he reached the western coast of the island, some fifteen minutes later, he scrambled up the rocky surface to a place where he had a
favourite small ledge. He sat down on this almost inaccessible spot and
looked down on the sea cascading up into the air, as the waves forced the
water up through a nearby cleft in the rocks. He sat meditating in the
sunshine on that day of wind and sun. He let the rays of sun penetrate
through his tunic and warm him through and through. He felt that rays
of love came to him always through his heart, from his Lord, and through
him to his brothers on the island, but he felt that those rays reached further than just this island. He felt rays of love, rays of prayer, like sunshine
rays reach out to the north. It felt too as if they were rays of light, lighting
up the darkness in the north of Alba. He realized he was being inwardly
drawn to the Picts. He watched the great waterspout as it angrily gushed
up from beneath the cliffs and then subsided again. Angry as the lash of
Druids' magic, he thought, thinking of Fraechan. He laughed a moment
and said to himself

"Yes, Druids' magic which can only be maintained for a short burst
and falls back to nothing."

He knew well, without being informed, that the High King of the
Picts in his fort at Inverness would, without doubt, have Druidic advisors. In fact, he soon found out that King Brude, High King of the Picts,

was foster-son to an arch-druid whose name he had not yet managed to discover. Columba sent forth his rays of love and light and prayer to that northern kingdom and prayed that God would guide them when the time was right to go forward and bring the Gospel there. He would need an interpreter. He would need help. He should not go alone. He prayed that God would enable his friends, Comghall and Cainnech who were of Cruithnian blood, to accompany him. He would write without delay, for the more he thought on this matter the more he felt that the guidance of God was upon him to start this venture soon.

Columba appointed his Uncle Ernan as his deputy to be Prior of the large monastery now for it had swelled to so many brothers. They had welcomed to their midst Aedán, Brithu, Molua, Berach, Finnichan, Malruo, Drostan, Lugne, Silnan, Berchan, young Ernan and Ferchno, Colchu and Ganarius among many, many others. Columba could almost hear resounding in his head, the voice of his old tutor and soul-friend Mobhi, reminding him that the success of any great enterprise for God depends totally on the prayer which has gone into the preparation of it. So Columba knew his first step must be to withdraw from his brothers to a more solitary place, where he could prepare alone with God. He asked Diormit to row him over with some provisions to the island of Hinba so that he could use the little cell that Ernan had built for himself there. And he gave himself to prayer.

Some weeks later, outside the door of this cell, Columba heard a familiar voice calling him.

"Columba!"

This was not a familiar voice from the monastery on I, but a voice familiar from many years before. He came out to the door of the cell. Four monks were standing there. Looking around at their faces, Columba's own face burst into a smile and he went up to each of the four of them in turn, welcoming them with the warmest embrace.

"Comghall! Welcome! Cainnech, more than welcome! Brendan, my friend! Cormac! It is good to see you!"

The four were full of news,

"We have been to your monastery here on this island of Hinba and they directed us here to your little hermitage. Will you come with us now you are here, to celebrate the holy mysteries for us in the church and will we eat together tonight and talk of our future plans?"

So they made their way down the hill to the small island monastery and gathered together the brothers there and made arrangements that

Columba should consecrate the sacred mysteries for them in the church. Brendan, Cainnech, Comghall and Cormac sat together in the front of the church. Brendan, the most visionary of the four, asked Comghall after the service was finished,

"Comghall, did you see what I saw during the divine service?"

"What did you see, Brendan?" Comghall asked. Brendan realized that Comghall had seen nothing, and so he explained:

"I saw a tongue of fire, flaming fire, very bright, blazing out of the top of Columba's head as he stood there before the altar consecrating the sacred oblation. I have very infrequently seen this above the head of any man. It stayed there during the whole of the service, rising upwards all the time like a pillar above his head. What do you think this means?"

Comghall shook his head and was silent a few moments.

"I do not know the explanation, Brendan, but I do believe this is a mark of the Lord upon the mission to the Cruithni. I thank you for sharing this vision of knowledge with me, for Cainnech and I propose to join with Columba in this important mission now. It is sad that you must return to Ériu and cannot come with us. Please be much in prayer for our success in this work for God. For the three of us and also for our two sailors: Diormit and Lugne the novice monk."

The first stage of the journey towards Inverness in the north-east, was a journey south-east, to the fort of Dunadd. Here, visiting some of his new Dalriadan churches on the way, Columba, Comghall and Cainnech visited Conal the King of Dalriada. Conal was delighted to hear of the mission and gave them full diplomatic status. During their visit of a couple of days he had scribes write messages to King Brude son of Melchon and he organised a bodyguard of soldiers to bring them. He also provided a small boat and an interpreter, for he said that the Cruithnian language as spoken by Comghall and Cainnech was in many ways different from the Cruithnian language as it was now spoken by the Picts in the north of Alba.

It was a long, long journey through glens and lakes with their boats. Their way lay between tall mountains, as well as along lakes. Beyond the tall mountains rose taller blue heights and then grey distant peaks behind them. Small white cascades of water streamed down the mountains and the clouds cast moving shadows on the green sides as the sun chased them. Their first big lough was Loch Linnhe, and Lismore Island the home of the hermit Moluag was at the mouth of this lake where it flowed into the sea. They visited Moluag first for his blessing. There were many continuous stretches of water, lakes and rivers, between I and Inverness, so sailing was a fast way to proceed. However, not every stretch of all the rivers was navigable, so on these small stretches they all got out and carried the boats between them. The boats made useful shelters under which to sleep at night if they did not find any hospitality in a village.

During the times when it was plain sailing, Comgall and Cainnech were delighted to give Diormit and Lugne a rest from handling the boat, and they enjoyed resurrecting their old skills. Columba used these times to instruct Lugne, who was an eager pupil and full of questions. Lugne asked:

"Father Abbot, do you look up to anyone the way we all look up to you?" Columba answered,

"Of course I do, I look up to Jesus Christ my Lord first of all, and to Bishop Ernan, and to the holy Ninnian and the holy Martin, the Bishop of Tours in France".

"Please tell me about Ninnian and Martin", Lugne begged. Columba delighted in enthusing the young novice with tales of the shining white house Ninnian lived in in Whithorn, and for the humility of Martin who lived in a hut in a field rather than in the bishop's palace. He told the story of how Martin, when he was a soldier, gave half his cloak to a naked beggar on a freezing day, and then had a dream in which Jesus boasted of the half-cloak Martin had given him. Lugne was able to quote the parable of the sheep and goats from the gospels where Jesus said "Inasmuch as you did this to the least of my brethren you did it to me" and Columba praised him for this.

Another day the young man asked,

"Why do we monks live in separate huts or cells and not share a house together?"

"A very good question" his abbot replied. "It is because it gives us time free of distractions, so it enables us to have time on our own to develop our life of prayer, the prayer that is contemplating the wonderfulness of God in stillness and silence, of communing with him in our spirits. And also it gives us the freedom from distractions which helps us concentrate well on our work as scribes: ink does not get spilt when there are no other people around to jog your elbow! And thankfully it cuts down bickering! We do live in community by worshipping together in church and eating together in the refectory, but we need for our spiritual development to be hermits for a while as well."

" Sort of half-hermits do you mean?" Lugne asked.

"Yes" Columba agreed. "St Martin taught this to Ninnian and it was taught to Martin by John Cassian who had studied the monks of the Egyptian desert. So we learn from each other the best ways of doing things. Learning from each other also keeps us humble!" It seemed strange to be talking of monastic life while traveling on boat through Alba! But Columba was glad they decided to bring this strong young novice, for instruction as well as for crewing.

As well as these peaceful sailing times, their journey was not without adventure. On one occasion the young warrior who was leading the soldiers, a man named Fintan from Dunadd, who had been assigned to them by King Conal, was reported by his fellows to Columba to be extremely ill. Columba hastened to the young man and found him, indeed, upon the point of death. He laid his hands upon him and claimed healing for him in the name of Jesus Christ the Good Shepherd and Healer. Fintan revived and smiled at Columba and allowed himself to be helped to stand again and return to his normal business. Not only his fellow-soldiers but also Fintan himself was deeply impressed with this healing, and Fintan years later became a good monk and follower of Jesus Christ.

On another occasion they met a man who staggered out of the woods and begged for food to feed his starving family. While some food was being fetched, Columba asked the soldiers to lend hm a knife, then he set to sharpening a stake for the man so that he could catch his own food from now on, as what was the point of only helping him for the time some food would last.

One eventful night Columba, Comghall, Cainnech, Diormit, Lugne and the soldiers were lying asleep beside a stream. Diormit with Lugne's help had previously hidden their boat for fear it should be discovered in the night and taken away while they were sleeping. He had hidden it in a little deserted village on the other side of the stream. The Holy Spirit revealed to Columba in the night the wisdom and knowledge that the boat was not safe and that it should be moved. So waking Diormit, Columba warned him to bring the boat at once and hide it much nearer to where they were sleeping. Diormit dragged himself out of sleep, woke Lugne to help him, and they managed to do this. Then again in the night, Columba woke Diormit, saying,

"Diormit come and see why I asked you to move the boat." Diormit sleepily opened his eyes and raised himself and looked across the stream and there was a blazing village engulfed in flames. Had they not known to move the boat, half of their party would have been without transport in the morning!

The long Loch Linnhe soon gave way to a small river which connected them with Lough Oich. This in turn soon came to an end and connected them to another river which they navigated for part of its way but had to carry the boats for part of the way over rocky patches, shallows and rapidly flowing cascades. This river led into the longest, largest, and deepest lake which any of the monks had ever seen before. They sailed from one end to the other, taking a whole day, for the length of the lake—which they were told by the soldiers was called Loch Ness—was so great.

It was in this area that they had their third adventure. Columba asked the monks and their military escort to bring the boats to the shore at a place where it was possible for them to clamber out and climb up onto the hillside. Columba said to them,

"Our arrival is awaited at the cottage of a heathen man who is dying. The holy angels are ready to bear his soul away, they just await me to come and give him baptism before he dies, for this man has had a wonderful natural goodness about him all through his life even though he has not heard of the Lord Jesus Christ. He is in advanced old age so let us hasten to him now."

Hearing this, their military escort, not having the same enthusiasm for preaching and baptising, suggested that they proceed onwards a little to scout and get the feel of the lie of the land and of what kind of reception they were likely to find when they reached King Brude's fortress. Columba agreed to this, and the soldiers set off.

So Columba, Comgall, Cainnech, Diormit and Lugne hastened ahead from Loch Ness until they came to the area where the man was living, an area called Airchartdan. There they were led to a serene and frail old man with grey hair, his name was Emchat. While his family stood respectfully to one side, Columba preached the word of God to Emchat who believed joyfully and requested to be baptized. As soon as Columba had baptized him with water in the name of the Father, the Son, and the Holy Spirit, Emchat's soul departed from his body and a seraphic smile was seen upon the face of the dying man. His son Virolec also believed and said,

"Please may I be baptized too? And my whole household."

Great was the rejoicing among the group of monks over this happening, and they felt that this was a good omen for their visit to the court of King Brude.

On their return, when they were nearing the spot where their own boat had been left by the River Ness, near the Northern end of Loch Ness, they found that there was a crowd of people gathered near the bank of the river. On inquiring what was happening, they found that these local people were burying a man who sadly had been seized while swimming by a beast who lived in the water, bitten very severely and had died of his wounds. His body had been hooked by its garments and helped out of the water by some local men and was now receiving burial.

At this point Cainnech, always a swift runner, came panting towards them, calling out:

"The boat has gone!". That this should happen just when the soldiers had not yet returned from their scouting trip, and they only had the one boat! Cainnech was followed shortly by Comghall, who said he had spotted the boat on the further bank. It must have have broken its moorings due to the current, for it was now on the opposite side of the river from where they had left it when they had proceeded to go and baptize the heathen man. Columba called out urgently,

"Would someone swim across and fetch our boat for we will not be able to reach our destination without it? Who among us is a strong swimmer?"

Without hesitation the young novice monk, Lugne, took off his cloak and plunged into the water. But unknown to the monks, the monster which had attacked the dead man was lurking in the depths of that river, keen for more prey. As soon as the beast felt the water disturbed by Lugne's movements, it came to the surface and with a mighty roar started swiftly towards Lugne as he was by now swimming across the mid-stream portion of the river. Not only the monks and Columba, but also the soldiers and the local people, were watching this scene in great fear and calling out to Lugne to warn him of the monster.

"Stop! Stop, Lugne! Come back!" they all yelled.

Columba, realizing there was no chance at all for Lugne to make the far bank in safety before the monster would catch up with him, prayed rapidly and immediately for help to God. He then made the sign of the cross in the air above the monster and called out in prayer, saying to the animal in a tone of great authority:

"You shall not advance further or touch that man! Go back with all speed!. In the name of Jesus Christ, begone!" Hearing these words of Columba's, the beast, in some supernatural way, appeared to have understood and it turned away as if terrified. Although it had been extremely close to Lugne at the time that Columba sained it with the sign of the cross, it turned and swam away as if frightened by Columba's prayer and all the voices. It dived underwater and nothing was seen of it again.

Lugne himself reached the far bank safely and entered the boat and paddled back to the others, mercifully unharmed and untouched and pulled himself up onto the bank, grinning to the monks who came to help pull the boat to a safe position. All of them were filled with wonder and glorified God for this miracle. The Pictish folk who had been burying their dead man were also amazed and full of wonder at what they had seen. Cainnech and Comgall instructed them in the Christian faith before they left the spot, and reported that this was well received. They felt as they proceeded towards Inverness that good seed had been sown and the beginnings of Christian churches were already beginning to be formed in this wild new country.

As they drew nearer to the fortress of King Brude, they met their military escort returning in their direction. Columba asked the soldiers provided by King Conal what kind of reception he should expect from the High King. Fintan shook his head dolefully and replied,

"Not a good welcome, abbot. We have been spotted already. There is much suspicion. They no doubt feel that we are a threat to them, and do not be surprised to find the gates closed against us. Would you like us to stay behind the trees and let just you monks proceed on your own to the gate? The interpreter can go with you."

"An excellent plan, Fintan, we will do as you suggest" agreed Columba, who strangely did not seem to be unduly worried about the reception he and his monks would receive. He had trusted in God through worse situations!

As they neared the fortress they were all impressed with the height of the almost perpendicular mound on which it stood, with the triple *chevaux de frise* and the tallness of the wooden defenses. When they did actually arrive at the outer walls of the fortress they found the gates were already closed against them, as Fintan had predicted. That must have been the clank of them being closed that they had heard as they were climbing the craggy hill. The tall Columba stood in front of the gates and called out in his magnificently loud voice,

"I come in the name of King Conal of Dalriada. I carry letters from him. I come in peace!"

Straightaway his interpreter called out these same words in the Pictish tongue. Yet the gates still remained closed. The monks showed their empty hands and opened their cloaks to display that they had no swords or spears hidden about their person and they reiterated again through the interpreter,

"We come in peace!"

Comghall and Cainneach joined in lustily for these were words which they could manage. But still the gates to the fortress stayed firmly shut.

"Have no fear," Columba said, "I know what we must do."

He walked right up to the doors and made the sign of the cross on them, and then having done so, knocked and placed his hand against them and at once the bars were forced back and the gates opened of their own accord with normal speed. As soon as they opened Columba entered and the monks and the interpreter with him, signalling back to the soldiers that they could emerge from their hiding places.

At this stage King Brude came out to meet Columba, accompanied by his advisors and had every appearance of giving Columba a very respectful and friendly welcome. The interpreter spoke his words and they were words of peace and friendliness. Through the interpreter again Columba gathered that Brude's first intention had not been to greet him in this manner, but this supernatural opening of the gates of the fortress had changed his attitude. He and his household were in some turmoil at present owing to the imminent death of one of the King's own children. Columba inwardly gave thanks to God for the miracle of the opening of the gates, praying in the words of the Sixty-second Psalm, *"My soul waits in silence for God: from him comes my salvation. He only is my rock and my salvation: my strong tower so that I shall never be moved."*

Immediately Columba offered to pray for healing for the boy, and asked what his name was, and was told it was Cennelath. Columba, Cainnech and Comghall were shown to his chamber, and looked down lovingly at the pale face of the teenager, and listened to his labored breathing. The three monks together laid hands on the lad, and prayed earnestly. After a while Cennelath sat up with an angelic smile on his face, and asked what was happening. The monks explained he had been healed by Jesus. The miracle of life restored by God's power once again had taken place.

So pleased was Columba by his welcome from King Brude, following the miracle of the gates, and then the healing of his son, that he was almost taken unawares by the surprise that awaited him inside the hall of the fortress. For beside the King's throne was a very familiar figure, a figure, small, old, and hunched, with dark brown eyes which narrowed as he looked toward Columba: Fraechan!

Columba had heard that Diarmit, son of Cerbal, had dismissed the arch-druid from his service and had presumed that he had made his way back to Bhreatain. What Columba was only just now discovering as he conversed with the interpreter was that the mother of Brude, son of Merchon, was also from Bhreatain, and Brude had been brought up there in the mountainous west, fostered by this Druid Fraechan, who was known in that British tongue as Broichan.

Fraechan had become no friendlier in the intervening years. However the Druid was powerless to stop Columba from accepting Brude's invitation to preach and explain the purpose of his journey. When the initial diplomatic work for Conal was completed, Columba stood up and preached to the court of the High King Brude of the purpose of the Creator of the World's coming to us in human form to show us the love that he bears us.

He spoke of the Oneness that lay behind the various divinities that the Druids worshipped. He spoke of the place where the deeds of Jesus Christ were written in a book, the Holy Book called the Bible. And he talked of the eternal life that was offered to those who have faith in him and become baptized as Christians. Above all he spoke of the Christian faith as being a way of life based not on fear but on love, and of this faith being open and offered to all, a free gift—not just a thing for certain people who have special knowledge, a special initiation. He made it quite plain too that the God who he believed in, who created the earth, protects his children and his power is far, far greater than the power of any Druid.

The longer Columba continued, the more Fraechan's face twisted in anger. Brude listened respectfully through it all, nodding carefully. He seemed interested but not deeply stirred. However Cennelath his son, now in full health, appeared to be listening very keenly indeed. It was no surprise to Columba but rather a joy, when towards the end of their visit Cennelath asked if he could be baptized as a Christian. His father Brude had no objection to this, and so the ceremony was conducted in an atmosphere of great joy. King Brude accepted that the mission of Columba was in peace and influenced by his son he also agreed to give complete permission to Columba and his monks to evangelize in his kingdom of Alba.

In the days that followed, as they talked long together, Columba felt the time was right to broach the subject of Dalriada, and Brude agreed to accept a peace with King Conal and to cease encroaching on his territory on the island of Mala and in various other areas. Brude was no fool. He realized that there were advantages to him in allowing Columba and his monks come and work among them. Apart from the miracles of healing that had already been witnessed in the land, he realized too that there would be teaching. That the Picts could become an educated people, they could learn to read and write. There would be great advantages for his country.

By the third day at Inverness, Fraechan appeared to have roused a little bit of support for his opposition to Columba and his Christian band. Columba, Comghall, Cainnech, Diormit, and a few others including the newly converted soldier Fintan, were singing God's praises out loud, with a small admiring crowd around them outside the fortress. As they were singing and worshiping several Druids came among them and did all they could to try to prevent the sound of God's praise being heard. They ran among the people who had been listening, shouting at them, and when Columba requested a translation, he found they were saying:

"Don't listen, don't listen to this! Don't listen to this silly heathen stuff that is coming out of these men's lips."

Columba's voice rose above the rabble, loud as a clap of thunder as he chanted the Forty-fourth Psalm. *"Our heart is not turned back, neither have our steps declined from thy way . . . Though thou hast sore broken us in the place of dragons, and covered us with the shadow of death . . . If we have forgotten the name of our God, or stretched out our hands to a strange god; shall not God search this out? for he knows the secrets of the heart . . .*

Awake, why sleepest thou, O Lord? arise, cast us not off forever. Wherefore hidest thou thy face, and forgetest our affliction and our oppression? . . . Arise for our help, and redeem us for thy mercies' sake."

Columba was aware that a final conflict with Fraechan was still to come. It was brought about by the arch-druid's own slave-girl. While Columba was making his simple meal last in the banqueting hall of King Brude's court, a female slave came up to him and gently tugged at his sleeve. Speaking in his own Gaelic tongue she whispered,

"Please help me Holy Columba, I have been Fraechan's slave since his days in Ériu, and I am sorely missing my country. He is not treating me well. Please have pity upon me and convince him to let me go free. I have people who will care for me if I can be released."

Columba looked at her and felt great pity in his heart.

"I will speak with Fraechan. Have faith, it will be done."

Anger rose in him at how this woman had been treated. The anger gave Columba the extra push he needed to confront Fraechan. First he tried requesting the arch-druid politely to release the slave. When Fraechan refused Columba let his full height tower over the bent and wizened druid and raised his voice. He still refused. Columba's anger was now roused to a greater fury,

"Know this Fraechan, know this: if you refuse to release this foreign captive for me, this Gaelic slave, before I return to my home from this province, you are going to die."

King Brude listened to this conversation but took no part in it. Columba strode out of the banqueting hall and went down to the river. In the shallows he reached for something under the water and then held his palm out to his companions,

"Do you see this white stone? Through this stone the Lord is going to bring about many cures of the sick among this heathen people." His fingers closed over the stone and he added,

"Fraechan, you know, has suffered a mighty blow just this moment. This has happened by angelic and supernatural means. He has been drinking from a glass cup which has now been shattered supernaturally. Fraechan is now gasping for breath and is very close to death. Let us wait a few minutes and see if messengers do not arrive from the king asking us to come immediately and help the dying Fraechan. I feel that in his present plight, the arch-druid is now ready to release the slave girl."

Even as Columba was speaking these words, two men arrived on horseback sent by King Brude. Anxiously they described the state Fraechan was in, which was a duplicate of the words Columba had just spoken.

"The King and his household have sent us to ask for your help for his foster-father Broichan, who is close to death."

Columba answered them,

"If Broichan first promises to free his Gaelic slave, then he will be healed. Let this little stone here be dipped in water and let him drink of the water and at once his health will come back. But if he refuses and opposes the release of this slave-girl from Ériu he will immediately die."

The two messengers returned to Brude's fort to report all his words carrying the precious little white stone with them. Columba and his companions stayed where they were by the river and waited anxiously to see would the slave girl be freed. Before sixty minutes had passed, the slave-girl appeared on the path leading from the fortress and ran to her countrymen with joy. The miracle of healing had indeed happened and Fraechan was now in full health.

Columba and Fraechan met each other once more on the final evening of Columba's visit to the fortress. Tension buzzed in the air between them still. Fraechan's scheming eyes narrowed as he asked pointedly,

"Tell me, Columba, when do you propose to set sail to return to I?"

Columba answered cheerfully

"We propose to start our voyage on the morrow if God wills."

A nasty edge sharpened Fraechan's voice as he threatened,

"You will not be able, for I have the power to create an adverse wind against you and raise up a dark pall of mist."

Columba's calm voice did not change as he replied,

"This does not frighten me in the least Fraechan. The omnipotence of my God rules over all things. He will not allow us to be thwarted."

Many people had been witness to these words, so when Columba and his companions were ready to set sail the next day, there was quite a large crowd come to see them off on the River Ness leading into the lake. Other druids were present, mingling among the crowds. These grinned as they scanned the horizon and saw that a mist was indeed rising up and the wind was gathering force, a storm brewing.

Columba barely raised his voice as he explained the position to the soldiers, reassuring them that all would be well. Then he boarded his own boat and encouraged his hesitant companions to do the same, and ordered the sails to be hoisted against the wind. They all followed his directions but in silence with solemn faces and without their usual laughter and shouting. This was no ordinary wind, Columba knew, but he knew too that his boat belonged to the Lord Christ and it was completely possible for it to sail against any wind with his help and their tacking skills. The sails raised like banners of hope, and off the two boats sped, tacking carefully, their sails straining, Columba's boat in the lead. King Brude and his people, and even Fraechan's druids, looked on in fearful amazement. Very soon after this act of faith the winds turned round and instead of an adverse wind they were gifted with a gentle and favourable breeze, a holy wind, which drove them right down the River Ness and the long length of Loch Ness speeding them on their way home to I.

Back to I, that little island of friendliness and holiness, the island Columba now looked on as his home. The island looked at him steadily and calmly as he approached it some weeks later, blue smoke rising from cooking fires in a friendly manner and dispersing in the air. The island looked like a green and grey jewel in a silver-blue sea, circled with a brown band of seaweed and ancient rocks around its base and protective rays of golden light seemed to surround it and yet be part of it. Columba realized that he had grown to love this island deeply, and he felt that the island was welcoming him home as a son.

14

Hinba

A.D. 568

Not only the island itself but his fellow monks gave Columba an up-roarious welcome home. Ernan too, who had come over to I from his island hermitage on Hinba for the duration of Columba's absence, to fulfil his duties as prior, welcomed him back warmly and with relief at his safe return. Ernan questioned Columba as they sat together in the church, for some soul-friending.

"Columba, tell me of the success of your mission or otherwise."

"Uncle, only God can judge of its success. But I report gladness that the hand of God was on our mission from the start. We had several con-versions and healings, and the Lord raised someone from near the point of death on our journey. On our journey back we also baptized a whole household full of people. The Lord protected us in mighty ways when we were confronted by a huge sea monster in a river. He opened the gates of the fortress to us which had been closed against our entry. Ernan, there were many, many signs of God's power at work and that he was going before us with his Spirit."

"How did King Brude receive your message?"

"He received it with respect and silence. I believe that although he has not received the Christian faith himself, he sees that we bring good news and he is happy for us to preach in his land, to his court, and to his family. His son Cennelath has been baptized a Christian and many others of the court as well. I believe myself that Brude will never convert, for he has been fostered by none other than the Arch-Druid from Bhreatain,

Fraechan. At the King's fortress he goes under his name in Bhreatain, which is Broichan. Brude has great affection for Fraechan and is very much under his domination. There is no chance that Brude will convert while Fraechan lives."

"Did you confront this Arch-Druid? Did he try any spells on you?" Columba smiled,

"Yes indeed. His magic is so like a sudden puff of wind that it spouts up like a water spout but falls back again. This is only a short-lived magic, no power in it. We were able to show him that God's power is far, far greater."

Columba then told him the full story of Fraechan's illness and healing and the release of the slave-girl, and their sailing against the wind on the River Ness. Ernan went on to ask,

"And your mission on behalf of King Conal? How went that?"

"That too was successful," answered Columba, "for King Brude has undertaken to cease his forays into Conal's territory. King Conal will be very glad of this news when I write to him now." Ernan looked at Columba and said,

"Columba—it will keep you humble to think that the battle that you had a part in at Cuildreimhne will be recorded in history; but all the many battles that you have stopped will go unrecorded! The dove is triumphing over the fox well now; but remember to use your fox-quality well; remember our Lord's advice to be wise as serpents and innocent as doves."

After the expedition to Inverness a rhythm and pattern to life once more was welcome indeed to Columba. There was one more thing which had been troubling him, and that was his desire to have his Mother Eithne's remains near to him instead of in Daire. How could this be managed, he wondered. After deliberation and prayer he raised the subject with Comgall. Comgall agreed to try to get the removal done with the least fuss and bother, and arranged to send a message when he was ready to set off with the casket—not from Foyle, but stopping at Rathlin Island which would be a safer place for Columba to meet them in his own boat., to bear the precious remains to a resting place near Columba on the beautiful island of I.

He was sad to have said goodbye to his friends Cainnech and Comghall, but knew that they had their own work to do, Comghall at his monastic school in Beannchor as well as his coming attempt to arrange the removal of Eithne's remains; and Cainnech at his monastery at Agha-boe. Columba was much in prayer for this project as his days took on a rhythm of manual work in the fields, and leatherwork, and smith-work, reading and transcribing books, praying together in the oratory at the regular offices, or hours, and time spent alone in his cell, which was the time for copying books, for rest and for his twice a day periods of con-templative prayer.

The peace of this period was broken by shouts one rainy early after-noon, and two monks rushed into Columba's cell out of breath and begged,

"Abbot, come quickly to Brother Diormit, he is very very ill!" Co-lumba did not wait to grab a cloak but ran to his attendant monk's cell, which was nearby. Diormit did indeed seem in very bad straits and was finding it difficult to breathe. There was a smell of herbal infusions in the cell, but this had not cleared his lungs. Columba put a hand on Diormit's brow which was very hot, and prayed as hard as he had ever prayed.

After some while there seemed to be a small amount of cooling on his brow, and Columba knew this was one of the occasions when all else would have to be let go of and time would need to be spent in battling against whatever it was that had attacked this man. So he stayed laying hands in prayer on his friend for the rest of the day, fighting this battle as if it were a spiritual battle against powers invisible to them. But Co-lumba knew the power of Christ and his name was stronger than all the wiles of the Evil One. Several monastic offices were said, and the psalms chanted without Columba's presence and his magnificent voice to lead them. Diormit's hut became their world for the present. But when the bell for vespers had started to ring, Diormit at last opened his eyes, and tried to sit up.

"Praise God! You are healed!" Columba exclaimed with relief and gladness.

A constant influx of visitors provided change and excitement in the routine of the monastery. Meals were always very simple with much fasting, particularly on Wednesdays and Fridays. But when a visitor ar-rived the fast was always dropped to offer hospitality. Columba believed in a stiff life but not in mortification to the extent that the monks' health would suffer, and they ate porridge with the addition of milk on Sundays. Sunday being a feast day, they could take eggs too and on very special feast days they would eat beef, mutton or fish. Porridge made with water and bread were their staples. Food that the farm produced was not by any means for their own use only, but was given to the poor around them on a regular basis.

Columba until the end of his life would never allow his monks to be the only ones to work hard. He would join them and work as hard as any in the labors of plowing, sowing, harvesting, grinding corn, baking, and building. He also believed that it was not right for any monk to be involved in these activities all the time. Each must be given a chance to work to perfect their calligraphy, and each must be given a chance to travel on missions to the outlying islands, whether by land or sea, bringing the Gospel to the Picts and the Dalriadans and for healing the sick and bringing alms.

At last the expected message from Comgall arrived, and Columba set off with Cobthach and Diormit to the Island of Rathlin, to meet with Comgall and transfer the casket. Rui and Fethuo sailed the large boat. This was done with much solemnity, and the two brothers set off for I once more with a lighter heart. But in spite of all the prayer that had gone into the task, all did not work out exactly as Columba had planned. Not only a squall but a fierce storm broke out and the ship was blown south-east to another small island. The island from their view of it was steep cliffs, with no landing place. The expert Rui and Fethuo managed to sail round to the land-side and there again although it was low land with no cliffs, there were rocks, and no obvious landing place. With difficulty they managed to find a small inlet and moor the boat to a rock there, and accomplish the landing.

When the storm had died down, Columba announced that this was his mother's way of making her wishes known. The little island was to be her final resting place, and place of resurrection. This small rocky island or *Eilach* had no inhabitants except for a few sheep. Columba could visit whenever he wished, for it was no farther than a day's boat-journey away, and might be an excellent place for him to make retreats away from the increasingly busy island of I, as he had done with Hinba.

The main element of their life together, above all when Columba himself was present among the brothers, was that he loved them as a father. In the evenings when all had returned from their work, and it was time to say the offices together and meet in the refectory, Columba would gird himself with a towel as the Lord had done, and wash their feet. He had it as a rule that any visitor to the island should have his feet washed and a good welcome given to him. Many a time he knew in his spirit with his gifts of knowledge and discernment that troublesome visitors were on the way—but these were treated no differently than any other visitor. A warm welcome, humble foot-washing, and a breaking of the fast for hospitality was offered to all, along with a place in their guesthouse.

Columba felt happy that the original twelve brothers who had sailed with him were proving hardy and strong. The trials they had been through had shown him that the choosing of God's Holy Spirit was above all the right choosing of the men. They were not chosen by him but were chosen by God, for God's work of which he Columba was but the humble leader.

The first death on the island was therefore not of one of the twelve, but one of the Saxon monks called Brito. Most of the brothers were away from the main monastery building, at work in the fields, and only Aidan was around to witness what had happened. Brito had been lying sick for some time and this was a sadness to Columba for this monk had been a monk of great goodness, who was zealous in caring for the poor, and who was thoughtful of others' needs in a very strong and sensitive way. Aidan saw Columba go to Brito's cell and visit him and bless him beside his bed for the hour of his departure seemed to be very close. Then he saw Columba come out of the cell and walk in the courtyard of the monastery and suddenly lift up his face and look into the sky in a very surprised way. Aidan was intrigued. What was Columba looking at? As Columba started walking again, Aidan came and knelt in front of him, beseeching him,

"Abbot Columba, father, what is making you marvel so much as you look up to Heaven?" Columba smiled at Aidan,

"I have been watching holy angels doing battle in the air against the powers of the enemy. And I am thankful in my soul that the victorious angels have now put the enemy to flight and they are even now carrying off the soul of our dear brother Brito, who has been the first among us to die on this island. He is now on his way to reach the joys of the country of Heaven. But Aidan," he added anxiously, "please do not reveal this mystery to anyone else here—at least during my lifetime."

"Of course not, Father. I understand. If more were to hear of this, you would have no peace. And already you are pressed hard by all the visitors, requests for healing, letters, and hard work. I will keep the secret while you live."

As if in proof of the truth of Aidan's words, that very day a new stranger arrived among them. Columba was sitting with Diormit on the top of a hill, and he noticed a white sail in the sound approaching the harbor. Diormit had noticed it too and said,

"That ship is taking so long to come. I wonder who it is."

"This is a Gaelic ship Diormit, and the man it is bringing is a man who has committed some great sins. I believe he is coming here to repent, and to repent in tears. Let us go and meet him for I know that Christ expects his sincere repentance."

So Diormit went to the harbor, where a man ran from the ship to meet Columba. The visitor knelt at Columba's feet, crying most bitterly as Columba had predicted. Columba was moved to tears himself as he heard the man confess his sins, completely publicly in front of all those standing around who had come to help with the boat.

"Stand up my son and take heart. The sins that you have committed are forgiven because God does not despise a humble and contrite heart."

He was given a good welcome. His name was Fechna and he was a wise man in his own community in Ériu. After a few days spent talking with Columba he was sent by the abbot off to the island of Ethe. He went peacefully to that nearby island, where Baithene, who was now the abbot of the monastery there, received him kindly.

Columba's prayers for his brothers, and for the people of this land where he was living in exile, were also added to frequently by his prayers for the people he loved in his own land. So often he would bring to God the needs of his family, and the needs of the struggling church in Ériu. As a pupil of Finnian of Cluain Ioraird who had studied with Gildas the Wise in Britain, Columba knew Gildas and his holiness by reputation. Thus he was overjoyed to have a letter one day telling him that King Ainmire, now King of all Ulaidh, had been elected Ard Rí of Ériu. Ainmire had invited Gildas to come to Ériu to strengthen the young church. He also knew that this action had been necessitated by the fact that once again the Gaelic Christians were falling back into old ways. Once again their faith needed strengthening. This was sad but the remedy for the fault was such a good one that Columba felt great joy knowing that the holy Gildas was walking among the people of Ériu now.

Columba's gift of foreknowledge so often was a help. He could predict when a whale was in the bay between I and Ethe, and he could warn those about to sail in which direction to pitch their journey. But many times his foreknowledge caused him great sadness for he could see in his spirit when people he loved were in pain or when bad things were happening in Ériu. Once he suddenly knew in one of his monasteries in

Ériu in Dairmhá that the abbot was overworking the monks, pressing them far, far too hard. He called some of his brothers to pray for them then and there, to call out to God and to pray that God would influence the abbot to go easy on them. Reports came to him by letter later that this prayer had been answered. The abbot, whose name was Laisren, felt led to announce rest and refreshment from the work for the tired and exhausted monks.

One of his sad foreknowledges concerned his uncle Ernan. Ernan felt a great desire to return at this time to Hinba to be solitary for a while. Columba knew and understood his soul-friend's need for solitude. For Ernan had a particular gift of praying to God out loud, and he wished to do his praying in a place where none would overhear. He felt his particular way of praying of calling out to God, shouting to him, beseeching him, was one which needed a deserted place. Moreover, he also had another gift which was to pray in strange tongue not understood by anyone around nor even by himself. This too he wished would not be overheard by his fellow monks. So Columba sadly gave the necessary permission for him to retire once more to Hinba to become a solitary in his little hermitage over there. As he and some other brothers showed Ernan to the boat, Columba felt a sadness in his breast and embraced Ernan most warmly. He stood and watched his uncle sit in the boat, his eyes with that familiar faraway look, his old face haggard from his mortifications but with a wonderful spiritual light in it—a face that had become very beloved to him over the years.

When the boat was out of sight, Columba turned to Diormit who was as ever loyally attending his master,

"This beloved friend of mine, who now takes his leave from me, Diormit, I do not expect to see face to face in this world again." A few days later when Columba had news that a boat had returned from Hinba and that Ernan was on board, he felt at first that this was one occasion when his gift of prophecy had failed him. He set out for the harbor to meet his uncle. However, although he saw his uncle's figure in the distance, he was not close enough to see his face, and by the time Columba had reached Ernan, the old bishop had fallen, to the horror of everyone. When Columba reached him, that blessed man had stopped breathing and none of Columba's prayers were of any avail to bring him back to life. Columba ordered the brothers to remove his body to the church and in great solemnity they bade farewell in their prayers to a man who had been such a tower of strength to them all. Columba asked one of the brothers who was skilled in stonemasonry to carve a cross and place it on the place where Ernan had died, and also another on his grave.

The whole monastery generally buzzed with life and activity these days. The permission of High King Brude to bring the Christian faith to his country had given rise to new missionary journeys. New brothers arrived from Pictish Alba, men who had been brought to Christ by the witness of the original converts from Columba's first journey to Inverness. This meant that they now had a plentiful supply of interpreters who knew both the Pictish dialects and the Scottic or Gaelic tongue that Columba and his monks spoke. Columba traveled to the Island of Skye and many other islands off the west coast of Alba. He also went to the main land-mass of Alba and founded churches in many, many places. At the times when he felt he could be spared, and when his spirit was in need of solitude he would go to the small Eileach, south-east of Mala and I, and pray there for some days, happy in the proximity of his mother's remains. The island had very little shelter, so he arranged on his next return to have some lay brothers dig an underground shelter there against the winds.

Columba returned from these expeditions full of joy at the way they had been blessed. But one day he found the joy of his return marred by the arrival of a letter. The letter bore news of the death of one of his most staunch and loyal friends, Brendan the Abbot of Birr. Already shocked by the death of both Brito and Ernan this new loss quietened and subdued Columba for some while. Shortly after that he announced his intention to go to Hinba. He needed to install a new prior for the monastery on Hinba, and then he knew that he needed quietness alone, away from everyone, even from his faithful attendant Diormit, to spend in prayer with God. While he stayed on the island of I the demands on him were so pressing that when he needed peace in which to be alone with his God, he had of necessity to go elsewhere. Columba generally chose to go to Hinba, but quite a few of his original twelve would make their hermitages on small wave-washed rocks in the channel between I and Hinba, the place of greatest danger from the sailing point of view, and there they would wrestle in prayer for weeks on end before returning to the main monastery.

So Columba withdrew to Hinba, to that little hermitage-cell that nestled beneath the tall, tall 'Paps of Hinba'. It had become beloved to him because of its association with Ernan. He had not been there long when with his gift of 'seeing', which had become much more a spiritual gift of knowledge, he knew in his spirit that King Conal of Dalriada was dead. Knowing that his part as Conal's advisor was an important one he brought the matter to God in prayer. That night he had an important dream or vision. He saw an angel holding in its hand a glass book which was the Book of the Ordination of Kings. The angel ordered Columba to read this book, and Columba balked for he saw that the next king in line after Conal in the angel's book was Aedán. Columba had already previously decided in his own mind that the most suitable successor to Conal would be Iogenan, a man of whom Columba was fond and whose kingly qualities he admired.

In the vision, Columba refused to read on; the angel scourged him and the vision came to an end. The next night the vision was repeated and the scourging too was repeated. By the third night when the vision came on again Columba realized he was beaten and humbly confessed that his choice of Iogenan was indeed his own choice rather than God's. He immediately made preparations to sail back to I and to meet Aedán, for he knew again with his seeing that Aedán would be coming to him to receive ordination as king.

On the short boat journey back to I, Columba meditated on the event. He humbly confessed to God his pride in being unwilling to follow his guidance at first. And he thought that even if Iogenan had appeared to be the more suitable candidate, Aedán would be able to be influenced by him and if willing to take his advice he could become a good Christian king. One of the reasons Columba was not happy about Aedán as successor to Conal had always been because he had lived in exile away from Dalriada, where he had taken a Pictish wife, and so was seen to have abandoned Christian ways.

When he arrived at the harbor there were many boats there, and he found that Aedán had arrived with quite a large retinue of soldiers. It was as well the weather was sunny and fine for there would be no room for this crowd in their small church or oratory. The coronation therefore must take place out of doors. And of course the crowning would have to take place upon the coronation stone that King Conal had told hm about, and that they had found near the burying place. Conal had told him it was very ancient and many stories about it were told: that it had come from Ireland, that it was from Palestine before that and had been Jacob's pillow when he had the dream of the ladder of angels, and another about a previous King of Dalriada, his ancestor, having borrowed it for his coronation and then died before he had a chance to return it. It would have to be sained and become a Christian holy stone, for as the angel's book had taught him, the crowning of a King was also an ordination, a Christian sacrament. So Columba asked Thorannu to inscribe a cross on the stone and he blessed it when this had been done.

So the coronation of Aedán took place on the now sained coronation-stone, not the first crowning and not the last. Columba gathered the monks around him for the ceremony and instructed them to be strong in prayer during it. As he anointed Aedán with blessed oil and made plain to him that this coronation was of God, he spoke prophecy.

"Believe without doubt Aedán, that none of your enemies will be able to resist you until the time when you first act deceitfully against me and my posterity. You must charge your own sons and let them charge their sons and grandsons not to loose from their hands the sceptre of this kingdom through wicked counsels. Let them do no wrong to me or my kinsmen in Ériu. I have been scourged at the hands of an angel on account of your crowning and this scourge will be turned to you and your kinsmen if they turn their hearts from God and the Christian ways. But if they follow the ways of God, he will be with them."

When the solemn anointing and crowning of Aedán was completed, Columba looked around at the men standing in a circle around him— soldiers as well as monks—and spoke to them, lifting his voice,

"I think that on the present occasion, you brave men, I do not require to deliver to you much exhortation on the subject of religion in general, to which (as I fancy I perceive) you give much greater attention at present than I have heard you have ever done in former times; but I have rather to urge you to be of one mind, and to perform the duty that you owe to Aedán, whom, by the will of God, you have elected to be your king. For it has been not so much by your request as by divine command, that I have been moved to place the royal crown upon Aedán's head." He looked round to see if they were attending to this, and was satisfied to see they were. Columba continued:

"Here, therefore, you have a king commanded to reign over you, not only by the will of man but also by the will of God. And it will be his office to administer with impartiality the government on which, by divine favour, you have now entered; to preserve the people in peace, so far as he shall be able to do so; to inflict injury on none and with all his might to hinder it from being inflicted. Your duty, on the other hand, is to live in loving concord and, content with your own possessions, never to invade the property of others; being mindful of how great benefits God, the greatest and the best, hath bestowed upon you in these times instructing you with his sacred doctrines; that you should be a people dear to himself, and peculiarly his own; and has given unto you a king, not only chosen of all, but also trusted to be loved and obeyed on account on his own singular virtue.

For if you should properly perform the things that it is your part to do, never turning aside from the cultivation of true piety, but always giving good heed to those urging you to righteousness; and if King Aedán himself (as we are confident that he will do) will always labor for the public weal, and will refer to the providence of God the honorable actions, which in his public administration he will perform, then you will have grounds to trust with strong confidence that the Heavenly Power will be present with and gracious to this kingdom, and that this nation, thus so enlightened with faith and religion, should be protected with the favour of Heaven, so that henceforth no enemy to your welfare at home or abroad need justly to be feared", Yes, all were still listening intently, so he continued to exhort them:

"But if, on the contrary (which evil fate may the good Lord avert), you fall away from the Christian religion and worship, graciously delivered unto you, and from the laws and institutions of your forefathers, and do not observe equity nor submit to the administration of the laws, tumbling headlong into all manner of inequity; or King Aedán himself, unmindful of the benefits conferred on him by God, should exercise his royal office otherwise than righteously, then know ye that this kingdom of Dalriada (unless by swift repentance ye shall turn away the divine indignation) shall undoubtedly be smitten with diverse plagues, with intestine seditions, and by the hands of enemies, and shall at length be overwhelmed with dire destruction. I beseech you, therefore (suffer me, I pray, effectually to persuade you) to beware, lest that any time becoming insolent through prosperity and provoking the wrath of the Divine Power, ye shall in the end expose your public and private welfare to the greatest of all dangers." The silence became even deeper as they took in these solemn words.

Over time a closeness sprang up between Aedán and Columba. Columba would, when King Aedán was far away, feel in his spirit when that son of his was in battle, and would summon his brothers to prayer. Their prayers were required on many occasions. The first occasion was one of great sadness, for the cousins of Aedán who had hoped to inherit the throne, the sons of Conal and Duncan in particular, were not accepting of the coronation of Aedán on I. They mustered the whole of the Conal Clan of their fathers, while Aedán mustered the whole of the Gabhran Clan to support him. In the year 574 the opposing factions met in their own lands of Kintyre, and the result, though victory for Aedán was also death to Duncan son of Conal the late king's son. Up to Columba's death he was summoned to pray for Aedan's wars on many occasions—for Aedan's invasion of the Orkney Islands, and for Aedan's war against the Miathi tribe, who lived on their high rocky fort in Clachmenan. He gave thanks often that distance was nothing to those in the spiritual realm, and even on one occasion asked his personal angel to rescue a man about to fall from a high roof in Daire, and knew that man was safe—what was to them a long boat-journey and even longer walk, was as nothing to the angelic beings.

Columba's own expeditions into the mainland of Alba became fewer, for his energies were completely taken up with organising his own monastery, and overseeing those on Ethe and Hinba and the mainland of Kintyre. However he did go on a preaching tour of the island of Skye, and he once again visited Inverness when he heard the news of the death of Brude son of Merchan.

Joy it was to Columba that Brude's other son, Gartman, had given his allegiance to the Lord Christ and Columba made the long journey to Inverness a second time to consolidate the work he had achieved there. He then proceeded south to Kingussie and some of the areas East of the mountains near the East coast of Alba. However Columba was aging, and he felt often the need of retiring to Hinba for times of refreshment. He longed for times of rest to help overcome the total weariness of body that resulted from driving himself physically, mentally and spiritually, and from mortifying himself and fasting more than his body was able to take.

Sadly these visits to Hinba, the purpose of which was peace, were not totally undisturbed by violence. Tales of the unchristian lives of some of the members of the royal family of Dalriada had become so frequent that he decided to excommunicate them. A good Christian layman called Colman had become a friend of Columba's. He had indeed been rescued from poverty by the abbot. Colman had suffered attacks and plunderings from his house by a certain Ioan, son of another Conal—not King Conal—of the royal family of Gabhran. This Ioan was in fact nothing but a pirate in spite of his royal blood. So Columba determined to excommunicate him. He made his way to the church of the monastery of Hinba in order to do this.

He had barely begun his words of excommunication when one of Ioan's companions, an unpleasant man named Lam Dess, rushed to the church door, spear in hand. One of the brothers, Findlaughan, was quick to see the situation. He immediately grabbed Columba's white abbot's cowl and put it on himself, leaving the abbot clothed like a normal monk and he, Findlaughan, appearing to be the senior by virtue of the distinctive white cowl. Findlaughan also walked to the front of the altar as if he were the one who was taking the service. Lam Dess threw his spear at this figure who he presumed was Columba. Miraculously Findlaughan was not harmed. The spear only pierced the cowl. Findlaughan gave a very good imitation of the scream of a dying man and fell to the ground. Lam Dess, presuming that he had died, ran off.

The brothers gathered around Findlaughan and Columba with anxious faces, but shouted with joy as they saw Findlaughan rise from the floor. They all gave great thanks to God for this wonderful miracle. But Columba's anger became hot against the pirates and the violent ways of these men from a country which was Christian in name only.

On a day of sunshine and gentle breezes, Columba saw the sunlight sparkling on the sea and looking over towards the mainland of Kintyre from Hinba where he was, he felt a great desire to visit his friend Colman. He sailed over and strode towards Colman's house. But on the way to the small house he encountered the pirate Ioan and several of his men laden with booty in the shape of Colman's livestock and sacks of grain. They were staggering along to the harbor to load these into their own ship, the pirates!

"Put down those sacks of grain this moment! Let go of those animals!" Columba called to him. Ioan refused to do so, and obstinately continued on his journey to the harbor ignoring the abbot. His men turned round and derided and mocked Columba. Columba followed him, remonstrating and trying to rescue the goods of his friend Colman, but the men just boarded their ship and Ioan himself called out rude things to the abbot, mocking him. Columba, carried away with his anger, strode into the sea after the ship until the waves were coming right up to his thighs, and raising his hands to heaven he prayed earnestly to God for help in this situation.

The boat made its way over the calm sunny water and Columba ran to a nearby hill to get a better sight of it so he could call out a curse upon them. He said to the crowd who had gathered to watch this drama,

"This miserable wretch Ioan, who has despised Christ and his servants, will never return to this harbor from which he has set sail before your eyes. Nor will he with his wicked accomplices reach any other lands to which he is going. A sudden death shall overtake him. Watch and see now if you cannot see now in answer to my prayers a cloud rising in the north-west which is going to unleash a violent storm which will sink him and his companions. Not one of them will survive to tell the tale."

Not one of that present company did survive; yet piracy continued in the land. Some of Ioan's companions in crime continued his ways, and having been informed of the reasons behind their leader Ioan's death, determined to avenge themselves.

15

Druimceatt

A.D. 574

Harvesting by hand is hard work. This day it was also hot work. Even the constant sound of the waves on the shore offering a refreshment to the ear was not sufficient to prevent the brothers, who were reaping the barley with their hand sickles, from feeling weary from their work. At last they heard after many hours of work, the bell sound across the fields and hills from the monastery. It was time to return home. They set out, but their footsteps were lagging as they went along, and their weariness increased as it was well past their usual time for having eaten food. Baithene had returned from Ethe of a purpose to help with the barley-harvest, and he was in charge of the monks this day. Baithene noticed as they passed a little hilly place in between the fields and the monastery that each monk in turn seemed to have a faraway look in his eyes and also a look of surprise and joy. The following evening on the way home from the fields Baithene noticed the same again.

By the third evening, Baithene too had this look on his face and he gathered the monks around him in a circle. They complied willingly for they were all very fond of this Prior of I and always looked forward to his visits. Baithene began:

"Now my brothers, you must confess one by one if you experience an unfamiliar and wonderful feeling at this particular place here, midway between the harvest and the monastery." The brothers all looked at each other inquiringly and then most of them broke into smiles. Cetea spoke first,

"Well, in accordance with your command I shall tell you what was revealed to me here. During the past few days, Baithene, and even now this minute as I speak, I've been sensing a perfume of wonderful fragrance. It is as if all the flowers in the world were gathered together in one place. I also feel, Baithene, a kind of fiery glow; it is not a painful glow but a pleasurable glow. I must in truth report that a wonderful incomparable delight floods my heart which at once brings me great comfort and gladdens me so that I forget all the weariness of harvesting and any sorrows that I have. Furthermore this sack that I am carrying on my back, which should be extremely heavy, seems to have become fairly light. I do not know how. On all the evenings on which I felt this, the whole journey through, the sack has given me no sense of heaviness or burden!"

The other monks were all nodding during this report, and one by one each of them told Baithene that they had felt exactly as Cetea had described. Cuimín asked,

"Baithene, did you feel this too? If you did, please tell us, what can it be?"

Baithene suggested they ask their father abbot, and when they did, Columba with an affectionate grin admitted that he had been praying for them all, having sensed their weariness in his spirit.

King Aedán requested Columba's advice. He had been proving to be a good king on the whole, a strong ruler.

"Columba, this Boromean Tribute is a millstone around our neck. I feel I could defend my own borders properly if my fighting men were not constantly away in the service of the King of Dalriada in Ériu. The Seven Erics of Kindly Blood I do not mind so much, for seven shields, seven steeds and seven bondsmen each year are a moderate tax for us to give, but if we could abolish the tribute it would make all the difference. Can you help me negotiate with the King of Dalriada across the sea in order to obtain our independence? It is time that we became our own country and not just an outpost of a smaller one across the sea, who is extracting this severe levy in fighting men that we can ill afford."

Columba considered for a while and then said,

"Aedán, I will write a letter to my cousin Aed. King Aed is now King of Ulaidh, so the King of Dalriada is one of his sub-kings. Aed is a Christian king who will understand our position and do what he can to help. I shall write to him straightaway and suggest a meeting between us all."

Aed had one of his scribes write a reply to Columba without much delay. In the letter, his tone was somewhat cool, but nevertheless he appeared willing to cooperate. He told Columba of a planned Convention to be held at Druimceatt, in the north-west. There were many items needing discussion and settlement. Chiefly Aed explained that he was sick and tired of the power of the poets, who were satirizing freely, travelling freely and availing freely of hospitality wherever they went. They were becoming a plague. He intended to put some kind of control on them if not to banish them altogether. There were other matters too and the kings of the whole province of Ulaidh would meet together at the Synod. Aed also added, for Columba's approbation, that he was continuing the tradition that had now started with the fair at Tailltu, whereby meetings to discuss things were becoming divorced from the old Druidical festivals at the solstices.

Columba noticed that in the letter Aed made no mention of the possibility of Columba coming with King Aedán to Ériu for the meeting. However he knew that Aedán wished his help. But he also knew that those like his kinsman in Ulaidh would know well of his vow never to see Ériu again. So Columba was in a difficulty. He thought long and hard, and prayed for guidance. He consulted, surprisingly, his attendant Diormit on what to do about this. Diormit, the Cairbre-man, had often very clever insight, and good common sense. Diormit laughed when he heard about the quandary and suggested,

"Abbot—the answer is simple! If you blindfold your eyes you will not see Ériu. Your body, your mind, your voice, will all be in Ériu, but you will still be keeping your vow not to see the land."

"Excellent, Diormit! But what about my vow not to set foot again on the soil of Ériu?" The resourceful Diormit still had an answer.

"That is a little harder, but not impossible. If we strap turves of Alba to the underneath of the soles of your sandals, you will no longer be treading on the soil of Ériu—could you manage that?"

Columba laughed and laughed.

"Diormit, what a ridiculously simple and wonderful answer! My admiration goes out to you. Why did I never think of that? Thank you!"

Columba anticipated the visit to Ériu with enormous pleasure. He hoped that his children and brothers in the monasteries that he intended visiting, would accept his blindfold. However, there would be little point in not visiting the places where he was drawn to in heart. In particular he felt drawn with a great uneasiness to the ridge of the baskets—Droim Cliabh in Cairbre, where the battle of Culdreimhne had been fought. After much prayer, he felt quite strongly that God was asking him to bring something to that part of Cairbre that would heal and cleanse the land of the bloodshed committed there. He decided to try and obtain some land in that part on which to build a monastery. Strong and sustained prayer he felt was the only thing that would bring complete healing to that area, and completely cleanse the blight of the killings, and a monastery there would be the ideal way of doing it. The one death of his own army had been buried with all due honors and prayer but it was only now after the thirteen years' interval that Columba felt ready to be able to say any priestly prayers of committal over the "enemy" dead.

He had just the man in mind for a first abbot and decided to bring this monk, Mothorian, with him to the Convention at Druimceatt and then on to Droim Cliabh afterwards where if the project was of God, the need for land on which to build the monastery would be met by God. Fired with enthusiasm for the project, Columba went to the forge and started work on a crozier for Mothorian; bells and chalices he had in plenty already. Mothorian accepted the commission with a kind of humble joy, his always happy face beaming with its habitual radiance.

Word that Columba was planning to visit the Convention at Druimceatt spread very fast. Columba found his guest-house was always full of couriers who had come with letters from the poets of Ériu, who all had got word of their impending banishment. They all beseeched him to visit Ériu and plead on their behalf. In particular Dallan, the Ollav or arch-poet, was extremely keen that Columba would be the one to represent their poets, being a fully-fledged poet himself, a qualified member of the Fili.

He also had a letter from his old battle-friend, Scandlan of Osraige. Scandlan was now being kept as a hostage by King Aed in Aontraim and was not happy with the treatment he had received, having been fettered, an unworthy treatment of a prince although a petty one.

Columba went to Dunadd and joined the King's impressive fleet of ships, full of attendants, warriors, clerics and horses and chariots, and he traveled with King Aedán. This gave Columba plenty of chance to persuade Aedán of the necessity of visiting Scandlan on the way. Scandlan was delighted to see Columba and asked him to bless him. Columba blessed him and spoke words of prophecy intending to be comforting to him,

"My son, do not be downcast but rather be glad and take heart, for King Aed, by whom you are imprisoned, will die before you do. After a period of exile you will reign as king among the people of Osraige for thirty years. Then you will be driven out of the kingdom a second time and have another short exile, but then you will be recalled by the people and reign for three seasons." The stout gruff warrior received this prophecy with contentment and admiration. Columba assured him that he would fight on his behalf at the convention.

And so King Aedán and Abbot Columba arrived together at Druimceatt with their band of attendant warriors and clerics, including Mothorian. True to character, they arrived late. Every man attending the Convention was already in place and so every head was turned and there was a great, almost communal, gasp as Columba entered with his black blindfold occupying the whole space of his cowl whose hood was up over his head. It was noticed that this black-faced, hooded abbot was being led to a seat by no less a personage than King Aedán of Dalriada himself. Aed's wife was seen to curb her two sons, Domnall and Conal. Conal made a public show of insult to Columba of which he with his blindfold was innocently unaware. But footsteps could then be heard and Domnall the younger son came and knelt at Columba's feet.

Aware that someone had knelt for his blessing, Columba asked a nearby person who this was.

"This is the younger son of King Aed," he was told. Domnall took hold of both Columba's hands and planted a kiss on each of them and asked for Columba's blessing. Columba managed to anger his former friend King Aed even more than he had done so already by blessing the boy with these words,

"This boy Domnall will outlive all his brothers and become a most famous king. He will never be delivered into the hands of his enemies, but will die a peaceful death in old age, on his own bed, and in his own home, amid a throng of close friends." Taking this as his cue, Aed then drew himself up and commenced his speech condemning the poets of Ériu, the condemnation about which the poet Dallan had written to Columba, beseeching him to come and save them.

Columba, had he not been also determined to come and assist his King Aedán at the convention and also to plead for justice for Scandlan in his prison, would without doubt have come to help save the poets alone, from his fellow-feeling and alarm that Ériu would shame herself by disowning this noble band. Columba knew well that they had indeed grown arrogant and unjust, but such petty misdemeanors were no cause for banishment. His task was to make sure that Aed's anger against the satire which had, Columba guessed, been redirected towards himself, would not lead him to an action that he would later regret.

Columba realized that he was not a moment too soon in his arrival and that Aed had probably deliberately started with the matter of the poets. Poetic blood flowed in his veins from his mother's family. He rose and boiled in anger, as he realized that his arrival was spurring King Aed on to greater and greater invective against the poets:

"These Fíli, these poets, have become no longer a small band of highly educated and talented writers of poetry that we can all admire. Now it has become a large band of overbearing, arrogant, exacting satirists." King Aed spat out these words with a vehemence Columba had never yet seen in him. Aed continued,

"Their manner of living as they wander the country eating the food of whichever chief prince or king they please, staying as long as they please, asking whatever price they please for their poems, has made them a scourge, these poets! Only last month a poet came to me and demanded in payment for his amhran, a royal brooch which was a beautiful heirloom of my family. This has gone too far! This band of tinkers must be banished from the land!" Ah, it has touched him personally, Columba thought, that explains his anger and vehemence.

As soon as Columba started speaking there was no longer any doubt at all in anyone's mind that this was indeed the famous Abbot Columba who had gone into exile to a small island on the west coast of Alba. Columba's majestic and loud voice stood him in good stead once again. As he rose, through the black mask of his blindfold, he lifted up his voice in his most elegant words and pleaded for his fellow poets.

"Shame on you, men of Ériu! Shame on you for violating our sacred tradition of poetry! Have you forgotten that it is Ériu's poets who have made her great in the world? What these men have is precious!" Columba pleaded,

"They deserve their recognition. However," Columba added, "it would seem that the bands of poets together with their own personal servants have constituted a heavy, heavy burden upon the kings and princes of this country with the hospitality that they have exacted. I would not deny this fact. My plea is that the poets be not banished, but that the order of poets should be reformed, should be better organised. Let the King feel he has sole control of the Fíli. Let the King maintain his own special bard, chosen from among the cream of the land. Let him not banish every poet from Ériu for if this were to happen, Ériu would die. Allow these men to share and teach what they have. Start schools of poetry in a more organised fashion than heretofore. Just organise these men and they will work for you and for Ériu if you will let them."

Columba listened to the debate that followed and realized that all the debate concerned methods of implementing his suggestion of organisation, and so no more word need be said by him. So he saved his voice and his presence for his next plea, and thanked God silently for the success of his speech, which had turned the tide, and banishment was no longer spoken of.

Next Columba spoke eloquently on a subject about which he was beginning to have strong views. He knew he would not gain sympathy from all quarters for this, but felt compelled by the spirit of Christ to fight to get exemption from military service for the women of Ériu. It had upset him greatly at the battle of Cuildreimhne to see the women of his kin with shields and spears and some with swords, on his behalf. He had been forming a resolve to try and rectify this outdated pagan custom as soon as he had a chance since that day. He did have a success in this although later it transpired that it was only a partial success as it did not get passed as a law, but was accepted in principle by many. Nevertheless his exertions did save many, many women from that indignity. Columba hoped and prayed that his successor as Abbot of I would be able to get this enshrined as law.

The matter of Scandlan was dealt with in comparative ease, and Columba waited with Aedán over the week until it was time to bring up the subject of the Dalriadan Kingdom in Alba.

King Aed did show respect and honor for King Aedán of Dalriada, and invited him to speak on the matter of the 'Eric of Kindly Blood', as part of the Boromean Tribute was sometimes called; 'Kindly Blood' meaning in this case their kinship, and the seven Erics was traditionally defined as 'seven shields, seven steeds and seven bondsmen' paid as tribute every year from the Alban Dalriadan King to the one in Ériu who had been in need of help to defend his borders. Also because of the kinship between the Dalriada of Ériu and the Dalriada of Alba, tribute in kind was paid annually in the form of livestock and in the form of fighting men.

The convention decided to the relief of all that the Alban Dalriada should be encouraged to independence, on condition that whenever the Dalriadan kingdom in Ériu, and also the provincial King of Ulaidh, should require extra fighting men that the men would be made available on a temporary basis. This was to work the other way around also, when King Aedán required extra fighting men to defend himself against the Picts, fighting men were to be made available from his kin, the Dalriada of Ériu. This new arrangement met with the approval of all.

When the convention had reached a break Colman Abbot of Snamluthir, a good friend of Columba's, set to thinking about Columba and his situation. He realized that Columba would be wanting to visit his monastic settlements such as Dairmhá, Ceanannas Mór, Sórd and Daire, but for the blindfolded man the journey on foot would not be a very easy way of doing such a thing, for King Aedán, with whom he had travelled to the Convention, was returning to Alban Dalriada on the morrow. So Colman decided to offer himself and his chariot to Columba, to bring him wherever he wished. So he approached Columba and said

" Columba, my horse and chariot, and myself as charioteer, are at your service if you need to travel elsewhere in Ériu. You are most welcome to this help."

And so Colman, Abbot of Snamluthir and founder of that monastery, acted as charioteer for his friend Columba, and was perfectly happy for Mothorian to be of their company. Colman had noticed this quiet monk who had a lovely radiance about him. Colman's first task, though, was to try to extract Columba and Mothorian from Druimceatt. For so many people had brought the sick and the dying and the disabled to be healed by Columba, having heard of his arrival in Ériu, that it was well-nigh impossible to walk anywhere around the green hill surrounding it, Daisy Hill as it was known locally. Colman tried to persuade Columba to come away with him straight away.

"No, Colman. Let me do the Lord's work for some short while first. I cannot leave those who are in pain."

So Columba laid hands on the sick who Mothorian had selected for him, and in order to save a little time, for darkness was beginning to fall after a while, he blessed a vessel of water and Colman would sprinkle this water on the sick people with a prayer. Many, too, grabbed the hem of Columba's cloak or his tunic as he passed by. Colman, Columba and Mothorian blessed those who were lying there and their helpers but did not wait to hear if there had been many miracles of healing. These rumors only reached their ears in the weeks to come.

It was in the cool of the first evening of this work that Columba noticed a cloaked figure come nearer. He quickly pulled up his blindfold, but then heard Aedh's voice "Columba shall we shake hands as we are friends again now?" Columba lowered the blindfold and the two men's eyes met and they fell into a manly embrace.

As Colman had put himself entirely at Columba's disposal, they planned a roundabout route, visiting Daire first of course, and then Rathlin Island and then revisiting the site of the battle of Cuildreimhne, the little church of Droim Cliabh nearby full of so many memories of his vigil before the battle, and then from there down to Dairmhá. When the three arrived at the monastery of Daire, a brother came out and welcomed them, kissed them and brought bowls of water to wash their feet. While the three of them were eating in the refectory the same brother, whose name was Berchan, came excitedly up to Colman and Columba. Excusing himself he explained,

"This is a miracle! This is a miracle! Your chariot wheels have no lynch pins in them. The wheels are just sitting at the end of the axles. How far have you traveled this day?"

"Well, a matter of three hours' driving on quite rough roads! From Druimceatt near Limavaddy," said Colman. Columba smiled and said,

"Let us praise God for this miracle. It was His grace alone that upheld us. It is His grace alone that upholds us at every moment of our life even though, as on this occasion, we are not always aware of it." Berchan told them new lynch-pins would be made and inserted immediately, and they thanked him warmly for this.

Visiting the church folk on Rathlin Island, Columba was obliged to help in a family dispute. Mothorian and Colman walked away a little together to allow Columba have privacy while a woman was approaching him. She explained that she found it intolerable and repulsive to have to sleep with her husband for he was such an ugly man. Columba tried to keep a straight face upon hearing this. The wife was unaware that Columba was smiling behind his blindfold, and said to Columba,

"I hate him for his ugliness. You cannot make me sleep in the same bed with this man."

Columba said to her,

"Woman, woman," gently, very gently, "woman do you try to disown your own flesh? Do you not remember that the Lord said that two shall be one in flesh? And so the flesh of your husband is actually your flesh. It is your flesh you are disowning."

The woman said in reply,

"I am ready to carry out whatever you require of me, however troublesome it may be, With just one exception, that you do not press me to sleep in the same bed as Lugne. I make no objection to taking on the whole care of the house or, if you bid, even to crossing seas or living in some convent for nuns." Columba replied,

"What you say would not be right. For while your husband is still alive, you are bound by the law of the husband. For what God has joined together it is forbidden to separate. What I suggest is that the three of us, myself, your husband Lugne, and you, fast and pray to God about this problem."

She then said, a little bit of faith coming to her,

"Yes, I know that it will not be impossible, for things which seem difficult or even impossible may be granted to you by God at your request. For your prayers are so powerful."

So, Columba did in fact stay awake that night and pray much for Lugne and his wife. The next day he asked to speak with her again and asked that Lugne be present as well. This time he asked her quite pointedly,

"Woman, are you ready today, as you said you were yesterday, to depart to a convent for women?"

She said,

"Now I know that your prayer concerning me has been heard by God. For the man I hated yesterday, today I love. My heart during this past night, I know not how, has been changed in me from hate to love."

Colman felt full of admiration for his friend who was willing to spend a night of prayer to help an obstinate woman, and to aid a couple in their marriage. What love and understanding, what faith he had! Colman again felt that he was more than willing to act as charioteer for Columba as long as he was needed.

After Rathlin Island they then proceeded to tour various churches and monasteries Columba had founded on the west coast, places like the now-named Glencolmcille, Rath Bhoth and Cill Mhic Néanáin. When they reached Droim Cliabh, Columba was overjoyed to find a strong, large, and thriving group of Christians. Praying and brooding there over his need for land on which to build the monastery, Columba's prayers were answered in a miraculous way. He was walking in prayer on a day of wetness and wind, Colman beside him as his guide, on the bank of the Codnach river, the main river at Droim Cliabh, when they heard screams and urgent shouts coming from down-river, the area of the ford, nearer the estuary of the river. Columba begged Colman to lead him to the spot to see if he could help. They found a chariot overturned in the river and two men hauling the inert body of a young woman to the shore. The men were silent and shaking their heads as there was no sign of life in her. Columba begged Colman to lead him to the woman, and he knelt beside her and prayed fervently, exhorting the men to join him in praying. At last there was some movement and the woman's eyes opened, and she straightaway realized that the blindfolded monk was Columba, her cousin, and she told him that she was a daughter of King Aed who had recently been married to a local Cairbre chieftain. After she was brought to safety and warmth in a nearby house, she insisted on thanking Columba profusely and sending messengers to her father. Aed himself arrived late the next day, and the two cousins were again in a state of friendliness towards each other.

"Columba, I thank you and I thank God for restoring my daughter to life. As a means of thanking you I wish that you will accept a gift of some of this land. I will give it to you and your heirs or coarbs in perpetuity, so that you can start a new monastery here."

Columba accepted the land gratefully, and the news that a new monastery was to be started there spread fast. As soon as Columba spoke to the people, many flocked to him and young men pressed him to allow them to become monks—among them the men who had helped Aedh's daughter. Because so many local men were clamouring to become monks, Columba told them he was about to found a monastery and leave Mothorian in charge as abbot. Local chieftains and princes agreed to pay tithes to support the new monastery. Columba left the monastery in a strong position with its own bell and chalice, that Colman was glad to see lifted out of his chariot, feeling that it was no wonder the lynch-pins had fallen out with that extra weight! Columba promised to expedite a copy of the Holy Gospels from another monastery such as Daire or Dairmhá as soon as it could be arranged.

The day before Columba and Colman set off again, they invited Mothorian to join them in a prayer-ritual to cleanse the battle field. It was a day of grey clouds, wind and showers, and as the wind blew sheets of rain in a sideways direction Columba could not help imagining that they were the hosts of Diarmit McCearbal's army, the ghosts still lingering there. The three monks labored long and hard in prayer and Columba solemnly gave the crozier he had made to Mothorian, and said:

"I entrust to you and the monks of this new Columban Rule Monastery the task of continuing to heal the land of the bloodshed and tragedy that has blighted it. Before you die, you must pass on this task to the next abbot and tell him to continue the tradition also after his own death, and so on, to every generation. An important task lies before us here". Mothorian replied with equal solemnity "I will undertake this task, the Lord being my helper."

Colman and Columba then said farewell to Mothorian and proceeded on in a south-easterly direction to visit Aghaboe and Dairmhá. However as they were passing near the monastery of Cluain Mhic Nós, both felt eager to see how the monastery of their dear friend the late Ciarán was shaping up. News of their impending arrival reached the monastery before they did, and when they arrived they found that many were gathered together with their abbot to give them a riotous welcome.

The Cluain Mhic Nós monks treated Columba as if he were an angel of the Lord, bowing their faces to the ground upon seeing him and kissing him with great reverence. They conducted Columba and Colman to the church, singing hymns and praises. But so numerous were his admirers that Columba was in danger of being trampled. The monks noticed this and quickly came with branches which they tied together to make an improvised litter and lifted him up and carried him towards the church. As he was being carried along, he felt a tug on his cloak. Not willing to take off his blindfold as was his vow, he prayed and perceived inwardly with the eyes of the Spirit that the person who tugged at him was a young boy. He took hold of the boy's neck and pulled him forward and stood him in front of him so that he could feel his face like a blind man would. All the people around were aggravated and said,

"Send that boy away! Banish him! Why should the Holy Columba have to touch this wretched boy? This is the boy who behaves worse than anybody in the school classes."

Columba smiled and said, "Let him be brothers, just let him be." He felt that the boy under his hands was trembling violently and he spoke to him softly, whispering,

"My son, is this true? Have you been disrespectful in class?" He felt a little nod under his hand and he said again,

"Do not fear my son. I will put this thing right. Open your mouth and put out your tongue." Columba felt the boy's mouth open and the wet tongue come out so he carefully made the sign of the cross on the boy's tongue and spoke a blessing. Then, in order to include the people aroumd him as the scene was now becoming slightly more public, he lifted his voice a bit louder and spoke a prophecy.

"Although this boy now seems contemptible to you and quite without worth, let no one despise him on that account. For from this hour he will no longer displease you, but will find great favour with you. He will steadily grow from day to day in good conduct and in the virtues of the soul. Wisdom, too, and good sense, will increase in him more and more from this day, and in this community of yours he will be a man of high achievement. His tongue also will be gifted now with eloquence from God to teach the doctrine of salvation."

Talking to the boy again he found out his name, and that his name was the same as Columba's beloved late uncle, Ernan.

After a happy visit to Cainnech at Aghaboe Columba spent time at Dairmhá during which he oversaw the building of a much larger church. He saw with pleasure the progress of the scriptorium and the number of book satchels hanging there, he decided that after one more visit to Ceanannas Mór and the small church at Sórd he would turn northwards, to visit Comgall and then seek a boat to bring him home to I once more.

Columba took leave of his spiritual children in their monasteries in each of the places he visited with the same words,

"See that you live together in love, harmony and gentleness with one another, in imitation of Christ, my dear children."

Colman tried his best to dissuade Columba from travelling further, and suggested they look for a boat from Ben Eadair, which was not far from Sórd, and had a good and busy harbor. He had a feeling that a further visit north might not be good, and his friend was already tiring. But Columba was not to be persuaded.

As if Columba's phase of miracle-working seemed to have, of a dark human necessity, to be followed by a display of what was left of his fox or wolf nature, he once again became involved in a dispute, and this time, sadly, with his dear old friend Comgall and his relatives. It concerned land, as was so often the case in Ériu, and two conflicting claims to it, at a place named Cúil Rathain, and ended in a small battle or skirmish, leaving Columba feeling a mixture of remorse, dejection and defensive self-righteousness. These feelings got pushed down to be dealt with at a future date when back in I—home in I!

Although Columba felt joy at being in his own country of Ériu once more, he did surprisingly feel a homesickness for the island of I. Not only that, but he longed to see Baithene again. For Baithene, not only his brother in Christ, his cousin by blood, and also his foster-son, had now added on the even stronger tie of having become Ciolumba's soul-friend since the death of Ernan. Columba felt the need of a serious talk with his soul-friend, to bring healing to the healer, for he knew that his soul was stained with many sins after allowing his pride and anger to take over at the incident in Cúil Rathain.

On the boat-journey back to I, Columba pondered these events. His heart leapt when, as the boat neared the harbor at the eastern side of the island, he heard the bell ringing for the office of sext. As soon as he was ashore he walked to the church his heart swelling with happiness as he heard the chanting of the psalms. He hastened past the guest house, the refectory. the monks' cells and the cookhouse with its smell of wood smoke, to join his brothers in their worship.

16

Place of Resurrection

A.D. 598

A monk sat on the seashore on a little grassy hillock among the wild flowers and shells. He was trying to divide his mind between prayers and watching the sea. He was expecting somebody and this somebody that he was expecting was a bird! This monk was Scandal, the same who had insisted on bringing their boat three times sun-wise around the rock as they embarked from Lough Foyle to reach the island of I. Columba had been busy writing in his cell, as nowadays in his eighth decade of life he seemed to do more and more often, writing, writing, writing, preparing Gospels and Psalters to send to his numerous churches and monasteries far and wide. Interrupting his work he called Scandal to him. Columba had smiled at Scandal and said

"Scandal my son, I have a very special task for you, and I feel you are the one person who could do this task. On the third day after this which now dawns you must keep watch on the west of this island, sitting above the seashore. For after three o'clock in the afternoon, a guest will arrive from the north of Ériu. The guest will be a large grey bird. This bird will be very tired and weary after flying far through the air on gusty winds, and its strength almost spent, it will fall on the shore before you and rest. You should look after it with great care. Lift it up gently and take it to a nearby house where it will be given food and a place to sleep. For three days and nights you shall carefully nurse this large bird, Scandal, and feed it well. After that when the three days have passed and it is refreshed it will not wish to make a longer pilgrimage with us but will return to that sweet district of Ériu from whence it came, its strength fully restored. One of the reasons for my giving you, Scandal, special charge of this bird is that this bird has come from the district of our kinsfolk in Ériu."

So here sat Scandal, sifting sand and seashells through his fingers and scanning the horizon every few moments. He felt as if he was idling away the afternoon, looking for a bird! As he sat there, Scandal wondered was there a special reason why the abbot had wished him to do this task for him? He scanned the horizon yet again. At last, in the heat of the afternoon, he thought he detected a little dot in the distance which was getting larger and larger. Concentrating well and fixing his eyes on that dot, he realized that it was indeed a large grey bird and that it was heading somewhat to the north of him. Running to the north to be at the right place to catch it should it fall, Scandal realized that this bird was a crane. The dreaded crane! The bird of evil omen! Scandal shuddered. However, obedience to his abbot came first. As soon as he reached the spot where the bird was likely to land he watched as the bird in fact hurtled to the ground a few feet away from him. He ran over to it. Mercifully the bird was alive but did in fact have not a broken wing but a wing which was feeble from exhaustion and from beating against the strong winds. It just seemed to be crumpled there its long legs dangling and its wings limp, as if it had no more strength.

Gently and tenderly, Scandal picked up the bird. He suppressed a shudder and made a big effort to be compassionate, in spite of the super-stition of his own childhood, of this bird being one of evil omen. He then walked to the nearest house with it in his arms, keeping the long beak well away from his flesh.

"Abbot Columba wishes this bird to have water and be fed. It is weary from its journey and can no longer fly for the moment. Will you help?" The occupant of the house was only too willing to help and soon the bird was drinking from a small pot and then nestling in a hastily improvised bed of rushes in the corner of the house, in the warmth and out of the wind. After vespers that evening, the abbot came smiling to Scandal and said,

"God bless you, my son, for your kind attention to our guest, the pilgrim. It will not linger in pilgrimage, as I told you, but after three days it will go back to its own country."

This did indeed happen, to Scandal's surprise, and also the surprise of the kind farmer who had helped nurse it. Brought out to the sunshine, having eaten and slept for those three days, it started a few halting steps and then flapped its wings. After a few lolloping short flights, the crane suddenly soared aloft, circled a few times and then crossed the ocean in a straight line as if it was indeed returning to Ériu. This day, as Columba had explained to Scandal, was a day of calm and suitable for the crane's pilgrimage. Scandal returned to his cell, meditating on the lesson he now realised his abbot wished him to learn from the episode. The bird did not seem evil at all, just tired and vulnerable, and grateful for his care. The old superstitions he had grown up with as a child suddenly seemed senseless and blown away with the wind of the Holy Spirit and the spread of the Christian faith in his homeland.

Since Baithene had become Columba's soul-friend, Columba paid him visits when he could be spared. Baithene was now abbot of a small community on the island of Ethe. On a day which seemed to be set fair, Columba set sail to the island of Ethe to visit his dear Baithene, particularly wanting to see him again because of the burden of guilt on his soul. On this occasion his companions seemed to think that his great gift of foreknowledge had deserted him for of a sudden a storm brewed up when they were only half way over to the island.

The crew became rather agitated. Columba sensed their fear and joined them in trying to bail out the bilge water. One of the sailors frowned at him and said,

"What you are doing now, abbot, is no great help to us in our danger! It will be much better for you to pray with us because we are going to perish if you do not!"

So instead of scooping out bilge water to pour back into the sea, Columba smiled sweetly and poured out a prayer to God. He stood up and stretched his hands out to heaven and prayed to the Creator of the storm, the Creator of the waves, the Creator of the wind, and asked that stillness might come so that their purpose might be accomplished and their lives saved. The sailors were astounded at how fast the waves calmed and the wind subsided. The effect of this made the sailors elevate Columba into some creature higher than he really was. Columba noticed this, and calling for their attention, said to them all

"Glorify God! For if anything out of the ordinary has been done, it has been done not by me but by God's power in and through me. Know my brothers that you too can be workers of miracles—you just need faith in God, in his power, and his faithfulness and his love."

By the time the boat had reached the shore, Baithene was there to greet them, his heart full of joy to see Columba again. "Come and refresh yourselves" Baithene invited the sailors. Later Columba withdrew with Baithene to the chapel, and there he unburdened himself to the younger abbot, his foster-son.

"Baithene I have much guilt on my soul. The wolf-nature in me has reared up again. It is to my bitter sorrow, and I heartily repent now, that I fought with my old friend Comgall."

"Fought?" Baithene inquired, "With words or physically?"

"Well it began with words, but ended in . . . a battle. My clan and his, over the church and land at Cúil Rathain. Even though I was in the right, I shouldn't have held out against Comgall's claim to its jurisdiction."

Baithene gently corrected Columba: "Even though you THOUGHT you were in the right."

"Yes. You are right. I realize now in the sight of you and the sight of God that I should not have let the quarrel get to a pitch of bloodshed, should not have involved my kinsmen at all. Baithene, I beg you to have no regard at all for my age in giving me penance for this foul deed."

Columba hung his head. Baithene shook his head, sad at what he was hearing, but knowing that neither he nor any other monk was exempt from the tendencies to fall back into their old, unredeemed nature.

Baithene bade Columba, after this time of soul-sharing and confession, a tender and sad farewell. Getting into the boat he found the sailors in a happy mood. These were but young monks, novices who had been taught the skills of sailing by Rui and Fethuo, two of the original twelve. However, almost as if to test them out, as they were again halfway between the island of Ethe and the island of I, a storm brewed up, a wild storm and a perilous storm. The young sailors called out to Columba,

"Pray for us! Pray to the Lord as you did on the way out!"

Columba sitting with a perfectly composed face said to them,

"Today it is not my place to pray for you in the peril that threatens us all, but that holy man Abbot Cainnech will pray for us."

The sailors looked astounded and cast querying looks among themselves and wondered if their abbot was ageing rather fast. However, the waves did indeed calm down and the wind subsided although Columba had done nothing. He had not lifted his voice in prayer once. They pressed Columba to explain this but Columba said, his foreknowledge returning to him,

"Cainnech himself will explain, for he is going to visit us in the next few days." Cainnech did indeed visit them shortly afterwards. One of the first things he and Columba talked about was the day of the storm, reckoning on their fingers what day it had been.

"Cainnech, thank you for your prayers" said Columba, "the day of the storm."

"Yes, Columba," said Cainnech, "I reckon too that it was three o'clock and we had just started to eat our meal. The bread was being distributed when suddenly, with the inner ear of my heart, the Holy Spirit just told me that you were in trouble on the sea. I felt that it would not be right to pray there and then, so I quickly hurried to the church. I had taken off my shoes for the meal and I only just managed to find one of them. I left the other behind in my haste and ran to the church, calling out to my brothers to pray too, saying to them, 'It is not for us to be dining at a time like this, when Columba's ship is in peril at sea. For this moment I know that he is calling on the name of Cainnech to pray to Christ for him and his companions in their peril.' After speaking these words to my companions I was already in the church door and fell to my knees there and prayed for a long while. Then I knew that the Lord had answered my prayer, for I felt the calming of the sea as a calming of my spirit."

Columba laughed and said,

"Cainnech, I knew that you were praying and I knew that God had heard your prayer. Even though I was in the boat I said aloud 'Cainnech I know that God has heard your prayer. Your running swiftly to the church with but a single shoe on one foot was a great help to us.' The sailors who were my companions in the boat thought that I was becoming a madman, talking like this to someone who was not present!"

The two laughed together and praised God in their hearts.

Two of the monks, Calcu and Ganarius, were helping their fellows Pilu and Virgno with the boat that, together with Malruth and Molua, they were going to sail to the land of Ériu with their father Columba. For Columba had determined, in spite of his failing strength, to visit Ériu once more. The news that Cainnech had brought him contained much, but not least it contained the news that Aed, the King of Tethba who had given him Dairmhá, had died. Other news was that his cousin and friend Aed the son of Ainmire was now not alone King of Ulaidh but had been elected Ard Ri of Ériu. Columba was very pleased. He longed to be present at the ordination of Aed as Ard Rí, even if he himself did not perform the ritual. He thought that his presence might help ensure that there were no Druidic rites being enacted, no pagan Fes, Columba felt it was imperative that he should sail to Ériu as soon as possible, his second visit since having been exiled to I.

Ganarius and Colcu turned to one another when the boat was out of sight and Colcu said sadly:

"His days of wandering will soon be over. I believe he drives himself too hard, his strength can hardly last. I become anxious for his safety each time he embarks on a ship, and I fear that I will not see him more."

"I become anxious too." Ganarius agreed.

"Yet he can call divine power to his aid whenever he wishes, you know," Colcu asserted.

"Did you hear of the time he rescued his friend Cormac at sea when his ship was in difficulty, and he was not even on the ship with him?" Ganarius asked. Colcu nodded, and added his memories:

"Ah yes, but did you hear how he increased the number of cattle his other friend Colman in Kintyre possessed; he blessed five little cows and in a few weeks they became a hundred and five?"

"Well, did you hear of the time he helped some brothers capture salmon for their supper? Not only one but two salmon. And not just ordinary salmon, but extraordinarily big," Ganarius replied.

"He knows things that are happening far away, too, like the time he knew a kinswoman of his in Ériu was in great difficulty in her delivery of a child, and through his earnest prayers she was delivered safely, right across the sea!" Colcu added:

"Yes, he not only knows what is happening to people, but he cares so much, and prays so hard for them, I wonder how he is not exhausted. He pushes himself so hard, eats so little, and gets only a small amount of sleep" Ganarius said admiringly:

"Of course God gives him supernatural strength, because he is so holy. Did you hear about the time he showed up the Druid's magic when he was staying on Mount Cainlea? This sorcerer had tried to show the people that he could take milk from the bull. Columba just said 'I am going to bless this milk and it will prove that it is not true milk but blood rubbed with color by an artifice of demons to deceive people. He did this of course to disprove the Druid's magic in front of all the onlookers."

Colcu agreed.

"Yes he has always been against superstition and some of the old ways. I was amused when he cured Scandal of his superstitions, by making him attend to a bird of evil omen for three days, feeding it and looking after it!" Ganarius said with a grin.

"Well, did you hear about the time he changed a bitter apple tree back in Ériu into a sweet apple tree?" Colcu contributed.

"That's nothing! He has done far better things than that. He has actually healed people of death. He has calmed the storms on the sea. He has changed bad water in a well to good water. He has actually got water out of the rock when people had nothing to drink." Ganarius boasted.

"Yes, he helps people whenever he can. And, you know, I think his great power comes from the times he spends alone in his cell praying. I happened to be passing his cell one day and looked in and saw his face. He was utterly still and silent and his face was showing the signs of peaceful bliss. I cannot help thinking that these times are when God fills him with his power and his spirit. Yet he does so little to help himself. He will not take life easier now he is older. I was so worried at first when he insisted on feeding only on nettle soup, just because he met an old woman on Mala gathering nettles for her meals. But thanks to my ruse of carving a hole in the stirring spoon and concealing milk there so that he could not see me add the milk, he thrived on that diet—until all was discovered! If only we were permitted to have our own cow then we would not need to be getting our milk from Mala; but of course he thinks it inappropriate for male monks to be milking female cattle, although many of us come from farming families!" Colcu grinned.

The two monks had reached the monastery by now and Ganarius warned Colcu,

"We had better keep quiet now. Our abbot does not like us engaging in idle chatter."

"Our abbot is not here at present, my brother, remember. Also I do not feel this is idle chatter. If our abbot had heard our conversation he would, I am sure, have wanted to remind us of our Lord's words, telling his disciples that greater things shall they do than he did in his life time through the help of the Holy Spirit. Our master always tells us that all power comes from God, and any miracle that is worked is not worked with an abbot's power, or a monk's power, or even a druid's power, but with the power of the God who created the earth," Colcu replied rather self-righteously.

After the coronation of Aed, Columba made a journey round some of the monasteries of his *paruchia* or family of monasteries. But it was not very easy to say which were his, for many called themselves Columban from admiration of him, and he founded many churches that later on had monasteries attached to them. Thus jurisdiction was a thorny subject. And so once again Columba's fieriness got the better of him, and he had a hand, albeit a smaller hand than he had had at Cúil Rathain, in the battle fought at Cuilfetha, near the weir of Cluain Ioraird.

After that, feeling empty and ashamed, weary and desperate for peace and a rest from his exhaustion, he went to Daire, attended by the faithful Diormit, who although he had long been a monk, insisted on attending Columba as much as he could, even more devotedly than ever since Columba had prayed him back from the edge of death. There in the church in Daire they and their fellow monks happened to sing the one hundred and thirty-first Psalm-

"O Lord my heart is not proud: nor are my eyes haughty. I do not busy myself in great matters: or in things too wonderful for me."

Columba felt deeply convicted by these verses, and impelled to return to I at the earliest opportunity in order to help make them true in his life. He longed to retire to a small cell or hermitage that he might also make come true the following verse *"But I have calmed and quieted my soul like a weaned child upon on its mother's breast."*

"Over to I, very soon," he thought, as he laid his weary body down, "Away from these enticing, whispering, oak trees, away from the trouble and turmoil of trying to administer a group of monasteries in a different island, away from temptations to meddle in too many affairs. Away to the small island that is now my accustomed home. But my real home is neither of these dear places. My real home is God." He drifted off into sleep.

A few days later he was safely back in I and singing his Psalms upon the eastern shore of the island before the other brothers were astir, as was his custom. He felt weary after his journey to Ériu, and great fervor went into his singing of the words,

"My soul has a great desire and a longing to enter into the court of the Lord."

Soon after this when he was back in his hut, he took out his quill-pen and made calculations upon a blank piece of parchment.

"As I thought! Thirty years!"

His face lit up with joy. Just then Pilu and Lugne were passing his hut and noticed his sudden joy, followed straight away by an equally sudden sadness.

"What is the cause, father, of your change from joy to sorrow? Can we help?" they asked. Columba saw them there and smiled, saying kindly

"Go in peace and do not ask the reason for my joy or my sadness."

The two were bitterly disappointed and knelt and begged him to share at least something of whatever vision had caused his emotion. Seeing that they were genuinely distressed, and that they were feeling with him in his own sadness, Columba relented.

"Because I love you both dearly, I would not make you sad. But first promise me not to betray to any man during my life the secret I will share with you."

"We promise," they both answered in unison and with sincerity.

"Today, my brothers, is the completion of 30 years of my pilgrimage in Alba. I am weary of it, and for the last many days I have been begging God to release my soul and bring me to the heavenly country. The joy you saw was the joy of my readiness to depart and my seeing of holy angels who were come to bring me to my heavenly home." Pilu and Lugne were spellbound by this and enraptured with the vision. Columba's voice now cracked as he continued.

"But suddenly the angels were held back. Held back by the prayers of my monks, and forbidden to come closer. It has been revealed to me by my angel, Axal, who is always by my side, that the Lord is granting me a further four years of life, hence my sadness. When these four years are completed, I shall depart happily and suddenly and without illness with these same angels who came for me today."

And they were four years of beauty and holiness, graced with an almost unearthly quality. Several other monks witnessed an unearthly light in his cell at night and again whenever he prayed in the church. Virgno in fact was commended by the abbot for keeping his eyes lowered

to the ground throughout this light, which protected him from being blinded. Colcu too noticed light, and spied through a keyhole, to Columba's disapproval. After that Columba had himself removed from his monks' presence, to Hinba. The Hinba monks too observed rays of light coming out through the chinks in the door his cell and through holes and heard spiritual singing such as they had never heard before.

Back in I, Malru came running to the monastery one Sabbath when Columba had forbidden the monks to venture to the west of the island for he wished to be alone. In great excitement he ran to his fellows and confessed that he was guilty. His brothers were perplexed at why he should be both radiantly happy and guilty! He explained:

"I am guilty of the crime of disobeying our father's command. I followed Holy Columba to a little hill to the side of the center of the machair—you know the grassy sloping hill with wild carrot and willow-herb which they call the Hill of the Fairies—there he stood with his arms outstretched in prayer and his eyes raised to heaven. As he stood there I gradually realized he was surrounded by beings of light, by holy angels who stayed and held conversation with him for a short while and then, as if sensing that they were being spied on, swiftly returned to the heights of heaven."

His brothers warned Malru,

"Do not speak again of this to any man. For the abbot is already having difficulty maintaining his privacy, and such a story will attract even more visitors to the island." A young brother asked,

"Why can we not help his privacy by building him a hermitage there, on the Western shore away from the monastery?"

"An excellent plan!" So they all set to work at once, using that Sunday rest time to do the manual work of digging earth and weaving wattles, and carrying stones to make a little hermitage in a grassy dip below the tallest hill and overlooking the western sea. This saved Columba the trouble and bone-jolting of the journey to Hinba and he delighted in his solitude in this little valley between the hills.

One morning of both sun and wind Columba awoke with a strong desire to walk once more to the south-west of the island and see the water-spout. After Lauds he decided to set out alone. First he made sure that the other monks were not following him in their desire to be helpful.

Their solicitude was burdensome to him, but he realized he must accept it in the spirit in which it was given.

He had been finding longer walks difficult, but he was driven on more by his inner spirit than by his gaunt thin body. His mind ever active, he composed poems as he walked, delighting as he always did in going over them again and again to find words for the end of each line which should end with the same sound, and so bring an even greater degree of music into the poem—or hymn, as his poems so often on the theme of God were really hymns of praise.

When he reached the spout, he was struck anew by its majesty, and sparked to reflections on the majesty of God. Tears came to his eyes, and he called out to God,

"Oh my Lord, forgive me that I have been too taken up with my own leadership of men to realize fully your wonder and majesty!"

He meditated on the fact that neither space nor time could contain God, the unbegotten, and started on a long poem beginning each verse with a different letter of the alphabet. He composed it in Latin, so that his Saxon, British and Pictish monks could all read it, as well as his own Gaelic monks. This occupied him for many weeks until he felt satisfied with it enough to commit it to parchment

"Ancient of days, enthroned on high . . ." He put as much teaching on God as he could into it, and hoped that the rhyming words and alphabetical beginnings to the verses would help his monks to memorise it, and thus they would still have solid teaching when he was gone from them, on the nature of God and the cosmos, the Creation of the world, on Heaven and Hell and Redemption.

His mood of inspiration was felt in the church as he preached to his brethren, and they followed him out of the church on another day of breezes and sunshine as he strode out as well as he could though stooped and slowed now by age. He circled the island, followed by his anxious monks, and when he had made the full circle, he stopped on a small rise, and looked around the island, his eyes growing misty with vision.

"This holy island, we all love so much, small as it is, will yet be highly honored not just by the people of Ériu but also by foreign and barbarous peoples; great reverence will be given to it. But it will not stay thus preserved in prayer and holiness. It will in more future times become once more uninhabited, and a place for cows from neighbouring islands to come and graze for their summer pasture, then be removed again by boat. All these buildings will rot and fall into disrepair even the stone ones that will arise after our deaths". Unhappy groans and murmurs were heard from the listeners. But Columba had not finished his prophecy. He continued: "Yet I see beyond that time. There will come another time afterwards and another man of vision who will take up my fallen cloak will come and many people will work at restoring what had been, and once more people will come here to be in a holy place where Christ is alive and exalted in his church."

When the fourth year was completed, all were aware of it, but none dared speak of it. The Easter celebration of the Holy Mysteries in the church that year was extremely precious. Columba already longed to depart, but did not wish to mar the happiness of the festival for the monks, and so prayed for a short postponement. Unable because of his physical exhaustion to walk very far, Diormit would fetch him in the little milk wagon and the old white horse who carried the milk churns to the harbor each day would snuffle affectionately at Columba's hand as he stroked it in a morning greeting. Diormit would drive the cart to the west of the island where the brothers were working and they would crowd round to exchange with Columba words of encouragement and maybe a laugh or two.

One Thursday in late May, a day of freshness and the smells of the earth's spring, Columba went once again in the wagon to visit the brothers as they worked. As they went down the track westwards on this Thursday, Columba knew for a certainty that it would be his last visit to the little grassy plain on the west of the island that they called the 'machair'. His bodily frailty was increasing. Wishing to spare the brothers the shock of a sudden unprepared departure he said to Diormit,

"Diormit, help me out of this cart and up to that higher ground over there. I have a message to deliver."

Diormit helped his master gently down and Cobthach ran over to help. The two monks supported Columba under the arms as he climbed the slope and stood beside him as he delivered his words, in case he would need them. They tried to persuade him to sit but he was determined to make this effort. Work had stopped now and all the brothers working in the place gathered round eager to hear their abbot's words.

"From this day, my little children, know that you will never again be able to see my face upon this plain. I longed to depart to the Lord during the Paschal celebration of the Holy Mysteries, on the Day of the

Resurrection of our Lord, but begged the Lord Christ to let me stay longer with you so as not to mar that holy and happy time."

He heard their murmurs and saw their anxiety, and tried to reassure them:

"Do not be anxious and frightened. My times—all our times—are in God's hands. As the blessed Apostle Paul said, 'as the outer body grows frailer every day, the inner spirit grows stronger. " He lifted his thin arms with difficulty and spread them wide as if to embrace the whole island, then continued speaking,

"May the Holy Trinity—God the Father, Jesus Christ the Son, and the Holy Spirit—bless you all, and bless this island and all who visit here in the years to come. May all who set foot on I be helped to come closer to God here, and to grow in holiness and Christ-likeness". Then he added,

"My brothers, do not be dismayed by the prophecy God gave through me. Our island will not fall into ruin for many years yet, and its revival will be glorious."

Then he looked at the brothers and as both an aside and a warning he added,

"From this moment, no snake shall be able to poison men or cattle on the shore of this island, as long as the inhabitants of this settlement observe the commandments of Christ."

In the days that followed Columba was much given to speaking of angels, and Diormit felt he was almost gone from them already. Saturday came, and he approached Columba gently.

"Father, have you strength today for our usual Sabbath task of blessing the grain in the barn?"

"Indeed I have, Diormit. Help me up." Columba replied, and they walked with great slowness to the barn. There were several piles of grain sacks still remaining from the previous year's harvest. Columba nodded in approval and said,

"They have done well—there will be enough bread next year when I have departed." Diormit shook his head sadly and tutted,

"During this year, Father, you have many, many times made us sad by your frequent mention of your passing." Sitting on a grain sack, Columba beckoned Diormit a small bit closer to him and said in a soft voice,

"Diormit I have a few secret words for you. Promise me not to tell anyone before my death." Diormit promised on bent knee, so Columba continued:

"Today is the Sabbath, which means 'rest'; and it is more truly a Sabbath for me as it is my last day in this life and I am starting to rest after my wearisome labors. I shall go the way of my fathers at midnight, for already my Lord Jesus Christ invites me to come to him." Diormit could not contain himself for sorrow and wept bitter tears there, still on his knees on the bare floor, the old abbot's arm about his shoulder as he sat on the sack of grain. Presently Diormit recovered and they returned to the monastery.

"Let me rest awhile here, Diormit," Columba gasped, tired from the journey which was normally short, and so had not warranted the harnessing of the horse. There was a small rock nearby and Columba was helped down to it by faithful Diormit. They sat there in quietness for a small while, Columba's breath being short. Columba's eyes were closed so he did not see the approach of one of his old familiar friends, but became aware of his nearness only when his head was laid gently on Columba's lap. Columba opened his eyes, and found himself looking into the eyes of the old white horse, who was looking at him affectionately and sadly with tears streaming down from his eyes.

"Go on! Get on! Leave him alone!" Diormit called to the horse, trying to shove it away, the Connaught farm labourer in him taking control. Columba restrained the horse and said,

"Let him be, Diormit," and he blessed the horse before returning to his cell to continue his work—his continual, unending work, the background to all else in his life—of copying the Holy Scriptures.

On the parchment in Columba's small neat script, were the opening words of the Thirty-Fourth Psalm, *"I Will bless the Lord continually: his praise shall be always in my mouth."* He labored on, loving the words, praying the words as he wrote, knowing their truth in his own experience. *"The angel of the Lord encamps around those who fear him: and delivers them in their need. O taste and see that the Lord is good: Happy the man who hides in him."* Getting near to the end of the page of parchment now, he saw that two more verses would fit. The bell for Vespers was already ringing when he had completed the tenth verse. *"Lions may suffer want and go hungry but those who seek the Lord lack nothing good . . ."*

"Baithene will have to finish it for me," he murmured. How true all these words had been throughout his seventy and seven years of life he thought, as with Diormit's help he attended vespers, and afterwards he lay down on his familiar rock with its pillow-stone at one end. He lay down and managed haltingly to say to Diormit,

"Diormit, one last message for you to all. I charge you, my children, to keep mutual and sincere love between you and to live in peace with each other. God will be your helper and I will be praying for you from heaven. Go now and rest Diormit."

Reluctant to leave Columba, Diormit was nevertheless still under obedience to him. He turned away his eyes lest Columba see the tears, and quietly left and went to his own cell nearby.

In Columba's last few moments of life he felt a sudden access of strength. Hearing the bell for Prime at midnight he rose up almost as if his body were no longer there, only his strong fiery spirit. He hobbled slowly but joyfully to the church arriving ahead of the other brothers. Diormit, having gone to the abbot's hut first and finding it empty, followed later, puzzled at his master's absence. He rushed to the church to make sure all was well . . . what was that bright light filling the small building? Diormit entered just in time to see his master kneeling in front of the altar—it seemed that there were columns of brightness on each side of him—and to see him crumple and sink down. Diormit and all his fellow monks held their breath and did not dare to move. They just gazed, for the moment seemed so sacred. Columba's body lay still, in front of the altar. Upwards from the still body, Diormit could swear he saw a large white dove, its appearance as if it were made of flame, but white flame. It started to ascend. Yes, a dove of white flame ascending heavenwards!

The End

Glossary

Ailech	Capital of Tirconnel, near Burt Co Donegal
Alba	Scotland
Amran	A praise poem
Aontraim	Antrim
Ard Macha	Armagh
Ard Rí	High King
Beannchor	Bangor
Ben Éadair	Howth
Ben Gulban	Benbulben
Bhreatain	Britain
Brehon	Lawyers
Cainnech	Canice/Kenneth
Cairbre	Barony of Carbury North Sligo
Caiseal	Cashel
Ceanannas Mór	Kells
Cill Mhic Néanáin	Kilmacrennan
Cluain Ioraird	Clonard
Cluain Mhic Nós	Clonmacnoise
Cnoc na Rí	Knocknarea
Coarb	Successor to an abbot

Colossus	Colonsay
Cruithni	Picts in Ulster
Cuildreimhne	Cooldrevny, plain below Benbulben
Cuil Rathain	Coleraine
Curragh	Boat of skins on a wooden frame
Curraghel	A coracle, or small round curragh
Daimhá	Durrow
Daimhinis	Devenish
Daire	Derry
Dalriada	Kingdom comprising Argyll, the Hebrides and Antrim
Droim Cliabh	Drumcliffe
Droim Ing	Dromin, Co Louth
Druim Ceatt	Daisy Hill, outside Limavaddy
Dún Sobhairce	Dunseverick
Ériu	Ireland
Ethe	Tiree
Fili	Poets
Gaelic	Irish
Gartán	Gartan near Letterkenny
Glas Naion	Glasnevin
Hinba	Jura
I	Iona
Inis Muredach	Inishmurray
Laigin	Leinster
Loch Cuan	Strangford Lough
Maigh Bhile	Movilla, present-day Newtonards
Mainister Bhuithin	Monasterboice
Mala	Mull

Midhe	Meath
Mumhan	Munster
Ollaves	Master poets, men of great learning
Osraige	Ossory
Ráth Bhoth	Raphoe
Scottic	Irish, to outsiders
Snamluthir	Granard
Sórd	Swords
Tailltu	Teltown
Teamhair	Tara
Tiobraid Árann	Tipperary
Tirconnel	North-west Ireland, present day county Donegal
Tulach Dubhglaise	Temple Douglas
Ulaidh	Ulster

Bibliography

Adamnan of Iona. *Life of St Columba*, tr. Richard Sharpe. (London: Penguin, 1995).

Annals of Clonmacnoise, The, tr. Conall McGeoghagan. (Dublin: Royal Society of Antiquaries of Ireland, 1896).

Annals of the Four Masters, The, ed. John O'Donovan. (Dublin: Brian Geraghty, 1846).

Annals of Tigernach, The, ed. Dennis Murphy. (Llanerch: Felinfach, 1993).

Annals of Ulster, The, ed. & tr. William M. Hennessy & B. MacCarthy. (Dublin: H.M.Stationery Office, 1887).

Bander, Peter, ed. *The Prophecies of St. Malachy and St Columbkille*, 3rd. Edition. (Gerrards Cross : Colin Smythe, 1974).

Bede, The Venerable. *A History of the English Church and People*, ed. & tr. Leo Sherley-Price, (Harmondsworth: Penguin, 1955).

Bieler, Ludwig. *Ireland, Harbinger of the Middle Ages*. (Oxford: Oxford Unkversity Press, 1963).

"Book of Glendalough, The" (H.2.18) poem by Cuan O'Lochain describing the banqueting hall at Tara. In George Petrie: *On the History and Antiquities of Tara Hill*. (Dublin: R.Graisberry, 1839).

Bradley, Ian. *The Celtic Way*. (London: Darton, Longman and Todd, 1993).

————. *Columba: Pilgrim and Pentitent* (Glasgow: Wild Goose, 1996).

Byrne, F. J. "The Ireland of St Columba". In J.L.McCracken: *Historical Studies—papers read to the Sixth Irish Conference of Historians Belfast 1965*.

————. *Irish Kings and High Kings* (London: Batsford, 1973).

Campbell, Marion. *Argyll, The Enduring Heartland*. (London: Turnstone, 1977).

Chadwick, Nora K. *The Age of Saints in the Early Celtic Church*. (London: The Riddell Memorial Lecture Durham University 1961, 32nd Series).

————. *Celtic Britain*. (London :Thames and Hudson, 1964).

Clerigh, Arthur Ua. *The History of Ireland to the Coming of Henry II*. (London: Kennikat, 1976).

Curtis, Edmond. *A History of Ireland*, 6th. Edn.(London: Methuen, 1936).

Cusack, Mary Frances. *An Illustrated History of Ireland from A.D., 400 to 1800*, Facsimile Edition. (London: Bracken, 1995).

Dillon, Myles. *Early Irish Society*. (Cork: Mercier, 1963).

Ellis, Peter Berresford. *The Druids*. (London: Constable, 1995).

Finlay, Ian. *Columba*. (London: Victor Gollancz, 1979).

Flanagan, Laurence. *A Chronicle of Irish Saints*. (Belfast: Blackstaff, 1990).

Gwynne, Aubrey, and R. Neville Hadcock. *Mediaeval Religious Houses—Ireland.* (London: Longmans, 1970).

Gwynn, Stephen. *Highways and Byways in Donegal and Antrim.* (London: Macmillan, 1899).

Hanson, W. G. *The Early Monastic Schools.* (Cambridge: W.Heffer, 1927).

Healy, John. *Ireland's Ancient Schools and Scholars.* (Dublin: Sealy, Bryers and Walker, 1897).

———. *History of the Diocese of Meath.* (Dublin: Association for Promoting Christian Knowledge, 1908).

Herbert, Maire. *Iona, Kells and Derry.* (Oxford: Clarendon, 1988).

Hickey, Elizabeth. *The Irish Life of St Finian of Cluan Eraird, Master of the Saints of Ireland.* (Meath Archaeological and Historical Society, 1996).

Hughes, Kathleen. *The Church in Early Irish Society.* (London: Methuen, 1966).

———. "The Cult of St. Finnian of Cluan Eraird". *Irish Historical Studies* No. 9; 1954/5.

———. *Early Christian Ireland—Introduction to the Sources.* (London: Hodder and Stoughton, 1972).

Joyce, P. W. *A Short History of Ireland, from the Earliest Times to 1608.* (London: Longmans, Green, 1924).

———. *A Social History of Ancient Ireland.* (London: Longmans, Green, 1903).

Lacey, Brian. "The Real Cause of the Battle of Cuil Dreimnepin Co. Sligo, the so-called 'Battle of the Book'." In ed. Martin A. Timoney. *Dedicated to Sligo: Thirty-Four Essays on Sligo's Past*, 83 to 90.

Lehane, Brendan. *Early Celtic Christianity.* (London: Continuum 2005).

Leslie, J. B. *Raphoe Clergy and Parishes.* (Enniskillen: Fermanagh Times, 1940).

Leslie, Shane. *Isle of Colmcille.* (Dublin: Catholic Truth Society of Ireland, 1910).

Macmanus, Seamus. *The Story of the Irish Race.* Revised edition (New York: Wings/ Random House, 1996).

MacNiocaill, Gearoid. *Ireland Before the Vikings.* (Dublin: Gill and Macmillan, 1972).

Maguire E. *History of the Diocese of Raphoe.* (Dublin: Browne and Nolan, 1920).

Marsden, John, ed. *The Illustrated Life of Columba.* (Edinburgh: Floris, 1995).

Menzies, Lucy. *St. Columba of Iona,* Facsimile edition. (Felinfach: J.M.F., 1992).

Monck-Mason. *Religion of Ancient Irish Saints.* (Dublin 1938).

Moody, T.W. and Martin, F.X. *The Course of Irish History.* (Cork: Mercier, 1994).

O'Corrain, Donncha. *Ireland Before the Normans.* (Dublin: Gill and Macmillan, 1972).

O'Croinin, Daibhi. *Early Mediaeval Ireland—400-1200.* (Harlow: Longman, 1995).

O'Donnell, Manus ed. & tr. *Betha Colmcille.* ed. Brian Lacey (Dublin: Four Courts, 1995).

O'Dwyer, Peter. *Towards a History of Irish Spirituality.* (Dublin: Columba, 1995).

Paor, Liam de. *St. Patrick's World,* Paperback edition. (Dublin: Four Courts, 1994).

Paor, Liam de & Maire de. *Early Christian Ireland.* (London: Thames and Hudson, 1964).

Ryan, John. *Irish Monasticism,* 2nd Edition. (Dublin: Four Courts, 1972).

Simms, G. O. *The Psalms in the Day of St. Columba.* (Dublin: A.P.C.K., 1963).

Simpson, W. Douglas. *The Historical St. Columba.* (Edinburgh: Oliver and Boyd, 1963).

Snyder, Henry L." Ireland from the beginning to the end of the Middle Ages". In *Irish History and Culture.* (Portmarnock: Wolfhound, 1979).

Sprott Towill, Edwin. *Saints of Scotland.* (Edinburgh, St Andrew, 1978).

Stokes, G. D. *Ireland and the Celtic Church.* (London: Hodder and Stoughton, 1886).

Stokes, Whitley, ed. *The Martyrology of Oenghus the Culdee.* 2nd. Edition. (London: The Henry Bradshaw Society, 1905).

Printed in Great Britain
by Amazon